D1263337

KILLING THE
COMPETITION

KILLING THE COMPETITION

KENNEDY SHAW

www.urbanbooks.net

Urban Books, LLC
78 East Industry Court
Deer Park, NY 11729

Killing the Competition Copyright © 2010 Kennedy Shaw

All rights reserved. No part of this book may be reproduced in any form or by any means without prior consent of the Publisher, except brief quotes used in reviews.

ISBN 13: 978-1-60162-237-2
ISBN 10: 1-60162-237-6

First Paperback Printing October 2010
Printed in the United States of America

10 9 8 7 6 5 4 3 2

Distributed by Kensington Publishing Corp.
Submit Wholesale Orders to:
Kensington Publishing Corp.
C/O Penguin Group (USA) Inc.
Attention: Order Processing
405 Murray Hill Parkway
East Rutherford, NJ 07073-2316
Phone: 1-800-526-0275
Fax: 1-800-227-9604

Prologue

Augustus Winn, editor in chief of the *Austin Daily Chronicle*, grappled for the phone in his darkened bedroom. He didn't bother with the light. A late-night call was never good, even in his line of business. It usually meant one of his reporters was on a hot lead or they were about to go to jail. He pulled the phone to his ear and grumbled a short hello.

"Augustus, this is Chandler Chase."

Okay, now that got his attention. Not only was Chase one of the most powerful and wealthy attorneys in the state of Texas, his only child, Kyra, worked for the paper as an investigative reporter. *Please*, he prayed silently, *let Kyra be all right.* "Yes, Mr. Chase." Better judgment told him not to mention the hour of the morning.

"My daughter is in trouble and I need your help."

Now Augustus was very up and very awake. "How? Why?"

"I can't go into details at the moment. I need you to send her away."

There was no further explanation.

"Do I need to speak with your superiors to make this happen or what?"

"No, sir, you do not." Whatever trouble Kyra was in had to be big, Augustus reasoned. He didn't want to get on Chandler Chase's bad side, either. That would mean the end of his job. "What do you want from me?"

"You can keep my daughter alive for one. Do I need to elaborate?"

"No, Mr. Chase. I just don't understand what I can possibly do outside of giving her an assignment. She normally comes to me with her ideas and I just go along with it. "

"She's not going to go unless it's a good tip. There was a cocaine scandal in a small town in Central Texas a few months back. Send her there. I'm sure you can come up with some kind of new slant for a news story."

"Mr. Chase, Kyra is going to ask questions. She still riding high on the public school funding story. She'll smell a rat."

He laughed. Even that sounded threatening. "She's my daughter. Of course she's going to be suspicious. I would expect nothing less."

Auggie sighed. Now he did turn on the lamp. Maybe all this was a bad dream and would fade away the minute light flooded the room.

Nothing. So all of this was true. He was actually talking to Chandler Chase at four in the morning. "How much time do I have?"

"Not much. I want her out of town by sunrise."

The line went dead.

CHAPTER 1

Kyra Chase parked her BMW Z4 Roadster in front of what she hoped was the sheriff's department. According to navigational system in her sports car, this had to be the building. It was the only one with both the USA flag and Texas flag flying high. Where were the police cars? She noted the vehicles surrounding the courthouse; none of them looked official. A few trucks, an SUV, and a mini-van, but nothing that screamed undercover police car.

The three-story building housed not only the sheriff's office, but the tax offices, the justice of the peace, mayor's office, and city council. She didn't think Wright City had anything that required a city council. Her graduating high school class had more people than this tiny town of 5,000.

Okay, girl, get your head in the game, she told herself. Being an investigative reporter for the *Austin Daily Chronicle,* she'd been in some tight spots in her career, but none that landed her in Mayberry, R.F.D.

Her day had started with a frantic call from her boss at five that morning, telling her about this crazy assignment. Sure, four months ago Wright City had had plenty of drama with the cocaine scandal, nine deaths related to the scandal, and the appointing of a new sheriff. But now as she gazed around the picturesque town, nothing seemed out of place.

Okay, to her everything seemed out of place, since she was born and raised in the Austin limelight. Downtown Wright City had two lanes of traffic, no tall buildings, and not a Starbucks in sight. She could just kill her no-account editor for suggesting this story about the residual effects of the cocaine scandal. Like someone would actually want to talk about the small community's most embarrassing moments.

On her drive to Wright City she'd wanted to turn around and head back to Austin, but her father's voice kept popping into her drowsy brain. As the only child of Texas's most famous attorney to the rich and powerful, she had an image to uphold. So she couldn't refuse an assignment; it just wasn't done. Besides, her editor had told her not to return without a story. For now, she was stuck in Wright City.

She looked at her watch. It was barely eight in the morning. Maybe the sheriff would be accommodating and she could be back in her townhouse by that evening, enjoying a fine glass of pinot grigio.

She opened her car door and got out. She took a deep breath, grabbed her purse and headed inside the courthouse.

She entered the building and gasped. Nothing was like Austin. Everything in the town seemed so laid back. There were no metal detectors in the courthouse. No surveillance cameras that followed her every move and no one asked for her identification. A sweet older woman directed her to the sheriff's office without knowing or caring about her reason for wanting to see him or if she had an appointment.

She walked up the steps to the second floor and was amazed. She expected this floor to mirror the one downstairs, but it was littered with doorways. The second floor not only held the sheriff's department, but also the dispatchers, tax department, and assorted county offices. She followed the arrow to the sheriff's office and knocked on the door.

It quickly opened and Kyra was shocked. Now, in her very public life, she had seen good-looking men before, but the man standing before her was gorgeous. His caramel brown skin, light brown eyes, and wavy hair were just the tip of the handsome iceberg. And this man was definitely all that.

He was taller than her five-ten form, by at least four or five inches. His athletic build was encased in a dark blue shirt emblazoned with "Wright City, Sheriff Department" and a pair of jeans just loose enough to make her mind wander, her gaze setting on a large gold belt buckle in the shape of Texas. Her traitorous eyes lingered just below his waist. He topped everything off with a pair of polished black snakeskin cowboy boots. An easy grin spread over his face. "Can I help you, ma'am?"

Ma'am. Kyra sighed. She loved a man with good

manners. "Yes, Sheriff. My name is Kyra Chase. I'm
an investigative reporter for the *Austin Daily Chronicle.* I would like to ask you a few questions about
the cocaine scandal of four months ago."

The smile quickly faded. He was actually scowl-
ing at her as he opened his office door. He motioned her inside before closing the door. After
she was seated, he took his chair behind his large
desk and let out a short breath. "I hate reporters.
For the last four months I've watched your lot
come to our town and dredge up memories everyone is trying to forget. I'm telling you this because
I'm fulfilling a promise to the mayor, nothing
more. I'm supposed to be nice to reporters, so I'm
telling you this once and only once. There's no
story here, Ms . . ."

"Chase," Kyra choked out. "Kyra Chase," she repeated, feeling like she was in the principal's office and she was about to be scolded.

"Well, Ms. Chase," he spat her name, "the story
you're looking for is back in Austin. Interstate 35 is
straight down Main Street and drive for about two
hours. Any information you need can be retrieved
from the Internet. Good day." He stood, walked to
the door, and opened it. "Drive safely."

She was too shock, to do anything but nod. She
rose, grabbed her bag, and left the office. The
sheriff might have won this round, but Kyra would
be better prepared for the next skirmish with Mr.
Handsome.

Sheriff Kevin Johnson shook his head and
slammed the door to his office. Another damned
reporter to ruin his day, but at least this one was

easy on the eyes and hard on the libido. Kyra Chase was as beautiful as her name. Her glossy black hair swung loosely about her shoulders. Her face had the minimum amount of makeup. Something about her screamed money. Maybe it was the small diamond earrings, or gold Rolex watch.

She was tall, which he liked, had meat on her bones, which he loved, but she was of the nosy lot, which he hated. One look into those pretty brown eyes and he'd almost lost it. She had honey brown skin, and he knew he hadn't seen the last of her. She had given up too easily.

The last thing Wright City needed was another nosy reporter waking up the details of the cocaine scandal that had claimed the life of the town's favorite citizen, six teenagers, the sheriff, a local banker, and almost his soon-to-be sister-in-law. With a story this big he'd expected reporters to descend upon his town like locusts, and they had, but it had been at least a month since any reporters dared show their faces, mostly due to his uncooperative attitude toward the media. Until today.

Since he'd officially taken office three months ago, Kevin had prided himself on helping the town with the healing process. He was helping with his brother's wedding, which was the day after Christmas, a mere seven weeks away. He didn't have time for one more nosy woman.

Kevin was also healing himself from a marriage gone bad. His divorce had been finalized over a year ago, and he hadn't let himself think about another woman.

It was those eyes. He had to do something to get those big brown eyes out of his head.

* * *

Kyra stomped down the stairs of the courthouse, not believing what had just happened. She shoved the door opened and continued to her car. "That guy's gotta lot of damn nerve! 'Austin is that way,'" she mimicked in the sheriff's baritone voice. "It's a good thing he's good looking or I'd . . ." Her sentence trailed off as she had no idea what she would have done.

Simply because Sheriff Kevin Johnson was just that good looking. Disgusted that her feminine side was taking over her thought process, she unlocked her car and got inside. Since it was such a nice hot day and because she was in hell, she decided to put the top down on her BMW Z4.

She reached for her cell phone and dialed Auggie's cell number. He picked up on the second ring. "Don't tell me you've got a story already." He sounded almost nervous.

"No, I just met with the sheriff and he's not being cooperative."

"All you have to do is bat those big eyes at him and he'll be putty in your hand. I've never seen a man resist your charms yet."

Kyra huffed. "He's a pain in the ass. As soon as he found out I was a reporter and from Austin he told me leave town."

"You're not on your way back, are you?"

"Are you kidding? My dad would kill me for leaving a job undone. That's not the Chase way. This is going to take some planning."

"When have you ever backed down from a challenge? Who got the chancellor drunk and let him spill all his embezzling secrets to a tape recorder?

Come on, Kyra, I know you're better than this. You're admitting defeat already?"

Her back straightened at the challenge. "No, I didn't say I was throwing in the towel yet. I merely said he was being difficult. Besides, I don't think my charms will work on this man. I'm going need some additional ammo. That, my favorite boss, is where you come in."

Auggie laughed. "If my sixty-year-old memory serves me correctly, I'm also your only boss. What do you need?"

"I need some background info on the sheriff; maybe there's another way to get to him. Maybe he's a deadbeat dad or something." She knew the likelihood of that was next to nothing. She'd already run a preliminary background check on him and it came back squeaky clean.

"Give me a couple of hours and I'll get back to you."

"Deal." Kyra closed her tiny phone and started the car. But where was she going? This place wasn't like Austin. When she needed some information, she usually headed to the Lion's Den, the local bar across from Senate building. In Wright City, she didn't have that option. She didn't even know if this town had a bar or even a liquor store for that matter.

Her stomach rumbled and she decided the first priority should be food. She decided a town this small probably had a mom-and-pop eatery somewhere downtown. She drove down Main Street and smiled when she saw a small restaurant. By the looks of the people going into Jay's Diner, it had to have the best food in Texas. She parked her car, entered the restaurant, and inhaled the aroma of good-smelling food. Her mouth watered as a slender woman led her to a table.

Kyra took a seat and smiled at the woman. Her smooth chocolate skin was pulled tight across her face. Kyra put her in her late forties. She glanced at the menu, recognizing many of her childhood favorites. "I just don't know what to get," Kyra admitted, looking at the menu. "Everything sounds so good."

"I'm Jay, the owner. I can honestly say that everything on the menu is good. Haven't had many complaints."

"Why don't you pick something for me?"

Jay looked at her. "I know you're visiting from Austin." She winked at Kyra. "News travels fast. Besides, I don't think there are many cars like yours in Wright City. I make a killer omelet."

"That sounds wonderful. Can you make an egg white omelet with turkey bacon?"

Jay's face wrinkled up into a frown. "I don't serve no health food here," she stated plainly. "I don't make egg white anything unless you're recovering from a heart attack, which I know you aren't. I'm not even going to discuss what's wrong with turkey bacon. Coffee?"

Kyra wanted some flavored coffee really badly. It had been almost two hours since her last cup. Her body was going through caffeine withdrawal. It might make up for that remark about the egg white omelet. "Would you happen to have some flavored coffee?" She prepared herself for a speech on the evils of not drinking plain old coffee.

"I have regular, French roast, decaf, and hazelnut."

Kyra exhaled and felt her entire body relax. At least she could have her coffee. "I'll take some hazelnut, please."

Jay laughed, writing something on a pad. "You sound like a crack addict beggin' for the next hit. I'll send the coffee right out. If you want to read about our town, the local paper is on the counter. It's complimentary. You can take it with you."

It never occurred to Kyra that Wright City had enough news for a newspaper. She would definitely have to visit the office to dig through the vault for information. "Is it a daily?"

"Honey, this is Wright City. It comes out once a week. Wednesdays. So you're actually getting the news fairly fresh since today is Thursday." Jay walked to the kitchen.

Kyra glanced around the busy diner. It was a small storefront, but every seat was taken. Ordered chaos, her father would call it, but Kyra knew he would love this place. Before she could think about getting the newspaper, another young woman handed her a large mug of coffee and the paper.

At that moment, Kyra did feel like a crack addict. The aroma of the coffee made her forget about all her troubles, including one arrogant sheriff named Kevin Johnson.

CHAPTER 2

Kevin let out a tired breath when that woman finally left his office. "Damn woman. I don't need this right now," he complained to the room. "I have to plan EJ's bachelor party. I don't have time to deal with some busybody reporter."

His office door opened and Nicolas Fraser walked in with two large Styrofoam cups of coffee in his large hands. Nick was a new addition to the department, thanks to Kevin's promotion to sheriff. Nick set one cup on Kevin's desk and took a seat. "I can hear you mumbling in my office across the hall. I saw that fine woman stomping out of here doing exactly the same thing. Now that was a tall drink of water," Nick said in his slow Texas drawl.

Kevin waved away the coffee. After the morning he'd had, only something from the diner would satisfy him. "Yeah, damn reporter from Austin. I'm tired of these big-city types coming to my town and disrupting everything."

"Said the man from Houston," Nick drawled.

"You know, Kev, I was born and raised in Houston. I'm still amazed you talked me into coming to Wright City as your deputy sheriff."

Kevin stared at his friend. "I was born and raised here, I can say that. You know this was the best thing that ever happened to you. You've been here less than three months and all the women are after you."

It was Nick's turn to laugh. "But they're not going to catch me. I just got out of the marriage from hell; there's no way I'm stepping back into that fire."

"I hear you."

"No, man. The way sister-girl stomped outta here, I'd say she's coming back and this time she's going to be ready."

"Ready for what?" Kevin wondered what his friend was up to.

Nick shrugged his broad shoulders. "I'm just talking, Kev. You know me. I think I know everything. But joking aside, I'm glad you talked me into coming here and being your deputy sheriff. In three months, I've stopped smoking and cut way back on my drinking. It's a wonder what a divorce can do."

"Not to mention a DNA test," Kevin reminded his friend.

"True that. Imagine my ex trying to pass that kid off as mine and me stupid enough to fall for it. Good thing I got you in my corner."

Kevin didn't want to walk down memory lane with Nick. They'd both been unhappy in their marriages and not known it. Nick more so than Kevin. At least Kevin's failed marriage had to do with his law enforcement career, not an extramarital affair. "I know you'd do the same for me."

"When that spitfire comes back, I'll make sure to stand guard."

Kevin knew she'd be back. "She should be on her way back to Austin and the nearest mall."

"Oh, that was low. She might not be the stereotypical city girl. She might be one of those earthy chicks. You know, they can only wear clothes that come from the earth, and everything has to be organic."

"Carrying a Coach handbag, wearing a special edition Rolex, and driving a convertible BMW Z4, I somehow doubt that."

Nick leaned back in the chair, smiling. "So you checked out her ride. Nice."

Kevin shook his head. "Let's go to Jay's. I need some food." He hoped food would also help him forget those big brown eyes.

"What the heck is she still doing in Wright City?" Kevin all but yelled at Nick when he pulled up in front of the diner. He'd instantly spotted the little black sports car parked on Main Street. "She should be halfway to Temple by now."

"You'd think she'd drive thirty miles in fifteen minutes. Looks like she didn't take your hint very well," Nick chided. "Maybe you should remind her when you go inside. Show her who's boss in this town."

"You wish. You just want to see an argument between us, but it's not going to happen. I've dealt with these daddy's-girl types before. Come on, let's get this over with." Kevin eased out of Nick's SUV and slammed the door. The men walked inside the diner and were led to a table.

Kevin didn't pick up the plastic menu. He already knew what he wanted, and it was Jay's specialty: a loaded omelet complete with green peppers, sausage, onions, and shredded cheese, with an order of hash-brown potatoes. He'd have to run an extra five miles for eating something so decadent, but it was worth it. After he gave his order, he glanced around, looking for Kyra. He knew she was there; the small hairs rising on the back of his neck told him she was near.

"Man, just go over there and tell her to get out of your town or you'll arrest her for disturbing the peace. You're the sheriff. You can do that."

"And I'd be out of a job this afternoon," Kevin stated. "You know the mayor's rule about the press."

Nick nodded. "Yeah, treat them better than your momma."

"Exactly," Kevin said. "Now, I can deter her as long as I'm rude to her. She should give up and go home." Even as he said the words, he knew it was useless. Kyra Chase had already gotten under his skin and she wasn't even trying. Someone neared their table and, judging from his sweaty palms, he didn't have to guess who.

"Good morning, Sheriff Johnson," Kyra said, smiling. She had a copy of the local newspaper in her arms. "I was just reading about your brother's wedding announcement. Congratulations."

Kevin nodded. "Shouldn't you be at a mall or something? I told you there was no story. Why are you still here?"

She didn't take his bait. "Don't you get it? I'm here. I have a job to do and I'm going to do it. Deal with it." Without being invited, she took a seat at the table and extended her hand to Nick. "Hello, I'm Kyra Chase. I'm an investigative reporter from the *Austin Daily Chronicle*. I'm looking into the cocaine scandal of the summer."

"You cut right the chase," Nick said. "No pun intended."

She smiled at him. "None taken. In fact, I'd be surprised if you didn't make fun of my last name. I've heard them all, so nothing you could say would shock me." She glanced in Kevin's direction. "I don't think I've ever actually been in a city that only had two lanes downtown."

Kevin knew he probably deserved that barb, but for her to actually take a dig at his expense was just too much. "Why don't you get going? You could be back in Austin for high tea or something just as upscale."

To her credit, she didn't take the bite out of him he deserved. After the briefest nod, she rose. "Well, I'd better get back to my breakfast. It was nice meeting you, Nick. I'm sure our paths will cross again." Her eyes narrowed at Kevin. "Sheriff." She left the table.

"Man, you guys are like a comedy act. Dude, you got it bad," Nick joked. "You know, I think your eyes actually lit up."

"I didn't know I was sitting with a woman,"

Kevin said, hoping Nick would just drop the subject of Kyra Chase.

"I'm not a chick, but I know when you got it bad. And, brother, you got it bad."

Kevin shrugged as the waitress brought coffee to the table. "She just irritates the crap out of me. I'll be glad when she leaves."

Nick open four packets of sugar and emptied them into his coffee. "You know, there's one way to get rid of her in a hurry, but I know you won't do it." After he put too much cream in his coffee, he stirred it and finally took a sip.

"And what's that?" Kevin drank his delicious hazelnut coffee. coffee straight. No sugar, no cream.

"Give her what she wants and she'll be gone before you can say *USA Today.* All she wants is information to complete her story and she doesn't have to get it from you."

Kevin thought about Nick's words. "Good, then I don't have to put up with her."

The waitress brought their breakfast and finally all conversation about Kyra Chase ended. Kevin laughed as he dug into his omelet. "If I'd known this is all I needed to get you to shut up, I'd have told Jay to put a rush on it."

Nick saluted Kevin with his fork.

Well, that went just awful, Kyra thought as she sat down at her table. In her absence, the breakfast angels had arrived with her food. It looked and smelled delicious. She took a bite of the omelet and thought she'd died and gone to heaven.

"I bet that tastes better than some nasty egg white omelet," Jay said as she refilled Kyra's coffee mug.

Kyra laughed, getting caught with her hand in the omelet jar. "Yes, Jay. This is delicious."

Jay smiled. "I only serve the finest food in Texas. I saw you and the sheriff had a few words."

"Seems like I had all the words," Kyra grumbled, taking another bite of omelet. "He refuses to talk about the scandal."

Jay nodded. "He has his reasons."

That much Kyra had figured. "I'm sure we could come to some sort of compromise, if he weren't so damn defensive. I can't go back to Austin without a story. So I guess I'm just stuck until I can come up with a plan."

"I'm sure you already have one in the works," Jay said as she walked to another table.

She did, but she didn't want to let Jay in on it just yet. Besides, Kyra was the stranger in town, not Jay. Until she could find an ally, her plan was her own. She finished her breakfast uninterrupted and came up with an idea since the sheriff wasn't giving her any help. She'd start at the public library and go from there. But first she needed to find a place to stay while she researched the scandal. After Jay informed her of the Wright City Inn, Kyra was on her way to the interstate.

She had left the restaurant without another glance at the sheriff or the deputy sheriff. *No use adding fuel to that fire*, she mused. Their paths would cross again soon enough, and she had to make sure she was prepared.

She arrived at the motel in a few minutes. *It looks clean,* she thought as she got out of her car. When she walked inside, she noticed a woman behind the counter working on her laptop.

The lobby, if one could call it that, was small but efficient. A plate of brownies sat on the table in the center of the room. Flowers were everywhere: on the table, on the counter, just about anywhere there was a flat surface. Kyra inhaled and she was not disappointed. These were fresh flowers.

"Can I help you?" The woman closed her laptop, smiling at Kyra. "I know who you are. The whole town is talking about that little car of yours."

"I need a room for a few days," Kyra said, checking out the woman's salt-and-pepper microbraids.

"I'm Jemma Caldwell. I'm the owner." She extended her hand to Kyra. "Welcome to Wright City."

"I'm Kyra Chase."

Jemma looked her up and down. "What brings you to our little town?"

"I'm here on business," Kyra hedged.

"About the new Wal-Mart?"

"No, I'm a reporter from Austin. I'm here to investigate the cocaine scandal of last summer. I need to do some research since the sheriff isn't very helpful."

Jemma surprised her by laughing. "I bet he gave you the sharp side of his tongue once he found out you were a reporter."

Apparently the sheriff's hatred of reporters was known citywide. "Yes, he did. Any reason why he dislikes the press so much?"

"He has his reasons," Jemma said, opening her laptop. "You said you were going to be here a few days?"

Kyra nodded, knowing the subject of the sheriff was now closed. "Yes, two days at least."

Jemma reached under the counter and handed her a set of keys. "Room twelve. It's at the top of the stairs. We'll settle the bill when you check out. My credit card machine isn't working right now," she explained.

She took the keys and thanked Jemma. Since she hadn't brought many clothes with her she was going to have to shop for some. "Any shops in town?"

"Wal-Mart, and there's a few dress shops down-town. If you want to do some real shopping you'll have to go to Waco. That's about thirty miles away."

"Not right now. I'll have to settle for Wal-Mart. Can you tell me how to get to the library?"

Jemma stared at her for a moment. "Are you sure about the library?"

Kyra smiled, trying to reassure the motel owner. "Yes, I'm quite sure. I can always shop."

Wright City Public Library was housed in a 1950s-style single-story wood frame house. It was painted bright red with white trim, and reminded Kyra of a fairy-tale grandmother's house instead of a place that housed books. As Kyra entered the building, she could swear she smelled her favorite chocolate chip cookies baking. A short, plump woman with fiery red hair and pale white skin approached her.

"Yes, dear, can I help you?"

Kyra stared at the woman. She could have been the Irish representative for tourism with that thick accent. "Yes, I was wondering if I can have a look at your old newspapers. I'm trying to get some information on the cocaine scandal of the summer."

"Aye, yes, that was awful," she said, clasping a hand to her generous bosom. "It was just such a mess. Teenagers were dying left and right. We lost a grand citizen, not to mention a doctor and the sheriff. But you're not going to find the information you need here. You should talk to the lawyer."

As if that explained everything. "The lawyer?"

The woman laughed. "Let's start again. I'm Margaret Mallory. I'm the librarian and you're that reporter from Austin."

"Right. I'm Kyra Chase. I'm a reporter for the *Austin Daily Chronicle*."

Margaret held up a chubby hand. "Yes, dear, I know. My eldest, Sean, lives in Austin. I read the paper online when I get a chance. Sean wants me and my husband to move there next year when James retires, but I just don't like it there. Too many people, too little space, and don't get me started about my daughter-in-law."

Kyra knew how people could ramble on if she didn't put a stop to it, so she tried her best to guide the kindly woman back to the topic at hand. "You were saying something about a lawyer?"

Margaret grabbed Kyra's hand and pulled her down the hall to her office. "Yeah, James Hinton is who you need to see. He was Donald Cotton's lawyer, for all the good that did him. You might get a better picture of what happened from him than the watered-down version the papers were reporting."

Kyra nodded, staring at the plate of extra-large chocolate chip cookies. She knew her nose hadn't failed her. Did every place of business have a plate of dessert waiting for her? Too bad she'd just eaten or she'd have been devouring those cookies. *Focus*, she told herself, *focus*. "Are you saying there was something else going on, Mrs. Mallory?"

"I'm saying not everything came to light. And that's all I'm saying. I prayed to the saints that someone would dig up the actual truth."

Now she had Kyra's full attention and her adrenaline was raring to go. "Direct me to this James Hinton."

Finding a parking space downtown was much easier than finding one at the Austin Galleria. Kyra had her choice of spaces, unfortunately, none of them were directly in front of the law office of James Hinton. She chose the one in front of the Tea Shoppe and got out. She slipped her sunglasses on and started walking down the uncrowded sidewalk.

"Excuse me, ma'am," a man drawled, stepping toward her. He was dressed in a dark suit, and wore mirrored sunglasses. "I'm new to town and was hoping there was a Wal-Mart nearby."

Kyra looked him up and down. He looked more like an old, school G-man than a visitor to this small

Central Texas town. "Yes, it's just down Main Street. Just keep going west; you can't miss it."

"Thank you." He bowed his head, turned on his heels, and left.

Kyra shook her head and watched him get into a dark sedan. "Okay, that was extremely weird. I've been in town four hours and I know where Wal-Mart is," she grumbled as walked down the street. There was only one way into Wright City and you had to pass Wal-Mart to get there.

CHAPTER 3

James Hinton's office didn't look like an attorney's office. It certainly didn't look like her father's place. In fact, the tiny storefront was a just a few doors from the diner. The closet in her master bedroom was bigger than this office. She opened the door and walked inside.

It had a little more space than she imagined. It was deep rather than wide. The walls were lined with wooden filing cabinets. Had this man ever heard of a computer?

"Ms. Chase, I'm James Hinton. Margaret said you wanted to talk about Donald." He extended a slender, cocoa-brown hand to her.

Kyra sighed. Would she ever get used to people telling her business before she could? She shook Mr. Hinton's hand. "Please, call me Kyra." She glanced around for a chair, hoping he'd take the hint.

He instantly pulled up a padded leather chair that was hiding in the corner. "James. Please have a seat, Kyra."

After she was seated, James took a seat behind his untidy desk. No secretary. His desk was the only one in the room. He was dressed nicely in a dark suit.

"Am I keeping you from something?" she asked.

James cleared his throat. "Nothing that won't keep." He caught her perusal of his clothes. "I've always prided myself on looking nice. I'm sure you're expecting Matlock in a cheap suit, but not here." He laughed as he reclined in his leather chair. "Now, how can I help you?"

Might as well get down to business. She reached in her handbag and retrieved her tape recorder. "You can tell me what kind of person Donald Cotton was. I've heard bits and pieces, but since you were his attorney, I thought you'd know more."

"Yes, I do. I knew Donald for about forty years. I moved here just after I'd gotten out of the Army. My wife was from here and convinced me to move here after my hitch was up. I met Donald right after we joined the church. He was one of the best friends I ever had."

Kyra nodded. That jibed with all the comments she'd gotten so far about this man. "What was he like?"

"He'd give you the shirt off his back, if that's what you needed. He probably helped just about everyone in this town at one time or another. Black, white, blue, it didn't matter to Donald. He just liked people, until that devil came to town."

That perked up Kyra's reporter's ears. "Devil?" She'd heard something about The Tank's club owners being involved with Cotton's death, but that would be two devils, not one. "Who?"

"Brenda Hamilton."

Kyra was more than a little confused. "Could you explain?"

"I could, but it wouldn't be ethical. Since Regan is the heir to Donald's estate and she's Brenda's daughter," he said ruefully. "I can say this: if Brenda Hamilton hadn't ever come to Wright City, this place would have been so much better and Donald would still be alive." He stopped speaking, holding whatever opinions he had about her at bay behind a closed mouth. She hated that.

Kyra felt there was a story waiting to be told and she was going to have to start at the beginning of the mystery to get the whole story. With her adrenaline pumped and raring to do some serious snooping, she stood abruptly, grabbing her tape recorder. "Thank you, James, for all your help. I appreciate the information."

He stood as well, nodding. "Anytime. If you need any more information, just let me know. I loved Donald like a brother."

Kyra left the office with the nagging feeling that James had a little more at stake than some brotherly love.

Since the story developing was as slow as molasses, Kyra decided to get acquainted with the town she was stuck in for the moment. She'd noticed a tea shop earlier, and how out of place it looked in the small town. Or was that her overactive imagination again?

Her cell phone rang as she walked past the small

storefront. She dug it out of her purse as she continued her walk. "Kyra Chase."

"Well, I've got bad news," Auggie said.

She knew what he was going to say and decided to save him the trouble. "Don't tell me, you came up empty on the wonderful sheriff?"

"How did you know?" Auggie huffed. "You know, I thought if I went back far enough there'd be something in his youth. Squeaky clean. Did all the right things. Went to college in Houston, became a Houston police officer, married, shot, divorced. Even the ex still likes him. They're on friendly terms. No daddy's babies out there. Nothing. His old boss still likes him and would take him back in a heartbeat."

She had a feeling this was going to happen. Perhaps she'd been around too many politicians to accept that Kevin was a clean as he was. But here was confirmation that he was doing exactly what he was trying to do. He was trying to help the town heal and would do everything in his power to stop her from doing her job. "Thanks, Auggie, I know you tried." She sighed. "I guess I'll just have to spread a little sugar on the sour sheriff."

She ended her call and continued walking. Downtown Wright City was quiet, being that it was Thursday afternoon. She passed an arts and crafts store, shoe repair, and a dress store. Across the street she noticed a sandwich shop, a furniture store, a temp agency, and Wright City National Bank. Then she saw it. Aunt Minnie's Antiques. Her mother loved antiques. She remembered many weekends spent shopping at antique malls around Austin. She had to go inside.

"Can I help you?" a not-so-old woman asked her. She had platinum blond hair pulled back into a ponytail. "I'm Susan Cosgrove, the owner. I know you're the reporter. My husband works in the mayor's office," she explained.

Kyra looked around the shop. "No, right now I'm just getting acquainted with the town. I love antique shops."

Susan walked behind her. "I'm open on Tuesdays, Thursdays, and Saturdays. I usually know anything going on in town, too. I know you're here about last summer. So sad. What a lot of secrets."

Kyra picked up an old silver picture frame. "How much?"

Susan shrugged. "Ten bucks."

Kyra dug her wallet out of her purse and gave the woman eleven dollars. "This will be perfect for my mom's picture."

Susan nodded and walked to the register. "I have plenty more if you're into that old stuff. No one around here appreciates craftsmanship of the sixties."

"Do you know anything about the tea shop?"

Susan motioned for her to come to the counter, so she wouldn't have to shout. "It's run by Clare Billingsworth. After her husband, Chad, ran off with the waitress at the Chicken Hut on the outskirts of town, Clare opened the shop. Chad never did love her, only loved her for her money. When Clare started putting conditions on the cash, he took off."

"That's too bad," Kyra said. "What happened?"

"The restaurant has flourished. Chad brought

his sorry behind back a few times, but each time she tells him no."

"That's good."

Susan bagged the frame and handed it to her. "I don't know why she doesn't take him back now. He's sorry for what he done."

Kyra shrugged. "You never know what really happened. Maybe she wasn't happy in the first place and now she is." Kyra had been down that road herself and didn't plan on making a return trip.

After she left the antique place, she decided to visit the tea shop for a light dinner. She looked forward to ending her first night in Wright City by going to bed early. Maybe with enough sleep she'd come up with a fantastic plan to have the sheriff eating out of her hand. She walked inside the shop and loved the place instantly. It would never compare to Jay's place, but it was a diversion.

"Can I help you, Ms. Chase?" a slightly chunky woman of about fifty asked. Her blond hair was fashioned into a swing bob and framed her face. She was dressed in jeans and a white cotton shirt with a black apron on top of it. She didn't look like the mousy woman Susan had described.

"It seems like everyone knows me before I can utter my name," Kyra said, extending her hand. "Yes, that's me. Please, call me Kyra."

"Clare Billingsworth," she said, smiling back at Kyra. "I'm sure Susan already gave you all my gossip. Would you like a seat?"

"Yes, please." She followed the woman to a seat. Being that it was late afternoon, there were a few customers in the place. "This place is nice. I wasn't expecting a tea shop in this little town."

Clare handed her a plastic menu. "Yes, I get that a lot. I like being different. Right after my divorce, I went to England to visit my daughter and fell in love with high tea. I learned all about scones, clotted cream, and teas."

Kyra nodded, reading the menu. She couldn't make up her mind about what to try first. She glanced at the specials and instantly made a decision. "I'll have the Cotton special."

Clare smiled. "That's my biggest seller."

"Is it named for Mr. Cotton who died last summer?"

"Yes, it is. If it weren't for Donald, I don't know what would have happened to me after my divorce. He convinced me to open this place. He was such a good friend."

Kyra sighed. "He sounds like a nice man. The story I'm researching has something to do with him and his untimely demise."

Clare wiped a tear from her face. "You make sure you write about how kind he was."

"Definitely. What's in a Cotton special?"

"All his favorites: chicken salad on wheat bread, potato salad, a slice of lemon icebox pie, and Darjeeling tea."

Kyra wished she could have met this man. There were so few true black male role models. From the information she'd gotten so far, she realized the world had lost a great man.

*   *   *

Friday morning, Kevin thought his world had returned to normal. It had been almost twenty-four hours since his last run-in with the meddlesome reporter. Maybe he would have an easy day leading into the weekend.

He was looking through paperwork needing his attention when Nick sauntered into his office and took a seat. He stared at Kevin, but said nothing, which drove Kevin nuts.

Kevin looked at his friend. "All right, I'll bite. What's up?"

Nick shifted restlessly in his seat. "Well, a call came in."

"Okay. That's what we do."

"It was from the store manager at Wal-Mart. A strange car has been camped in the parking lot since yesterday afternoon. He wants us to check it out."

Kevin nodded, not really seeing the problem. "Send Derek or Josh. Either one of them can handle a simple abandoned vehicle." Kevin resumed reading his report.

Nick cleared his throat. "Well, there is a hiccup to that. Derek just called back to say that the man in the car was dead. Two bullets to the head."

"What? You walk in here like there's nothing wrong and we've got a dead body. Who's this guy?"

"He wasn't a local. His name was Samuel Andelli and his driver's license had an Austin address."

"Austin? As is Kyra Chase, Austin."

"Think there's a connection?"

Kevin hated to admit it, but his gut told him

there was a direct correlation between the nosy reporter and the dead man, since they had arrived in Wright City within hours of each other. "If the sharp pain in my stomach is any indication, I'd say yes." Kevin stood and grabbed his Stetson and the keys to his truck. "Come on, let's go look at the stiff. Then we're going to pay Ms. Chase a visit."

Nick stood and rubbed his large hands together. "Oh, this is going to be so good."

That morning, Kyra woke to the annoying sound of her cell phone ringing. Why was someone calling her this early on a Friday? It rang again as she sat up in bed and took her off eye mask. She answered it before it could ring again. "Hello?"

"Is that all you have to say?" Kory Reed, her best friend since college, all but yelled into the phone. "I heard you were out of the office for an undetermined amount of time, according to Auggie. I get back from hearing the liars in DC and this is what I have to come back to? More lies!" She continued reading Kyra the riot act.

Kyra laughed. Kory would always be a drama queen, no matter how inconsequential the situation. "Kory, breathe."

"I know. I know. But, girl, you know it's some real nuts out there. Auggie won't tell me where you are. Neither will your dad. Where are you?"

Kyra wanted to tell someone, but remembered Auggie's instructions and the serious look on his face. "On assignment."

"Not you too," Kory huffed. "I can get that from Auggie. Is it that big a story?"

"It could be," Kyra admitted. "I just don't know who's feeding me false information. What are you doing?"

Kory sighed. "Not much. Working on the have column. Auggie is riding me to get it in early." She always referred to the society column as the haves column and the people who read it as the have-nots. "You know the mayor's daughter is getting married next month. Who plans a big wedding in downtown Austin on Christmas Eve?"

"The mayor's not-so-pretty daughter," Kyra said. "That's one way to make sure you're on the front page of the society section. How else could she guarantee all that coverage? I just hope this marriage lasts longer than her last one."

"We're betting six months; five months longer than the last."

Kyra chuckled. "Put me down for three months."

Kory laughed. "Okay, so you're not going to tell me where you are. Is it a place with a lot of gorgeous men?"

She thought of the sheriff. Yes, Kevin was all kinds of sexy, and so was his deputy. "You could say that."

"Yummy, eye candy. Any prospects?"

"No, afraid not. That's more your department. Men tend to run away from me."

"Only because you make them. Quit being so damn honest all the time."

"Sorry, that's just way I roll. No time for lies. Talk to you later."

Men wanted only two things from Kyra: her fa-

ther and her money. Two things she wasn't prepared to give up.

When Kevin and Nick arrived at the scene, the
coroner was already there waiting for them. Kevin
parked near the crime scene and got out. He in-
spected the car and immediately noticed the shots
were clean. The glass hadn't even shattered, which
meant the shooter knew exactly how to aim the
gun. It also meant the caliber was small. He
glanced at the nondescript victim and the interior
of the car. A few scraps of paper littered the floor-
boards. He picked up a scrap that caught his eye.
Andelli wasn't much to look at. He wouldn't stand
out in a crowd. Medium height, dark hair, dark
eyes.

"Sheriff," Derek Hall said in his Texas twang,
"the car is a rental out of Austin. I have a cousin
with the FBI and she's at the Austin office."

Kevin pressed his lips together, trying not to tell
his deputy to hurry with the story. Derek was
known for not telling a concise story. "What does
your cousin say?"

"Well, I got her to run Andelli's name through
the computer to see if the government had anything on him."

"What did you find out?"

"It's more like what I didn't find out. He has
some kind of security clearance. My cousin, Julie,
says the clearance he has is for NSE." The National
Security Evaluators was a group of government assassins who normally worked outside of the United
States in the name of freedom.

"Why is someone from NSE here? Rumor has it that agency is more like an extermination team." Kevin couldn't keep the sarcasm out of his voice. "Why on earth would a government hitter be here?"

Derek nodded, his bright blue eyes staring at Kevin. "That was the odd thing. Julie says sometimes they take contract jobs."

"So he does a little killing on the side?"

Derek nodded. "Yeah. Jules is going to get back to me if she finds out if he was working. That would be the only explanation of him being here. But who would he actually be after?"

Kevin had a pretty good idea, but he didn't know why. He would soon. He walked over to the coroner. He'd known Justin Barker most of his life. "So what do you think, Justin?" He watched the man assess the body.

Justin stood and looked Kevin in the eye. "I think this man has been executed. I watch those mafia shows, I know how this works. The victim has two nine-millimeter bullets in his head. This was very professional. He's been dead almost twenty hours. I'd say he bought it yesterday about five." He pointed to Andelli's forehead. "See the entry wound?"

Kevin nodded. "Yeah, it's a clean shot."

"If you look really close you can see where the second bullet entered his brain. I don't know why they would waste a second shot. The first one probably did him in." Justin signaled for the requisite body bag. Soon his assistants were loading Andelli's corpse onto the stretcher. "I'll send you the preliminary autopsy report this afternoon."

"Thanks, Justin." Kevin signaled for Nick to join him at his truck.

"What's up, Kev?"

"We're going to question the reporter. Something doesn't sound right, and I think Ms. Chase has the answers."

CHAPTER 4

K yra had just emerged from the shower when she heard an angry knock on her hotel room door. She secured the sash on her silk bathrobe and answered the summons. Never in her wildest dreams would she have imagined the sheriff and his deputy in her doorway.

"Ms. Chase, I'd like to ask you a few questions," Sheriff Johnson said rather deadpan, as if women answered the door dressed in a bathrobe and nothing else every day. "You think you could spare a few minutes before your shower?"

That man has a whole lot of nerve. She looked him up and down and liked what she saw. He was sexy. *Damn it.* There was something incredibly erotic about a cowboy of color. "Actually, I just stepped out of the shower. Could you give me about five minutes to dress in something more appropriate than my birthday suit?"

Sheriff Johnson merely looked at her like she was the scum of the earth. "Three." He tipped his hat at her. "Ma'am." He closed the door in her face.

Normally, Kyra would have opened the door and read him the riot act for being such an ass. But she only had a few minutes to get dressed or she was sure he would arrest her for obstructing justice. After slipping on some undergarments, she reached for a pair of jeans and a T-shirt. She was just slipping on a pair of casual shoes when a very hard, determined knock nearly scared her out of her mind.

She stomped to the door and jerked it open. "You know, you could use a few etiquette lessons," she snarled at him as she waved him and his deputy inside.

Sheriff Johnson looked at her. "Really? I guess that's your department, huh? Those high-society rules don't apply here, Ms. Chase. I'm within my rights."

She noticed both men were still standing. They were waiting for her to sit down! Kyra sighed. Southern gents to the end. She sat on her made-up bed. "I'm sorry I only have one chair. One of you gentlemen will have to sit on the bed with me." She smiled as Nick quickly claimed the chair.

The sheriff cleared his throat and glanced around the room. He didn't take a seat. "Ms. Chase, how long are you planning on staying in Wright City?"

"Call me. Kyra. The length of my stay depends on you, Sheriff. You give me what I need, I could be gone today."

He ignored her sarcasm. "All right, Kyra. Do you know Samuel Andelli?"

"No, should I?"

"Yes, you should. He's from Austin," the sheriff said.

Kyra counted to ten. "Contrary to popular belief, not everyone in Austin knows one another. There are over a million people in Austin. What makes you think I would know this man?"

"You were seen speaking to him yesterday. Medium height, medium build, dark hair, dark eyes, dark suit."

Kyra didn't see how one thing led to another. "Okay, someone asked me directions."

"To Wal-Mart?"

"Yeah. He said he was new in town."

"And he didn't look familiar to you?"

The sheriff was riding her last good nerve and she was ready to throw him off. "For the last time, I didn't know this man. If I'd have known him I would have told him to get out of this town quick."

Sheriff Johnson took the insult for what it was worth. "There's nothing wrong with Wright City. I was born and raised here. My deputy sheriff is from Houston and he loves it here. Right, Nick?"

"Yes, sir, Sheriff. I love this place. Great for healing," Nick said, winking at Kyra.

Kyra laughed. "Okay, now that the tourism board is finished, what makes you think I know this dead guy? Did he work at my newspaper?"

"No, your name was scribbled on a piece of paper we found in his car. Did your conversation yesterday involve trading names?"

No, he did not. "What kind of girl do you think I am? You think I just hand my name out to anyone

I meet? Well, I don't. I don't know this guy and have no idea how he got my name."

The sheriff looked grimly at her face, as if he was discerning whether she was telling the truth. "Are you running from something in Austin?"

Kyra gasped at the insinuation. She hated playing the parent card, but the arrogant sheriff left her no options. "Do you know who my father is?"

He shook his head. "Is this a joke or something?"

"No, Sheriff. My father is Chandler Chase. And before you say something insane like, 'duh, who's that?' I will tell you. My father is one of the top defense attorneys in the state. He mostly handles celebrities, namely athletes and high-profile politicians, and businessmen. I was raised in the limelight of Austin, and with Chandler Chase being my father, running is not an option."

"Well, I guess you told us, huh? You might want to give Daddy a ring to tell him that I will be calling. Better yet, you might want to retain him for counsel."

"You're not seriously going to charge me with that idiot's murder just because he had my name on a piece of paper. If you look in my car, I have your name on a piece of paper too. If you turn up dead tomorrow will I be charged with your murder as well?"

He actually smiled. It was a small, tight smile, but one nonetheless. "If I turn up dead tomorrow, then yes, you should be charged. You're the only one in town with a grudge against me."

"Are you sure?"

Nick erupted in laughter. "Okay, guys. That's

enough. You're making my side hurt from laughing with those questions." He looked in the sheriff's direction. "How about I take over and you can take a break?"

The sheriff nodded and headed for the door. "Be my guest." To Kyra he said, "Don't make any plans to leave town." And he was gone.

Nick sat on the bed. "Look, Kyra, the cards are pretty much stacked against you, circumstantially speaking. We both know your dad would have the case thrown out in a hot minute. Until we sort this mess out, just chill, okay?"

Kyra narrowed her gaze on the handsome deputy. Now that she'd had a good look at him, she guessed he was much closer to forty than the sheriff. He was still nice to look at. "In other words, you're asking me to cut the sheriff some slack and not be such a reporter."

Nick smiled. "I said it with only the best intentions. You need a story, and the sheriff wants the town to move on from the cocaine scandal. I'll help you in any way I can. I do like it here and don't want to see anyone else get hurt. This guy getting whacked liked that tells me something bigger is going on."

Kyra didn't like the sound of that. "What do you think is actually going on?"

Nick looked at her. "Since you and the dead man arrived in town within hours of each other, and your name, physical description, and license plate number were on a piece of paper in the strange man's car, my cop brain tells me this was more than coincidence. I think that man was sent to kill you."

"Nick, you can't be serious!" Kyra sat on the bed, just as her feet decided they didn't want to hold her up anymore. "Why would anyone want to hurt me? Yeah, I did an exposé a while back, but that's old news now. Chancellor Carson Jacobs is on house arrest awaiting his trial."

"Due to your news story, right?" Nick sat down on the bed beside her. "I think someone in his camp might have been sent to take you out. Don't you have to testify?"

"No, Daddy took my deposition so I wouldn't have to. Plus, the state has copies of all my research. So it's a done deal. Jacobs is going to jail."

"Revenge," Nick said coldly. "I could see him still sending someone after you. But the one thing I don't get is who killed the killer? And why?"

Kyra didn't like the direction of the conversation. "Oh, great, so now you think there's someone else out there gunning for me too. This was supposed to be a simple assignment, and it has turned into the biggest disaster of my career." She took a deep breath, deciding to channel some of that negative energy elsewhere. She exhaled and repeated the process.

"Kyra, are you having some kind of anxiety attack?"

She opened her eyes and stared at him. "No, I'm doing some breathing exercises to help calm my nerves." She breathed in and out. "I'm forcing all the negative energy out from my body when I exhale and allowing positive energy to enter when I inhale."

Nick laughed. "Better not let Kevin hear you say that. He's not one for stars, karma, and all that

earthy stuff. He'll think you need a psych evalua-
tion."

"If it will help get me out of this town, I will
gladly agree," she said dryly. This time she actually
meant it. "But I know I can't leave. Check that, I
won't leave. I have to find out what's going on and
if I brought the trouble with me."

Nick nodded. "That's the way you do it. I know
enough about your dad to know you'd never walk
away from something unfinished."

Kyra's brain buzzed with possibilities. She'd
have to make different arrangements if she was
going to be stuck in this town for who knew how
long. The room was fine, but she was going to
need more space. "Yes, Nick, I'm going to stay
until this is finished. You know anyone who'd be
willing to rent a house or something to me?"

Nick shrugged. "I don't personally, but I bet the
sheriff does." Nick smiled slyly.

Kyra sighed. "Oh, please, let's not bother him
with this." The last thing she wanted was to have
another conversation with Mr. Personality. "I'll ask
around. This is between us, Nick, okay?"

He smiled. "Sure, Kyra. This should be fun."

"What?"

"You'll see." Nick walked to the door. "Let me
know if you need any help." He opened the door
and left.

Now what was she supposed to do? She had protection, but it was in her car. She'd been in tight
scrapes before, but she'd never had anyone ready
to kill her on command. She could let the fear
rule her or she could take it by the horns. She decided to control her own destiny. Kyra reached for

the antique hotel phone and called the front desk. When was the last time she'd used a rotary phone? Jemma answered the phone on the first ring and Kyra didn't waste any time asking for help. "I'm going to be in town longer than I had originally planned. I was wondering if you knew of any place I could rent."

"Not many places around here," Jemma said. "Most of the apartments are snapped up quickly. If you don't mind living in a house where two people died, I know of a place."

"Good. I'll be right down." The dead didn't bother her; it was the living that did. Kyra ended the call, grabbed her purse, and headed downstairs. Luckily, the sheriff and Nick were already gone when she made it to the reception area.

Jemma was sitting behind the desk, working diligently on the laptop, talking on her cell phone, and checking in a guest. *Talk about a multitasker*, Kyra thought. Jemma smiled when she noticed Kyra standing at the counter. "Well, that was fast," she said, handing the weary traveler his room key.

Kyra nodded, needing to get the show on the road. "Yes, if I'm going to rent a place, I'm going to need to get some things to make it seem a little more like home. Now, who got killed at this place?"

Jemma smiled at her. "Actually, he was a sweet man and is part of the story you're digging up. His niece owns the house now and she's renting it out. She lives in Fort Worth, but she's still in town. She was hurt in a kidnapping attempt a few months ago," she explained. "She's recuperating at her mom's. I'll give you the address." Jemma scribbled a few lines on her personal stationary and handed it to Kyra.

"Thanks, Jemma. I really like it here at the hotel, but it looks like I'm going to be here awhile, so I'm going to need more space."

Jemma laughed. "Probably for all those clothes you big-city women own. I'll never understand why a person needs so many clothes."

Kyra diplomatically decided not to reply to Jemma's ramblings. Kyra was one of those women who had a closet full of clothes and always complained of needing more. "I better call this Ms. Hamilton." She waved as she walked to the door.

"Tell her I said hello," Jemma called.

Once in the safety of her car, Kyra relaxed. She had to get used to this small town thing. These people definitely believed in saying what was on their minds. It was like being around her father non-stop.

Kyra dialed the number and made an appointment with Regan Hamilton to see the house in an hour. Plenty of time to get her phone call with her father over with. No one kept Chandler Chase waiting, not even his only child.

Her father picked up his private line on the first ring. "Chase."

"Hey, Dad." Kyra mentally cursed herself for such a horrible opening. "I thought you'd be in court or something today. I was going to leave you a message." She knew he was representing one of the area's professional basketball players on a domestic violence charge.

"She dropped the charges. Are you all right?"

That's weird, she thought. Her father seldom

asked about her welfare. Why would he now? "Yes, Dad, I'm fine. I thought the paper said the guy hit her in front of witnesses."

"Another case of gold digging," her father said on a laugh. "The truth came out in her deposition and the threat of putting her on the witness stand. She was trying to get back at him for breaking up with her. I'll never understand these women. Where are you?"

"On assignment," Kyra told her father.

"Good."

"Good?" Kyra was surprised at her father's voice. He actually sounded relieved. "Well, I've run into some trouble. I'll be staying here until I can get this mess straightened out." She hated to tell him the last part. "Oh, by the way, the sheriff may call you."

"Sheriff Kevin Johnson," her father announced.

Why was she surprised? "He already called? I can't believe this. That idiot actually thinks I'm connected to a seedy hit man. What did he tell you?"

Her father laughed. "You sound like my clients, baby girl. He didn't tell me anything, I was on a conference call. But by the tone in his short message, I could tell the sheriff would prefer it if you left town. What did you do to him?"

Typical Chandler Chase. Always on his high horse and blaming her before he heard all the facts. "I'm a reporter, so he hates me just because. I know he doesn't want me here, but I'm his closest link to the murdered hit man. So I'm going to stay here until I figure out what exactly is going on."

"You know a Chase never runs," Chandler said.

"I know, Daddy. No matter how awful the sheriff is to me, I'll stay until my job is done. Besides, Auggie will have my hide if I came back without a sensational story."

"That's my girl. Don't let some hick sheriff run you out of town. I can do a little snooping around so you can have some ammo on him."

"That's a nice thought, but I already checked him out and Auggie couldn't find a thing, either. He's as clean as a whistle."

"Oh, that's too bad. I hate it when that happens. Maybe I should come and visit this sorry excuse for a town? Maybe I should have a word with the sheriff?"

"No, Daddy. I'm already having enough trouble with the sheriff. I don't need you down here, too."

"All right, just be careful. Don't trust anyone. You still got the gun I gave you last year?"

"Yes, it's in my glove compartment," Kyra lied. She hated guns, and never used the nine mil. It was beautiful as guns went, but she still hated it. The SIG Sauer was locked in a box in the trunk of her car.

Her father cleared his throat. "I'm going to be busy the next few days. I'll call you from my spare cell phone. Don't call me. I have to go. I'll be in touch. I got a press conference announcing the charges have been dropped against my client."

Kyra turned her phone off. Just once she'd like to hear her father say, "I love you," like a normal parent. She headed for the address Regan had given her. It was a street of one-story frame houses, probably much older than her thirty-five years.

The old neighborhood seemed inviting. A stranger would never have known that two murders had been committed on this quiet street.

She stopped at 315 Third Street and parked behind a dark blue Chevy TrailBlazer. This had to be Regan's SUV, Kyra hoped as she got out of her car. She glanced around at her surroundings just to be on the safe side, praying another hit man wasn't waiting behind the immaculately manicured hedges for her. No, no hit man in sight. But how would she know? It wasn't like it was on TV.

A slender woman met her as she approached the front door. Her smile was bright and she wasn't alone. An older woman stood behind her, inspecting Kyra from head to toe. The younger woman extended her hand. "I'm Regan Hamilton, Ms. Chase." She pointed to the woman behind her. "This is my mom, Brenda. Please come inside."

Was this the women James had referred to? Kyra followed the women inside and noticed that Regan limped. Maybe not limped, but she definitely favored her right side. Regan's mother helped her into a chair. There were two other chairs in the room, but Brenda sat next to her daughter. "Regan was in an accident a few months ago and she's still healing. She really shouldn't be out of bed, but she's hardheaded." Brenda smiled at her daughter.

"Mom, please. I'm sorry, Ms. Chase, but she's right. I'm not supposed to be out of bed, but I wanted to personally show you the place. Jemma told me why you were in town."

"Please call me Kyra. I know about the deaths and it doesn't bother me. I'm a reporter."

"From Austin, according to Jemma."

"Yes. I need to stay in town longer than I had originally planned. The sheriff seems to think I had something to do with the recent trouble, so I need to stick around. Is he always so . . . thorough?"

Regan smiled. "Yes, that's Kevin. He takes his responsibilities very seriously. Elias is the same way. That's Kevin's brother. He's my fiancé."

"Congratulations."

"Thank you. Elias and I are very excited. We're getting married the day after Christmas."

"Does he live here as well?"

Regan shook her head. "No, he's in Dallas. Our story would take way too long to tell you. Let's get back to the house. Mom will show you around and answer any questions you may have. It's unfurnished, as you can see."

Kyra loved the house instantly. The new hardwood floors shined. Love had gone into each new fixture of the tiny house. The small kitchen had all new appliances, along with new cabinets, and a large stainless steel sink. The floors had been also redone with black-and-white ceramic tiles, reminding Kyra of an old-school diner. Never in a million years would she have thought she'd be willing to live in a two-bedroom house with no garage, no media room, and only one bathroom! "I'll take it. Is it first and last, with a deposit?" Kyra reached into her purse for her checkbook.

Regan shook her head. "Since you don't know how long you'll be here, why don't we play it by ear? How about we do month to month?"

Kyra was taken aback by Regan's attitude. In

Austin, any landlord would tack on more and more charges because she didn't know how long she was going to be in town. "Thank you, Regan. I appreciate your understanding my situation."

"Actually, you're the first person who actually wanted to rent the place since it's been refurbished. I love this house and practically grew up here. After my uncle died, I couldn't bear to sell it." Regan darted a glance at Brenda.

Kyra felt the love in the house by the way Regan had redone the place. "I understand. My dad is the same about our house in Austin. My mom passed away last year and it's really too big for just him, but he says he can't bear to part with it. Too many memories."

"Do you have any other questions?"

Kyra noticed Regan's skin had started to look funny. Her medium brown skin now had a green undertone, which meant she was seconds from tossing her cookies, or passing out. *Probably too much exertion for her*, Kyra mused. "Just point me to the nearest furniture store."

Regan's mom finally spoke. "We'll have to continue this later, when Regan has more strength. Why don't we do this Monday at Jay's Diner around lunchtime? That'll give me three days to get the papers ready for you."

Kyra nodded, noticing that Regan had slumped over in her chair. If her breathing weren't so labored, Kyra would have sworn that Regan was dead. "Sure thing, Mrs. Hamilton. Is she all right?"

"She will be in just a few minutes." Brenda reached inside her large purse and pulled out a bottle of water and some pills. She patted Regan's face until she opened her eyes and gave her the medicine.

Kyra felt helpless. She wanted to help them but didn't know how. Brenda seemed to have the situation well under control. Regan was once again alert. Groggy, but alert. Kyra wondered about at the extent of Regan's injuries and what had caused them.

Kevin sat at his desk, once again in control of his world. He didn't know what it was about Kyra Chase, but that woman got under his skin like no other. Not even his ex-wife, Ravena.

He reached for the file of the murdered man and sighed. He'd seen enough dead bodies during the summer, but it looked like things were just getting started. Samuel Andelli was a government assassin. So who killed him? Was it competition? Was he actually going to have to hunt for another killer?

"Sheriff, there's a phone call on line one and I think you'd better take it," Nick said, standing in the doorway. He was wearing a sly smile. "It's Chandler Chase returning your call, and he doesn't sound too happy."

Kevin picked up the phone, and motioned for Nick to get back to work. "This is probably going to take awhile. I'm sure he's ready to send the coalition down here to get his little princess out of this mess."

Nick shook his head. "Man, you got it bad." He left the doorway without another word.

Kevin pulled the phone to his ear. "Hello, Mr.

Chase. I'm Sheriff Kevin Johnson. Thank you for returning my call so quickly."

"First, you can tell me what you're doing to keep my daughter safe. Second, you can explain to me why you're questioning her like she's some sort of common murder suspect."

Kevin rubbed his head. Yes, this was going to be a really long conversation. Chase had a reputation for cutting through all the crap and getting to the heart of the matter. In this case, the heart was Kyra. "She's not being held against her will, sir. I only inquired as to how long she'd be in town. I'm within my legal rights. She's integral to the case."

"And what are you doing to keep her safe?"

"I have to follow up on a few leads, but she's safe here," Kevin lied. He had nothing, no idea why Andelli was there to kill Kyra.

"What does this hitter have to do with anything?" Chase drilled him like a witness for the other side.

"I was hoping you could tell me. Any information you could tell me, Mr. Chase, would be helpful." Kevin had a feeling this killing had ties to the capital city.

"I have some of the best investigators in the state on my payroll and I haven't turned up anything yet. Granted, I've only had about an hour, but the minute I get something solid, I'll get back to you. Meanwhile, you'll keep an eye on my daughter if you value your job. And if you fail you will lose more than just your job."

CHAPTER 5

After getting the dial tone from Kyra's famous father, Kevin decided to cut out early. He needed space to think this thing through. He could study reports at home and that was exactly what he was planning to do. He'd been the official sheriff for exactly three months and each month had been filled with the cocaine scandal he was trying to forget.

He grabbed his briefcase and headed for Nick's office. Nick was surfing the Net, probably looking at his stock quotes, his normal activity. "You know they say a watched pot never boils," Kevin said.

Nick laughed. "I'm not checking quotes, Kevin. I was looking for anything on Andelli. There has to be some kind of tie to Kyra."

"And I'm sure no one would post that information on the Net." Kevin leaned against the doorway. "I wouldn't trust anything I found in cyberspace."

"I know. I have some friends in the system who

can verify anything I can find. Which hasn't been very much. I can't even find anything on him on the underground sites and don't ask me how I know about them."

Kevin held up his free hand. "Okay, man. I'm heading home. I have the coroner's report on Andelli. Maybe something will jump out at me. There has to be something we're overlooking. Either that, or Kyra is lying to us."

"You know the latter is not true. You actually would love it if she was gone back to Austin, but I have it on good authority that she's still in town."

He didn't like the smug look on Nick's chiseled face, but Kevin wasn't going to rise to the occasion, at least not now. "Well, as long as she's out of my hair, everything will be fine." Kevin headed for the stairs.

His cell phone rang as he exited the courthouse. He glanced at the caller ID, and was thankful it was his brother, Elias. He was enjoying his new post as Deputy Manager of the Dallas branch of the DEA. "Hey, EJ, what's up? I know it's Friday, but you don't usually get here until late. Don't tell me you on your way down here already." Elias was also engaged to Regan Hamilton, who was in Wright City recuperating from an accident. Elias usually came to visit her every weekend, since moving around wasn't an option for Regan.

He laughed. "No, I just talked to Regan and she finally rented the house to some stranger in town. I'm just protecting my woman. You know anything about some reporter named Kyra Chase?"

"Yes, I know that woman," he said through gritted teeth. "She's been in this town two days and already there's been a murder." He unlocked his truck and tossed his case onto the passenger seat.

"What? Who?"

"That's the crazy part. He was a major hitter sent down here to kill her. Andelli."

"Did she kill him?"

Kevin slid behind the steering wheel and closed the door. The air had a bite of a fall breeze so he didn't have to immediately start the air conditioner. He wanted to be able to talk freely with his brother and he could in the security of the truck. "No, but I feel like there's some kind of connection between them. She claims it's because of some investigative story she did about the school fund going missing, but I think there is something else attached to it. I just don't know what."

"Man, when it hits the fan, it really hits the fan," Elias quipped. "Now she's renting the house for an undetermined amount of time."

"What?" Kevin knew his day was only going to get worse. "Why won't this woman just leave?"

"Now you just said she's got some kind of tie to the dead guy. Anybody claim his body yet?"

"No. I even called the addy he had in his wallet, but I got nothing. Now I got this reporter in town wanting to dredge up the memories of the summer, when everyone is just trying to forget."

"You know there is a way to get rid of her, if that's what you truly want," Elias accused.

"Not you too. Have you been talking to Nick?"

"No, I can hear it in your voice. This woman has you seeing red, got your blood pumping, and your motor going. Why do you think you haven't dated since moving back to Wright City?"

"Because I don't want to date," Kevin said simply. And it was true, for the most part. His marriage had fallen apart long before the divorce was final. He didn't want to relive that heartache again.

"Kev, you're my brother and I know you think you failed us by getting divorced, but you didn't. This woman sounds like exactly what you need. The women in Wright City would fall at your feet if you gave them a second look. This woman has arrived and managed to push all your buttons in a very short amount of time."

Kevin wasn't trying to hear all that. He'd already knew Kyra was different. She'd awakened some emotions he had thought departed with his divorce. "You were saying something about a sure way to get rid of her."

"Give her what she wants."

"Say what?"

"Oh, yeah. You got it bad." Elias's laughter reached through the phone lines, irritating Kevin all the more. "I was referring to her reporting gig."

Damn. Elias got him on that one. Kevin was going to have to stay on his toes and keep those feelings buried where they belonged. "You were saying?"

"Let her interview you. Don't give in so easily, though. Make her work for it, and maybe she'll get enough to make her want to leave. If that's what you really want her to do."

Kevin sighed. "Okay, EJ, I'll admit she's pushing my buttons in a way no woman has before. But that doesn't mean I'm ready to start dating."

"You don't have to marry her, Kev. You're just

trying to get her out of town. The more resistant you are, the more she's going to think you're hiding something big."

"You know, her father is Chandler Chase," Kevin said.

"Oh, man, he's the next Johnnie Cochran. Forget about it and send her packing, man. Even if you can hold her in Wright City, he'd be down there like nobody's business with a gang of television cameras, and I know you don't want that."

"I've already talked to him. He's concerned for his daughter's safety and he wants me to keep her in town. If I didn't know better I'd think this has something to do with dear old Daddy."

Elias gasped. "You think someone is after him, so they're going through this man's only child and heir to the Chase fortune?"

"What Chase fortune? I mean, I knew most of his clients were celebrities, so I figured he was well off," Kevin said.

"This man has major dollars. He's worth several million, I know."

"So why is his dear baby girl doing the reporter thing? I'd assume she'd be window dressing for Daddy's office. She's not bad to look at."

Elias let his brother's slip of the tongue ease by without saying a word. "She's just like her dad. Has to make her own way. Her last story landed the chancellor of the public school fund on house arrest awaiting sentencing."

"Yeah, I knew about that," Kevin said. "I'm leaning toward Daddy. I think I'll check him out when I get home."

"You'd better be careful, man. If he thinks he's on your radar, you're going to be on his."

Kevin started his truck. "Tell me something I don't know."

Kyra was starving.

After an afternoon of researching and realizing that she would have to talk to the sheriff, she was ready for, no, deserved some food from the diner. She headed straight to Jay's. She was going to have to start working out to combat all that fattening food, but not anytime soon.

She entered the restaurant not surprised to see the building packed with people. It was a Friday night. Didn't people cook dinner anymore? Then she realized it was also high school football season. Who'd cook then go to a football game?

She was surprised not to see Jay buzzing around and taking orders. A young woman with sable skin and a slender build greeted her.

"Table for one, Ms. Chase?"

Small towns. Would she ever get used to everyone knowing her business before she could tell it herself? Just once she'd like to be able to introduce herself to someone in town. Kyra smiled at her hostess. "Yes. Thank you." Kyra found herself saying that phrase more and more with each passing day. Did she ever say "thank you" in Austin? Probably, but here she actually meant it.

She took a seat and glanced around at the crowd. Most of the patrons were looking at her. Kyra figured the news had made the rounds that she was a reporter from Austin. Dismissing all that, she reached for the plastic menu and read her choices.

"I hear you're renting the Cotton place," Sheriff Johnson said as he sat across from her. "I hope you don't mind me sitting here."

She looked up into those light brown eyes and knew those eyes would probably be her downfall. "Of course not, Sheriff. I'd enjoy the company, even if it is you."

"My name is Kevin."

"My name is Kyra."

He smiled. "Okay, now that that's out of the way, I guess you plan on staying awhile." He signaled for the waitress.

"I didn't think you were giving me many options. Plus, I still have a job to do."

The waitress arrived at the table, all smiles aimed directly at Kevin. "What can I do for you, Sheriff?"

He looked at Kyra, smiling as if he could read the thoughts running through her mind. "Kyra will have a glass of tea, and I'll have water."

"Of course, Sheriff." The waitress scrambled away from the table.

"You know, if your budget is that tight, I could spring for you to have a glass of tea," Kyra said.

"That's not why I don't drink the tea," he said.

She waited for him to elaborate, but when he didn't, it only infuriated her more. "You can't just stop like that. It's rude."

He laughed. "Yeah, I guess it was. I try not to drink sugar."

The waitress returned with their drinks. After

she set the beverages on the table and took their dinner orders, she left the table.

Kyra took a sip of the tea and cringed. She too didn't drink sugar as a rule, except for her coffee, but the overly sweet tea was growing on her, much like the town. "I like it."

He opened his bottled water and took a drink. "Yeah, Mom swears by Jay's tea. We have diabetes on both sides of our family, so I try to watch my sugar intake."

"Well, that explains your cranky attitude."

"Okay, maybe I deserved that one," Kevin said. "And to show my goodness, I'll spring for dinner."

"Oh, no, Kevin. That's not necessary," Kyra said. "You don't have to pay for my meal."

"Let's just say I owe you," Kevin said. "So when are you moving in?"

"I don't sign anything until Monday. Being that it's the weekend, I would say it'll be Tuesday before I can get utilities turned on. How do you know?"

"My brother is engaged to Regan."

"Oh," Kyra said, not really understanding what one thing had to do with another. Then it hit her. "Oh, I get it, he wanted you to check me out. And since we have such a stable friendship you decided to track me down." She was kidding, of course.

"Something like that. You're not too hard to track with that sports car zooming through town. All the teenaged boys are going to start circling you real soon."

"A little young blood can be beneficial to a mature woman's health, you know. They have great stamina."

"You speak from experience," Kevin said, finishing his bottle of water.

Lord, that man looked good. "Not really." Kyra was in way over her head with this man and his slow Southern charm.

"Well, that's good to know." He signaled the waitress for another bottle of water.

"Is there any other reason you tracked me down? Don't tell me that you're actually going to let me interview you, so I can get out of this place?"

"You mean you're ready to leave already? I'm really hurt, Kyra. How about we pick this up on Monday? The beginning of the week might not be as hectic as the weekend. Saturdays are usually crazy at the courthouse. We'd probably never get anything done. Monday morning at ten o'clock, I'm willing if you are, Kyra."

Her name rolled off his tongue like it was meant to be there. He made it sound lyrical, poetic, and just plain sexy. Oh, she was so in over her head.

CHAPTER 6

Kyra unlocked the door to her hotel room, walked inside, and flopped down on her bed. She still couldn't believe the events of the night. She'd initially hoped to get a lot of research done, but instead she ended up talking to the enemy over dinner.

Sheriff Kevin Johnson was on his way to becoming her friend, or at least an irritating acquaintance. He'd agreed to an interview on Monday. At least she had a few days to get some questions together. That also meant she wouldn't be back in Austin before next weekend. And that was if everything went well. That was if they solved the case of the murdered hit man.

Things fell into place too easily for Kyra to believe it was spontaneous. He showed up at the diner unexpectedly and sat with her! They ate together like they'd been doing that for years. *Kevin's probably just waiting for me to let my guard down to charge me with Andelli's murder,* she thought.

She took a deep breath. She had to get a grip on

reality. Even though he had a slow, easy smile and great manners, she still had to be objective. She had to pretend that this was just another story and he was just another subject.

With that in her head, she walked to her briefcase and gathered the papers she'd copied earlier that day. She was going to be ready for the sheriff, even if she had to stay up all night to do it.

Her cell phone rang just as she settled down with her reading. It rang again before she could answer it. "Hello?"

"Girl! Some guy came to the paper asking for you today."

Kyra was confused, but her brain soon cleared. "Oh, it probably has something to do with the case with the chancellor."

"That's what I thought, but he didn't look like that. He reminded me of one of those government police people. You know, like the FBI, CIA, someone like that. You know I don't get freaked out that easily, but that guy got to me."

Kyra looked sideways at the phone. Kory wasn't making any sense. "So what happened? I take it the guy left."

"Yeah, that's the really funny part. Auggie told him that you were missing."

Now that was really weird. "What did this guy look like?"

"I told you, like a contract killer. Dark suit, military haircut, and sunglasses. You know, like in that Will Smith movie, *Men in Black*."

"Oh." Kyra's brain buzzed with possibilities. "What on earth is going on?"

"What are you going to do, girl?"

"I'm going to talk to Auggie."

"Don't tell him I called you," Kory warned. "He's been chomping at the bit the last few days. Whatever is going on is big. When that guy walked in the office, you could feel the tension in the room. I was worried so I called your dad."

"And?"

"He told me to keep quiet about you if I valued living. Kyra, you know I'm your girl. You'd tell me if you were in trouble, right?"

She'd known Kory since she started working at the paper and they had become friends instantly, sharing a love of shopping and men. "Of course, Kory, I'd tell you," she lied.

For some reason, the two men she'd respected the most wanted her out of Austin and wanted to keep her location a secret. "I can't really say what's going on right now. I'll fill you in as soon as I get a handle on it. Promise."

"You know I've been in DC the last ten days. All I've heard is 'promise' or 'trust me,' so try again."

Kyra laughed. Her friend could always make her laugh. And she needed a good laugh right now or she was going to start crying. Something wasn't right. "Okay, you got me. Hopefully, I'm doing the right thing. And as soon as I can, I will tell all, Kory."

"I guess that's all I can ask of you right now." She took a minute to catch her breath. "You know you're missing the annual sale at the Galleria this week. I saw those shoes you were eyeing before I left for DC."

Kyra remembered the shoes. They were a pair of designer stilettos. Gorgeous shoes, but a hefty price tag. She just couldn't justify spending that amount of cash for a pair of shoes. Now since being in Wright City, she hadn't thought of those shoes once. "I know I won't be able to make it."

"I can pick them up for you," Kory offered.

"No, I don't want them," said Kyra. Usually she would have jumped at the chance to add to her wardrobe. Something had changed.

"Girl, what's up with you?"

"Nothing. There are more important things than shoes, Kory." *Like being in a town where everyone knows your name.*

"You haven't met a man, have you?"

"It sounds like a disease when you say it. But no."

"It is a disease. Men are bad."

Kyra knew her friend was just being sarcastic. "One day, Kory Reed, you're going to find a man who's just perfect for you."

"I hope I'm still alive by then. Stay in touch." The line went dead.

Kyra pushed the button on her cell phone and put it down. Kory's call just added more questions to her puzzle. She'd have to be crafty to get any information from her dad. Was someone threatening him by claiming to get to Kyra? Her father hadn't done anything illegal. His reputation was spotless. He didn't have a mistress, or had any investments that went bad. Had he fathered a child out of wedlock many years ago and now it was coming to light?

She glanced at the bedside clock, noticing the time. It was near ten o'clock, too late to call her father. His schedule was like clockwork: from nine to ten P.M., he worked out, ten o'clock he watched the news without distractions; eleven to twelve he made notes for his secretary for the next day. No one dared interrupt that timetable, not even his only child.

So she did the next best thing. She called her boss.

"Where's my story?" Auggie grumbled. "You've been there a few days, so I know you've been gathering info."

Kyra knew reverse psychology when she heard it. "You know, I'm about to wrap it up tomorrow. I should be home tomorrow evening."

"That's not possible. I thought the sheriff told you not to leave town."

"And how would you know anything about that?" Kyra was beginning to smell a rat. "Auggie, what the hell is going on?"

"Hey, look, gotta go. You stay there and get the story right. Remember to use only the company credit card and not your own. We don't have time for redos." He hung up.

"Well, I guess he just answered my question," Kyra told the room. "So I guess I might as well play along if I want to find out what's going on."

Saturday morning, Kevin was glad he had followed his gut feeling the previous night. He'd spontaneously decided to track Kyra down, which hadn't taken much effort. Normally, Friday nights he made an appearance at the high school football games, but last night was different.

Last night he had played a game of his own. EJ

would be proud that Kevin had laid out a plan for the reporter. Monday morning would be soon enough to start it.

Nick sauntered into the office with a copy of the autopsy report on Andelli, most likely. He handed it to Kevin.

"Two shots to the head. Nothing that said who shot him." Nick sat down in front of Kevin. "I like puzzles, but this is so crazy none of the dots connect anywhere."

Kevin understood his friend's frustration. "It would be nice if there were a large arrow pointing to a clue."

"Not funny. But Kyra didn't know him. He's a contract killer. Who killed the killer? Who would be that good in a town this size?"

Kevin shook his head. "I wish I knew. I keep thinking, why would someone send a killer here? Why not wait until she's back in Austin? It would be easier in a larger city. The murder would be lost in the cracks."

Nick nodded. "That's what I was thinking. It would be so much easier to get her walking to her car in a parking lot, than here, where a stranger would be noticed. You think there's a time limit on it?"

Kevin shrugged. "I don't know, Nick. There are too many possibilities to examine them all. When she comes in Monday for her interview, I'm going to question her more thoroughly. Some things aren't adding up about Ms. Kyra Chase."

Sunday morning, Kevin entered his house after his morning run, dripping wet with sweat. He'd run an extra five miles. As he walked through his four-bedroom house, he had the feeling he wasn't alone. Someone else was in his house.

He reached for the gun he'd hidden in the hall closet. Some habits he'd acquired as a detective in the Houston Police Department were hard to stop. He kept a gun in his closet, the kitchen, and his bedroom.

He walked quietly down the hall to his home office where he heard the noise. With practiced moves, he stepped quietly down the hall. His gun was aimed at a man rifling through his desk drawers. "Damn, EJ, I was gonna blow your head off!"

"Then why give me a key to your house, if I can't come in when I want?" He continued his search, not bothered in the least that his brother had aimed a gun at him.

"I thought you were a burglar." Kevin engaged the safety on the gun, then placed it in the closet. There was no such thing as being too safe. "What are you doing here?"

"I was looking for the confirmation number for the plane tickets."

Kevin plopped down in a chair. "I feel like I'm talking to a crazy person right now. What the hell are you talking about?"

Elias looked at him sideways. "Man, I'll be glad when you either bag that reporter or send her packing. She has your attitude all messed up."

"Don't be a jerk. I'm not bagging her anyway. Start from the beginning."

Elias sighed and stopped his search. "Okay, a few weeks ago I made honeymoon arrangements for Regan and me, for a week in Hawaii. But now I need to switch it two weeks, 'cause she mentioned this other island she thought was nice too. But to make any changes, I need the confirmation number. Since it's supposed to be a surprise, I can't have this info at the house or Mom or Chris might blab."

Kevin nodded. Now it made plenty of sense. "Okay, search away. I'm going to go shower."

Elias resumed his search and Kevin left the room. He walked down the hall to his bedroom. He stripped out of his sweaty clothes and took a shower.

When he'd dressed in jeans and a shirt, he walked down the hall to check on his brother. EJ was in the living room watching TV.

"Are you eating at Mom's today?"

"Yeah. Dad's grilling steaks, right?"

Elias nodded. "Give me a ride back to the house."

"How'd you get here?"

"Chris dropped me off on his way to McDonald's. Mom decided she didn't want to cook this morning."

Kevin licked his lips. "Man, a bagel sandwich sure would taste great right now."

"He's bringing you one."

Was he really this predictable? He was going to have to change things up and fast.

Monday morning Kevin arrived at work early. He was definitely going to be ready for Ms. Kyra Chase. He took a bite of his PowerBar, knowing he was going to have to be on his toes or his nemesis would see through his little game and probably call her daddy. Then the trouble would really hit the fan.

His private phone line rang. Since not many people had the number outside of his family, he let it ring a second time before answering. "Hello?"

"Sheriff, this is Chandler Chase."

That got his attention. Kevin put the PoweBbar down, but took a healthy drink of orange juice before answering. "Yes, Mr. Chase, how can I help you?"

"I've just got some information that I'm passing along. This is strictly off the record."

Kevin's skin did a little dance every time he heard that phrase. "Depends on the information."

"I hear another hitter is in your area. Brent Adams, about six-two, one-eighty, brown hair, and brown eyes."

Kevin reached for a pad and scribbled the information. "Is he after Kyra?"

"Yes."

When Chase didn't elaborate Kevin rolled his eyes toward the ceiling. *Why can't anything ever be simple?* This man was so much like his daughter, making him fight for every answer. "Are you going to tell me why?"

"Not right now. It's a very delicate matter. You just make sure my baby girl doesn't get hurt. I'd come there, but I would do more harm than good. They'd kill her in front of my very eyes just to make their point."

"How did you come by this information?" Kevin

knew it probably wasn't legal and Chase wouldn't admit it to save his soul.

"That's very privileged information. I've given you everything but the color of his underwear. Surely a man as smart and experienced as your former superiors claim you are can find this man in a town the size of Wright City."

So he'd already run a background check on him? Why wasn't Kevin more surprised? "Yes, sir, I was on the SWAT team in Houston and I was very good at my job. Actually, Kyra is coming in for an interview for that story her editor sent her here for."

"You just make sure you keep her in Wright City until I tell you differently."

Kevin looked at the phone as it buzzed at him, mocking him. "Does anybody tells this man no?" He shook his head as he placed the phone back in its cradle.

Nick stood in the doorway, smiling at him. "If that look on your face is any indication, I would say that was Chandler Chase on your private line."

Kevin nodded. "Yeah, I'd love to know how he got an unlisted phone number. He gave me some info about a visitor in town."

Nick walked further into the office and closed the door. "You know all that man has to do is snap his fingers and information magically appears. Who's the visitor?"

"Another hitter. Some guy name Brent Adams. Chase said he's arriving today, gave me a pretty thorough description."

"I don't get it. He told you who the hitter is, why

he is in town, and what the guy looks like. Why doesn't he just hire some guy to protect his daughter and just be done with it? This seems like he's going to a lot of trouble."

"I don't know. He told me to keep her here until he tells me otherwise."

Nick chuckled. "Let me see if I have this right. Chandler Chase gives you the name of the hitter, his description, and when he's coming to town, and then has the nerve to tell you to keep his daughter here until he tells you to let her go?"

Kevin leaned back in his leather chair. "Yeah, in a nutshell, that's it."

"He must have balls the size of the Liberty Bell."

Kevin had only spoken with Chandler Chase twice and already he could tell this man was a force to be reckoned with. He hoped he would never find out just how much of one. "Probably."

Kyra walked in Jay's Diner at little after eight in the morning. She'd figured everyone was at work by now and she would have her pick of seats. Instead, the diner was still crowded! Apparently, everyone depended on Jay for their breakfast. A young woman approached as Kyra reached for the free newspaper.

"Table for one, Ms. Chase?"

"Yes, thank you." Kyra folded the thin paper and placed it in her handbag. She followed the young woman to a small table in the corner of the restaurant. From her vantage point she could watch people without being too obvious. After Kyra was seated, the young woman recited the special of the day.

"Today's special is Jay's Special, which includes an omelet, bacon, hash browns, biscuits, gravy, and a fruit cup for $4.95. Would you like one?"

Kyra didn't think she could eat all that. She really needed to start cutting back on all this rich food or she wouldn't be able to fit into any of her jeans. On the other hand, she couldn't hurt Jay's feelings. "Yes, please. Also a cup of coffee and a glass of orange juice."

"Sure thing, Ms. Chase. Won't be too long." She left the table and headed to the kitchen.

While she waited, she took out the paper and began scanning the headlines for any information concerning the scandal of the summer. She loved reading the *Wright City Record*. It was what a newspaper used to be. Full of human interest stories, heartwarming stories, a few stories about national politics. She hadn't realized how much she missed writing those kinds of stories.

She missed the story behind the story. *Maybe that should be my angle to the cocaine scandal.* Nine people had lost their lives, whether by murder or an overdose of drugs. There was a story to be told.

"Here you go, Ms. Chase." The woman set the very large plate before Kyra, then placed a mug of steaming hot hazelnut coffee to the side. "I'll be right back with your orange juice." She was gone again.

Kyra started in on the omelet. It was light and fluffy and she'd probably gained five pounds with just that little taste. Jay should have been cooking at a five-star restaurant in some major city. She picked up a thick piece of toast and put a scant amount of butter on it. She was getting ready to eat it when Jay appeared with a glass of orange juice, shaking her head in disappointment.

"Kyra, you know that's not enough butter. And before you start whining about all the weight you think you'll gain, you can always jog with me. I generally start about four."

Kyra gasped. "You don't mean four in the morning?"

"I do. A little more butter isn't going to hurt you. I told you I don't serve diet food. Never have, never will. Food is like a good lover: it should be enjoyed, savored, and you can't wait until the next time." Jay narrowed those dark eyes at her.

Normally, Kyra didn't bend to pressure unless it was her father, but something about Jay made her want to please the restaurateur. Kyra put more butter on her toast. "At least tell me this is margarine or butter substitute."

"Nope, pure butter," she said, smiling. "I don't believe in substitutes for anything."

Kyra was intrigued by the statement. "Not even in the man department?"

Jay laughed. "No. With me it's the real thing or nothing. That's why I'm divorced." She sat down across from Kyra. "My ex thought being married wasn't no reason for him to stop dating. So I left him when I was six months pregnant with our son and drove to the first place I liked. I never looked back."

Kyra wasn't expecting that. "Wow. I don't know

if I would have the guts to leave like that. Your ex never came looking for you?"

"Oh, yeah, he tracked me down right after I had Brandon. He told me I had to come back and that I couldn't raise our son on my own. I refused, and he refused to give me any child support. He thought that was going to hurt me and make me come back to him. You see, I married up, as the people say. He was a high-powered attorney in Austin, but I didn't love him. I was substituting material objects for love. He bought me nice things, but he didn't give me love."

"You're from Austin? Oh, my gosh! You have to tell me the rest of the story."

Jay grinned. "Only if you eat your breakfast."

"Deal." Kyra was dying to find out who this mystery guy was. She doctored her coffee and began eating while Jay continued the story.

"Well, by the time Brandon was born, my sister Raelyn had moved here. She was also surviving a bad relationship and wanted a scenery change. Between the two of us, we made it. Then Brian, my ex, made the mistake of trying to sue me for total custody."

"How on earth could he do that?"

"He thought I'd taken some stupid pills, I guess. He'd paid a few people to say that I was a bad mother, but I had an angel on my side. Donald testified on my behalf and that was the end of that. So, for my trouble, I was going to sue him for back child support, but he didn't want that going through the courts and offered me a huge settlement, if I let him see Brandon."

"So what did you do? Who was this Donald?"

"The person you're investigating. Donald Cotton had been a savior to most of the people in this town. Although he had no children of his own, he loved helping kids the most. He loved Brandon and helped me and Rae a lot. He was killed because he thought he was helping two men start a business, but they used him and killed him when he found out what was really going on. You're renting his house." Jay wiped her eyes with a napkin.

Kyra waited a beat before asking her next question. "How did you start the diner? Are you a trained chef?"

"I started the diner because I love cooking. I never dreamed it would have taken off like it did. My sister owns Rae's across the street; it's a sandwich shop. Her husband owns the bar next to it."

Kyra looked down at her plate, which was now empty. Had she really eaten all that food? "Wow, Jay, that's awesome. I have to ask. What's your last name?"

"That's another sore spot with the ex. When I left him, I resumed using my maiden name. So Brandon doesn't even share his father's name. But to soothe your curiosity, I'll tell you. It's Pullet."

Now Kyra was really thrown for a loop. If this Brian Pullet was the same Brian Pullet she'd known for most of her life, this was too bizarre. She vaguely remembered him being married. "Brian is my godfather."

"I know that." Jay stood. "Right after the first time you walked in here, I called him. I recognized you instantly. You look just like your mother. You have Chandler's tenacity, but you have her charming personality. I kept in touch with her."

"You know, he never remarried. He has a picture of your son on his desk," Kyra reported. "This just seems so fantastic. No wonder Daddy is chompin' at the bit to get down here."

"I'll just bet he is. I've put it all behind me now. I have this place. Don't let anyone ever tell you what you can't do." She headed back to the kitchen.

Kyra sipped her orange juice. Pieces to an unsolvable puzzle slowly locked into place. Her father had a lot of explaining to do. Did he know she'd run into Jay and eventually learn about Brian? Was he hoping she'd find out something else? She sighed with all the possibilities.

"Would you like some more coffee?" Jay asked. "You look out of sorts. I hope it wasn't my fault."

"No, Jay. Life did it. To both of us. I'm trying to find out what exactly is going on around here and why my editor would send me to Wright City in the first place."

CHAPTER 7

After such a revealing breakfast at the diner, Kyra hurried to her appointment with the sheriff. She hoped she was ready for whatever Kevin was going to throw at her. She walked to the second floor and knocked gently on the partially opened door.

"It's about time you got here," Kevin said, opening the door so she could enter the room. The chairs in front of his large desk were covered with papers, mostly computer printouts, newspaper clippings, and some legal pads. He cleared one of the chairs and motioned for her to take a seat.

"Looks like someone was doing some homework," Kyra said. She was definitely glad she dressed casually in jeans and a T-shirt.

Kevin sat in his leather chair behind the desk. "Yes, I did. Most of it was about you." His voice had an accusatory undercurrent to it. "You've had quite a life, Kyra Alexandra Chase. You graduated with honors from the University of Texas with a Bachelor of Arts degree, got a Master's degree from UCLA, was crowned Miss Austin, became president of the Young Democrats, and have been linked romantically to several professional athletes, a country singer and my personal favorite, a state judge. That must have made Daddy happy."

She really didn't like his tone or the sarcasm. Or the fact that he was digging up her past. "Have I committed a crime I'm not aware of, Sheriff?"

"Why, no, Kyra." He smiled. That slow grin split his face, making him look as sexy as hell. "I just like to know who I'm talking to. And since your daddy is calling me on a daily basis, I need to know what exactly is going on."

"That makes two of us." Kyra reached into her handbag and took out her trusty notepad. She also had her tape recorder for occasions like this. No one could ever say she misquoted anyone. "So, can I still interview you, or do I need to call my daddy and tell him to get his butt down here to bail me out of jail?"

"You haven't been charged with a crime. Yet. Unfortunately, being a nuisance isn't against the law. How about let's get this over with so you can go harass someone else."

Kyra tried to hold her tongue. She really did. But when confronted with an asshole, patience was one thing she had in short supply. "Might I remind you that you suggested this? If you have a better disposition later in the day, which I highly doubt, I can come back." She rose to prove her point. There was more than one way to skin a handsome sheriff.

"Sit down," he said, not in his sweet, syrupy Texas drawl, but in a commanding voice much like her father's. "You're not going anywhere until I tell you different. Got it?"

Kyra was a suspect. She sat down with a thud. "You can't seriously tell me you're actually considering holding me here against my will. Talk about small-town justice."

He rose to his full height and closed the door. "There's nothing wrong with our justice system. Maybe it's you."

She hadn't wanted to argue with him. It would only make her assignment that much harder and probably impossible to complete. She took a deep breath. "Look, Kevin, why don't we just start over? If there's something you want to know about my connection to the hitter, just ask me. We both know you don't want me here and I can only take so many days without a real coffee fix."

He glared at her with those light brown eyes, assessing her every move. "All right, Kyra. Why don't we start with your father?"

"Daddy?"

"Yes, Daddy." He took a note pad out of his desk and searched for a pen. After the third search under all the papers on his desk, he was successful.

"What does my father, who has never stepped foot in Wright City, have to do with this? My father doesn't know those kinds of people."

Kevin leaned back in his chair. "Don't be too sure."

"Does your father know any hit men?"

Kevin laughed. "My dad. No way."

"So what makes my dad so different from your dad? Is it because he's an attorney?"

"No, it's because . . ." He dropped the sentence.

"Okay, let's skip it for now. When are you meeting Regan?"

She had forgotten that quickly that Kevin and Regan were almost related. "Around lunch time." Kyra glanced at the generic clock on the wall. With all their bickering and stalling they'd wasted nearly an hour. "So, any more questions about my father?"

"Is he really worth over ten million?"

"Why? Do you want to date him?"

Kevin's slow, easy grin quickly went to a scowl. "I assure you, Kyra, that I'm neither gay, nor a down-low brother. I was just curious how he amassed such a fortune and he's not even sixty."

Kyra smiled. She loved telling this story. "He's fifty-four. He grew up dirt poor in Corpus Christi. Married young, had a family young, worked his way through college and law school with no fewer than three jobs, and still graduated at the top of his law class. His first job was at Hibbert, Maddox, and Klein. He made partner within ten years. My father loves to learn about things. One of his golf friends was a stockbroker and he started dabbling in the market. His really big break came when he defended Josefina Cortez. You know, the restaurateur charged with murdering her husband and his mistress. That really put him on the map. After she was found innocent, he got more clients, and a few years later he started his own firm. He has five attorneys working under him."

Kevin nodded as she told him the story. He probably had all the information on a computer readout somewhere. "Well, he's certainly the success story if I ever heard one. Ever thought of writing a book about him? I'm sure it'll sell like crazy. There aren't enough positive African American stories out there."

Was he actually complimenting her father? "Why, thank you, Kevin. Actually, he's in negotiations with a publisher right now."

"Are you going to write it?"

"Me? Goodness, no. News stories are my thing. Plus, I think I'd be too biased. I'm very proud of my father, but he does have his bad side, too."

"That just makes him more human." Kevin stood, walked around the desk, and took a seat on the edge. "Now that we've had the arguing and small-talk hour, how about we get this over with?"

About darn time, she thought. "Great," Kyra said. She glanced over her notes quickly, deciding how to start the delicate question-and-answer session with Kevin.

"Before you start grilling me, would you like a tour of the courthouse? It might give you a better feel for the story, along with living in the house that was central to the investigation."

"That sounds like a great idea." She rose and grabbed her handbag. "I don't know who you are, but I'm glad you're here."

Kevin stood and laughed. "I guess I have been a son-of-a-gun to you lately. Let's just say I realized you're just as human as I am." He opened the door and motioned for her to precede him out of his office.

After he closed the door, the first stop was the Nick's office. "Nick, I'm going to give Kyra the tour. If anything comes up, I have my phone with me."

Nick smiled as he nodded. "Sure thing, Kev." He winked at Kyra. "Don't forget to show her the evidence room."

Kevin's body stiffened at the mention of the room. "Don't start." He closed the door and they headed on their way.

Kevin could have strangled Nick and would do so as soon as he got rid of Kyra. He hoped Kyra wouldn't ask about it. But the skin crawling on the back of his neck told him that she would.

The next stop was the dispatch room. He introduced her to the two women taking calls. "This is Karen Green and Rachel Smith." The ladies gave Kyra the once-over, then they winked at Kevin. He'd be paying for this for a long time. "This is Kyra Chase. She's a reporter from Austin."

Rachel laughed. "Everybody in town knows this woman and her cute little car. If I were a hundred pounds lighter, I'd have to take a spin in it. I don't think I could fit in it right now."

Kyra laughed. "Some days, I don't know how I get into it either. But I do like to drive fast." She glanced in Kevin's direction, then she said in a stage whisper to Rachel, "Don't tell the sheriff."

Kevin shook his head and closed the door to the dispatch room. "You really drive that fast?"

"You have my driving record. You tell me."

Of course her driving record was spotless. No doubt her father had a hand in that, too. "Either your daddy is well connected or you're just talking."

She started to walk down the hall and called

over her shoulder, "A little from column A and a little from column B."

Kevin picked up his pace to catch up with her. "Can you ever give me a straight answer? It would make life a lot easier."

"Ditto, buster."

Kevin stopped. "Ditto?"

Kyra walked back to him. "Yes, ditto. You've danced around the pole with me a time or two yourself."

"Okay, you got me. I'm the sheriff. I'm supposed to suppress information. You're a reporter. Your life is an open book. Do you want to continue this or what?"

"Yeah, we can continue this. Show me the evidence room."

"I can't." Kevin hoped she'd respect his short tone, like most people did.

"Can't or won't?" Kyra stepped into his personal space. "I bet Nick would show it to me."

"Yes, I just bet he would," Kevin said shortly. "Don't you dare go anywhere near that room with anyone but me." He looked away for a heartbeat. "It may not be safe."

Kyra looked confused. "Okay, either tell me exactly what's in there you don't want me to see or I'm going in with the first deputy I find."

Kevin had few options at the moment. Outside of killing Nick the first chance he got, he would have to show this irritating woman the "evidence room." The evidence room was anything but. Actually, it was a room where some of the members of the deputy sheriff's department went for a little office romance. How could he explain that to Kyra without it sounding like a come-on?

An idea popped into his brain. Even his brother would approve of this one. And he wouldn't have to pretend that much. He was attracted to her. "All right, Kyra. Remember when we get in there that you begged for it."

"Oh, I like the sound of that," she said.

Kevin didn't like the sound of her voice. "Come on, it's down the hall." He started toward the dreaded room and hoped he wouldn't find anyone already using it.

They stopped at the door at the end of the hall. Kevin tapped lightly on the door and was relieved when he didn't hear anyone reply in return. The understood hint was to leave a key in the lock. "The evidence room, Kyra. Come inside."

Kyra entered the room. She laughed as he followed her inside. "It's a make out room. Do the taxpayers know they're paying for this?"

"Actually, I didn't know it existed until a month ago. Seems it has a history all its own. It's been in use for years."

"Oh, that sounds like the room at the capitol building in Austin. I think every major building has a room like that. It might not have such a creative name as the 'evidence room,'" she said, laughing.

Kevin wanted to kiss that smirk off her face, but his cell phone chirped to life. "Sheriff Johnson."

"Kev, we gotta problem," Nick said.

"What is it?"

"Did you kiss her yet?" Nick taunted. "Was it good?"

"What's the problem?" Kevin asked, trying to keep Nick on track. Sometimes he was worse than a woman.

"Abandoned car at the Stop & Shop on Highway Seven."

"Why are you calling me about that? Send Jason or Derek," Kevin said, watching Kyra walk around the small room. There wasn't much to see: a very worn couch, a table, and a small refrigerator. Not the most romantic place.

"I did. They just called in."

Something wasn't right. He heard it in Nick's voice. "What?"

"They found another body. Two shots to the temple. Execution style."

Another murder. He hadn't solved the first one. Now they'd found another body. "Any ID?"

"Yeah, but you'd better get back your office, 'cause you're not going to believe what I have to tell you."

"Another hitter?"

"Bingo."

CHAPTER 8

Kyra listened to Kevin's side of the conversation that he was having with Nick. It didn't sound good. She watched as he clipped his cell phone to his belt and let out a tired breath. He looked at her with those gorgeous eyes. This was not going to be good. Kyra held up her hand. She'd seen that look on her father's face countless times: her graduation from UT; her first engagement party, the second engagement, third engagement, and just about any other important function in her life. Kevin was about to dump on her. "I know what you're going to say," she said. "You have to go."

He had the nerve to look surprised. "Well, yeah. My deputies found a body."

Just great. "Am I being charged with this murder as well?"

"I only said they found a body. How did you know the victim was killed?"

He was quite serious, she realized. Light brown eyes scowled at her as she considered her answer.

"I didn't know. I guess since the other death was also a murder, I just assumed."

He opened the door and motioned for her to leave the room. "Well, since I don't have all the information yet, the answer to your question is no, I'm not charging you. But I don't have to tell you not to leave town, right?"

Kyra looked sideways at him. "Are you kidding? I'm on the edge of a sensational story. You couldn't even make me leave right now. Is the victim local?"

"No, I can say he's not local." They started walking back to his office.

Kyra's reporter's brain was on full alert and needed more details. "Can you give me more than these few crumbs?" They entered his office, where Nick was waiting.

"No, I can't. We're going to have to take this up later. I'll be in touch."

Kyra knew she'd been dismissed. Nick and Kevin traded confused looks, waiting for her to catch the hint. "Oh, sure. I'll either be at the hotel or at the Cotton house."

Kevin nodded. "Yes, and I have your cell number."

"Well, I didn't give it to you," Kyra said.

"Well, your daddy did. So, as I said earlier, I'll be in touch."

"Got it." Kyra closed the door and headed down the hall. She wanted to know who was dead, but knew it would come to light soon enough.

Kevin shook his head at the closed door. "Can you believe that woman?" he asked Nick. "Does she need a ton of bricks to fall on her head to leave?"

"No, man, but she's a reporter first. A second murder probably has her ready to jump at the first clue. You'd better warn Derek and Jason not to talk to anyone with the press including her. I can see this escalating out of control and it could just be some freaky circumstances."

Kevin grabbed his Stetson and his truck keys. He wasn't the conventional sheriff, because he drove his own truck, not the official police car. "How freaky would it be if it's the guy her dad just told me was on his way?"

Nick followed him down the stairs and out the door of the lobby. "What are the chances this guy is already here?"

"The bigger question, is who is killing the hit men once they arrive here? Is there something I'm just not catching?"

They drove to the Stop & Shop and spotted the plain sedan surrounded by police cars and the coroner's meat wagon. "Is that what I think it is?" Kevin asked.

Nick laughed. "Yes, that's a BMW Z4 belonging to one Kyra Chase. I didn't think her leaving like that was her style. I wonder how she got the information so fast."

"I don't know, but from now on, no one talks to that woman without my authorization," Kevin said through gritted teeth. "I'm going to give her a piece of my mind." He stopped the truck and got out. *I ought to arrest her for undermining my authority.*

Nick stopped him before he could reach for his handcuffs. "Kevin, think about what you're doing.

Do you really want to antagonize the daughter of one of the most influential attorneys in Texas?"

His friend was right. The last thing he needed was Chandler Chase accusing them of jailing his daughter just because she was a freaking nuisance. "Thanks for talking me down. That woman has me seeing red ninety percent of the time."

"Man, you know what would release some of that pressure," Nick drawled. "I bet if you kissed her just once, all this so-called dislike for the hot reporter will be over."

Kevin sighed. Nick was worse than his brother. "Why don't you kiss her then?"

"Because Kyra and I aren't the problem. You and Kyra are the problem," Nick pointed out. "Let's go check out the stiff."

Kevin had momentarily forgotten his reason for being at the crime scene. "Lead the way."

They approached the scene and Kevin ordered all nonessential personnel to leave the area. With a deadly look, Kyra hopped into her little sports car and drove away.

The coroner already had the body in its own Ziploc-like bag. Another dead body, the last thing the town needed. Kevin walked to Justin as he assessed the body. "Okay, Justin, what's the verdict?" He kneeled beside the body.

"Two bullets to the temple. Extremely close range. He's been here for at least twelve hours." Justin scratched his thinning blond hair. "I don't know about you, but I think if I saw someone with a gun coming at me, I would have done something beside sit there like a bump on a log."

"What do you mean?"

"There was no sign of a struggle. Even the window was down. It almost seems like he didn't feel any threat." He motioned for his assistant to zip the bag and take it away. "Do you want to waste county dollars on an autopsy?"

"For an execution-style killing?" Kevin thought of the first death last week. "No, don't waste it. Any ID?"

Justin nodded and retrieved a plastic bag holding a wallet. "Brent Adams, age forty-five, place of residence is 4598 Haltom Place, Austin, Texas."

"Damn," Kevin muttered. Chase has been spot on with his description of Adams. He reached for the bag. "Let me know when someone claims the body."

"I don't think that will be possible," Justin said.

"What now?"

"In his wallet, adhered to his Texas driver's license, was a document stating wherever he met his demise, he wanted to be cremated and buried in the county cemetery."

"We don't have a county cemetery," Kevin said stating the obvious. "You're telling me this man doesn't have a next of kin listed in his wallet?"

Justin nodded. "That's what I'm telling you, Kevin. Sorry I don't have more information for you."

"Yeah, hold off sending, him for cremation for a couple of days. Keep him on ice until I tell you different."

"I can do that."

"Thanks, Justin."

Justin nodded and walked to the meat wagon. After Kevin watched the coroner's car head for the highway, he turned to Nick. "So what do you think?"

"You know exactly what I think. Either someone around here has a hit man fetish or there's a serious leak at the courthouse."

Kevin didn't like either possibility and neither made any sense. "I only knew about the second hit man. Your theory doesn't explain the first one. Come to think of it, it was the same MO. Different locales, but the cause of death is exactly the same. Gunshot to the head. You think it's someone in town?"

"Kevin, be serious! Who's going to know about these guys? These are internationally known hit men. They have nothing to do with Wright City."

"I hope you're right, Nick, because after this summer I've seen more dead bodies than I ever want to see in my lifetime." Kevin shook his head. The summer had seemed to be a nightmare that wouldn't end. Now he was already looking at two more deaths. He had to find something that linked the murders. They only thing the men had in common was their prey, Kyra. "Let's search the car and see if we come up with anything before the tow truck gets here."

"Sounds like a plan." Nick opened the passenger door and got to work. "Holler if you find anything."

Kevin opened the driver's side door and started searching under the seat. He didn't have to look long. He pulled out a snapshot of Kyra. "Can you believe this?" He turned the photo over and read Kyra's vitals to Nick. "Man, they have everything but her favorite color on the back of here. Chandler has some explaining to do."

"Yeah, if he knew the hitter, why not warn his daughter? Why warn you?"

"He thought I'd be able to stop him. But someone beat me to it." The more Kevin thought about his dilemma, the more he realized that the truth lay with Kyra. "I'll have to let her interview me so I can interview her and find out what the heck's going on."

After Kevin ordered her to leave the murder scene, Kyra had a little time to kill before meeting her new landlord at Jay's. She decided to visit the *Wright City Record* and look through the old papers for information about the cocaine scandal of the past summer.

She entered the small building and took a deep breath. It smelled like a newspaper office. Or at least what she'd always dreamed one would smell like. Her office in Austin reminded her of corporate America. Computers everywhere, people barely speaking to each other personally. Everything was usually related to her by e-mail.

"Can I help you?" an older woman asked. "You look lost. You need some copies of an obit?"

"I'm sorry." Kyra looked at the slender woman. Her brunette hair was pulled back in an efficient bun.

The woman stared at Kyra, then smiled. "You're her, ain't you?" She hit her hand to her pale forehead. "Of course you are. You're that big-city reporter everybody in town has been goin' on about. I know what you need." She pointed a skinny finger down the hall. "You need the morgue to learn about what happened last summer. It was such a mess, kids dying everywhere, poor Mr. Cotton gunned down in his own house." She shook her head. "It's just down the hall. We keep all our old papers there."

Kyra nodded and followed the woman's direction. She thought the woman would let her peruse the old issues of the *Wright City Record* alone, but when Kyra reached the room marked MORGUE, she realized she wasn't alone.

"I'm Daphne Hughes. I'm the receptionist, runner, guarder of all that's good, and just about anything else Carter Record needs."

"Carter Record owns the paper, I take it."

"Yes, he does. Paper's been in his family for the last seventy or so years. He's not as dedicated as his daddy, but he tries his best. Maybe you can meet him later." Daphne opened the door and walked inside the room.

Kyra sneezed as the dust settled. She glanced around the room, checking out row after row of newspapers stacked on the metal racks. The racks were from ceiling to floor and they were jam-pack. "You guys ever heard of microfilm? Or even scanning them into the computer?"

"Yes, actually we are in the middle of putting them into the computer. This is the last section. You should have seen it before we started, you couldn't have walked in here." She walked to a section in the back of the room. "This is from last summer. Let me think," she said, closing her eyes and tapping a forefinger to her head. She opened her eyes and stared at the ceiling for moment, then looked at Kyra. "I believe Donald died right at the beginning of the summer, but the story really begins months earlier."

"How so?" Kyra asked, looking at the stack of newspapers. The morgue at her office in Austin only had a few months of papers. Sometimes the Internet was a curse.

"Well, kids had started dying earlier in the year, but no one ever connected the dots until the sheriff's brother started investigating Donald's death. The kids were getting badly cut cocaine from the local club and were suffocating. I think it was about a dozen or so kids who died. It was such a horrible time."

"Oh, my gosh," Kyra whispered. She'd only read about a few deaths, but had no idea so many had been kids." She thought of Kevin and could understand why he didn't want any more reporters in town.

"Yes, it was quite an awful time for everyone. But thanks to Kevin and his brother, the town can move on." She handed Kyra a stack of newspapers. "If you want to study them in the outer office, there's a vacant desk. It's the one without any pictures on it."

Kyra thought that sounded like a great idea. "Daphne, I have a noon appointment, so would it be all right if I come back?"

"Sure, no one will bother your stuff. Tell Regan I said hello. I'm glad you're renting Donald's house. He was such a wonderful person. He died much too soon. Wright City will never be the same."

Kyra laughed. Everyone in town knew all her business before she could utter one word. The more she learned about the close-knit community, she found it didn't bother her one bit. "Thank you. I still have some time, so I think I'll just start reading."

Daphne smiled at her. "That sounds like a good idea." She left Kyra alone to gather her newspapers.

After she had accumulated about a dozen newspapers, Kyra went to the vacant desk Daphne mentioned. True to her word, no one bothered her. Not in the true sense. People stopped and introduced themselves and welcomed her to Wright City, maybe offered her coffee, but no one really bothered her.

Kyra was so engrossed in her reading, she would've missed her appointment with Regan, if Daphne hadn't reminded her. She'd spent the last hour reading the stories she couldn't write in Austin. Stories about the people behind the sensational headlines. Like the mayor's son, who now owned the club the former drug dealers were operating out of, and made it more community-friendly. She read about Regan continuing her uncle's dream of the Safe Haven, a place where kids could hang out after school. The stories that were usually buried so far back in the paper, no one bothered reading them.

She made it to Jay's with a few minutes to spare. She watched Regan and her mother enter the restaurant.

Regan looked much better than she had the last time Kyra had laid eyes on her a few days before.

She was dressed in jeans and a sweatshirt, and her mother was in a Reebok wind suit. Regan walked slowly to Kyra with her mother right behind her for support.

Kyra felt helpless when it came to Regan. She'd read the paper's account of how Regan was injured during a kidnapping attempt, and the list of her injuries. She could imagine how painful it was for Regan just to walk, but still she persevered. A lesser person would have just given up. Kyra stood and pulled out a chair for her landlord. "Hi, Regan, Brenda," Kyra said, getting another chair for Regan's mother.

"Thanks," Regan said weakly. "I guess I'm moving really slowly today."

"It's okay, Regan. I mean, if I'd gone through the severe trauma of getting shot, I'd still be flat on my back."

"Some days, that sounds pretty good. But if I didn't keep trying, Uncle Potbelly would haunt me to the end of my days."

"I'm sorry, I have to ask. Uncle Potbelly?"

"My uncle, Donald Cotton. That was my nickname for him. He was rather portly," she said, smiling. "Sometimes it's hard to believe he's gone. It seems like a bad dream."

She watched Regan wipe tears away with a paper napkin. "I'm sorry, Regan, I didn't mean to upset you," Kyra apologized. "I didn't mean to bring up bad memories. My mother passed away last year, so I know how you feel." Kyra fought back her own tears.

Regan quickly recovered. "I'm sorry. Let's talk about something else or we'll both be crying."

Brenda took the lease agreement out of a brown envelope. To Kyra's surprise, it was only one page. "I know what you're thinking," Brenda said. "We're doing this open-ended."

Kyra briefly glanced over the document, took out her favorite pen, and signed it. She handed over a check for $700 for the first month's rent.

Brenda took both items, placed them back in the envelope, and closed it. She gave Kyra a set of three keys. "One is to the back door, one is to the front door, and one is to the shed in the back."

Kyra took the keys and put them in her purse. After such a productive day, she was ready to move into the house, but right now, something else took precedence. Being in Jay's at lunchtime was a mistake, but since she was already there, she might as well make trouble while she could. "How about some lunch? My treat."

CHAPTER 9

Later that afternoon, Kyra entered her hotel room completely exhausted. After eating lunch at the diner, and making sure the utilities would be turned on the next day, she had returned to the newspaper office for more research.

While at the office, she hadn't planned on meeting the owner, Carter Record, but she had. Carter didn't look like a small-town editor. He was walking around in a custom-tailored Armani suit, expensive Italian leather shoes, and a Hugo Boss tie. She knew clothes and could spot a designer's work anywhere. But his clothes weren't what raised the curiosity bug. It was his behavior.

He had questioned Kyra like she was a common criminal on the lam and he was lead prosecutor.

She opened her laptop now and Googled Carter Record. To her surprise, there were over ten pages about him and his very public life. He'd recently returned to Wright City to take over the paper when his father died of a heart attack five years ago. It seemed his entire life had been chronicled by the Internet, except for a five-year gap for the years 1999–2004. Where was he before he returned to Wright City?

Shaking her head, she turned off her computer and starting reading the newspapers. After all, she did have an assignment to complete. She had to have something to report to Auggie when he called her wanting a progress report.

A hard knock on the door woke her a few hours later. She stumbled to the door and wrenched it open, ready to read someone the riot act for interrupting her nap. She wasn't prepared for Kevin, dressed in jeans, a button-down shirt, and tennis shoes!

"Kevin! What are you doing here?"

"Well, it's nice to see you too, Kyra," he teased. "Can I come in or do you want me to state my business out in the hall?"

She stepped aside to let him in. "Please come in, Kevin." After she closed the door, she faced her opposition. "What can I do for you?" *Or to you*, she hoped.

"We were in the middle of our interview when I had to leave. I thought we could pick it up now."

"Now?"

"Now." Kevin glanced around the small room, his eyes settling on the mound of newspapers on the corner of her unmade bed. "Is there a problem?"

If she said yes, he'd claim he'd offered her a chance but she didn't take it. "No problem. Just give me a minute to wash my face and I'll be ready."

"I was thinking about dinner at Jay's," he offered casually. "You know, I could eat dinner and you could hammer me with questions."

Kyra tilted her head to one side. "Is this a date?" She laughed walking to the bathroom and closing the door.

Kevin cleared his throat. "I'd prefer to call it information gathering."

"Sounds like a date," she said louder, so he could hear her. "My granny used to say if it quacks like a duck." She quickly splashed cold water on her face and dried it with a fluffy towel.

Please, let him make a move. She left the bathroom and walked right into Kevin who was pacing the small length of the room. "You know, you make this room look tiny."

He shrugged. "Ready?"

"Ready?"

"Yes. Ready. Are you ready to eat?"

Kyra sighed. "Yes." She was so hoping for something else. "I could eat a horse."

"Well, Jay doesn't serve that, but I'll see what I can do." He smiled slyly and nodded to the door.

Kyra grabbed her purse and walked out into the hall. Kevin followed her, closed the door, then held out his large hand. Kyra was about to ask him if he'd lost his mind, when he said, "Keys."

"Oh." She felt really stupid. He was just showing off his good manners. Regretfully, she dropped her keys in his hand.

He quickly locked her door and they were off. Kyra walked toward her car but stopped when she heard Kevin swear. "I can't get into the sardine can. We'll go in my truck."

Well, what happened to those Southern manners?

"Oh, no, buster. You didn't ask me anything. I thought we'd go in separate cars."

"No."

She smiled in triumph. "So this is a date."

"No."

"Is too. You came to my house. Picked me up and now we're going in your truck. And to top it all off, it's Monday night. Ask anyone, that's a date."

Kevin walked to the driver's side of the truck. "You're opening your own door. It's not a date. Get in."

Kyra stood there, waiting for him to do something, since he was the man with the manners, but he only started the motor. Finally, because she wanted to know more about the man who could get her engine started with just a smile, she walked to the truck, and slid into the passenger seat without another word.

When they arrived at Jay's, Kyra's stomach did all her thinking for her. She had every intention of ordering baked chicken, but the word "fried" somehow slipped out of her mouth when she recited her order for the waitress. She felt her head nodding at the prospect of hot, buttered corn on the cob, and mashed potatoes. She was going to have to buy a treadmill pretty soon to combat all these high-fat meals, or she was going to look like a very fat but contented cow.

Kevin chuckled, lifting up his water glass. "You look like you just lost your designer purse. It's okay. I know you women worry about your weight. I can find a way to work it off you." He took a long sip of water.

"Really? I'm listening."

"I run in the mornings."

"Not you too. What's wrong with the people in this town? No one ever heard of a gym?"

"Yes, I've heard of one. There's one near Wal-Mart, but I prefer to see nature when I'm exercising, not the latest talk show with the stereotypical baby daddy mess."

"I'm not into talk shows, reality shows, or any that stuff. I'm a History Channel girl."

"No way."

"Very way."

He smiled. "Me too. EJ, that's my brother, always gives me a hard time for watching it, but there's some interesting stuff on there. They should make it required viewing in school."

Kyra laughed. If she'd mentioned that same fact to her boss once, she had mentioned it a million times. "Hey, you don't have to sell me on it. I totally agree with you."

He sat back in his seat and grinned. "Wow, is this the first time we agreed on something or what?"

"Pretty much."

Kevin leaned back in his chair, watching her like she was about to take flight. "Well, maybe a celebration is in order."

Kyra knew what kind of celebration she was thinking of, but knew the sheriff probably had a five-mile jog in mind. "How about another time? I have some research I need to complete."

He nodded, watching the waitress bring their food order. "Is this something like washing your hair?"

The young woman placed their food between them in record time and left. Kyra wanted to answer him, but the aroma of Southern fried chicken was just too much. Her brain could only focus on how good the food was going to taste.

"I guess that's my answer then." Kevin stabbed at his food. "This has gotta be the quickest truce known to man."

As Kyra chomped on the meat, she heard some of what Kevin said. "What are you talking about?"

"Your pitiful excuse for not wanting to go to the Dairy Queen for a shake."

Kyra was relieved. "I thought you wanted to go for a night run or something. Honestly, I do have research to do."

He smiled. "Oh, so I guess I'll have to enjoy some ice cream alone. It won't be the same," he teased.

Kyra took a bite of her food, reasoning the cost of that ice cream shake. She was already in deep infatuation with Kevin and he hadn't so much as kissed her yet. She was going to be putty in his hands pretty soon. "Catch me letting you have dessert by yourself."

"Good. I'll find out what kind of woman you really are."

"What?"

Kevin leaned across the table. "You can tell a lot from a woman by the way she eats her ice cream."

"Really?" That was almost her undoing. Surely, Kevin knew what he was doing to her. "I would ask why, but I think I'd be asking for trouble."

"You'd be right."

* * *

When Kevin entered Dairy Queen holding Kyra's hand, the crowded restaurant suddenly became quiet. Maybe it was because he was walking into his second-favorite restaurant in town with the big-city reporter. Maybe it was because they both had silly grins on their faces. Maybe it was simply the fact that the newly divorced sheriff was walking in with a woman at all.

He didn't have much time to decide what was what. He spotted his younger brother with his gang of girlfriends. Chris untangled himself from the young girls and made his way to Kevin and Kyra, just as they slid into a booth across from each other.

"Kev, I can't believe you're in here." His brother sat next to him, his stare fixed on Kyra. "I'm Chris, by the way. I'm Kevin's youngest brother. You must be the reporter everyone in town is talking about."

Kyra looked back at him. "Guilty."

Chris nodded. "You're hot! I've heard about your car."

Kyra laughed. "I don't know what it is about that car, but guys go nuts for it."

Chris shot a look at his brother. "It might be something else as well. Just look at Kev. He seldom mingles at the Dairy Queen with us commoners. Normally, he gets his food to go." He smiled at his brother and left the table without another word.

Kyra glanced around the small room. "I don't think I've ever been in a place like this. It feels nice. Not as homey as Jay's place, but it's nice."

Kevin gazed across the table at her. Kyra was a beauty, true enough, but tonight in the bright, harsh lighting of the Dairy Queen, she was the most beautiful woman he'd ever seen. "Wait until you have a chocolate fudge sundae. Once you wrap your tongue around some of this chocolate, you won't remember why you ever went to Jay's in the first place."

Kyra cleared her throat. "Well, Kevin, I guess I'll have to take your word for that. I'm having frozen yogurt."

Kevin knew what Kyra needed. Or at least he hoped he did. He rose and stood near the booth. "Sure, frozen yogurt coming right up. Plain vanilla okay?"

She looked him up and down, waking up those damn dormant hormones again. "Why don't I believe you?"

"I could ask you the same question."

"I don't know what you're talking about."

"You will." He walked to the counter to order the ice cream.

With Kevin safely out of her line of vision, Kyra took a deep breath. Then another. She said a quick chant of self-empowerment and courage before he returned. She had a feeling Kevin wasn't going to order the frozen yogurt and she had to be strong enough not to give in those dreamy brown eyes and that sexy smile.

She watched as person after person greeted Kevin and glanced in her direction. What was it about this man that had everyone acting like he was a movie star on a surprised visit home? Was she jealous?

He strode to the table with two chocolate sundaes. To call that creation a sundae was almost a misnomer. The dish was piled high with ice cream, and drizzled with chocolate, peanuts, and a mound of whipped cream. She could feel her arteries clogging the closer Kevin got to the table. He placed one in front of her. "They were all out of frozen yogurt. So I got you one of these. I hope you don't mind."

Kyra looked at the mound of ice cream. This place and this man were going to be her downfall. "No, this is fine." She reached for a plastic spoon and went to work. "Oh, this is good."

He sat back in satisfaction. "See, I told you. Probably one of the better things you've had in your mouth."

Was it her or was everything he said relating to sex in some way? Maybe it was her level of frustration with Kevin, the lack of a story, and the need for a caramel mocha latte. "Pretty close."

He laughed and continued eating. Between bites, he asked her about her life in Austin. "I bet you really miss the limelight."

"Not really. When I first arrived here, I didn't think I was going to make it one day, but I've survived." She wanted to tell him about Jay being married to her godfather, but didn't feel it was her place.

"When I got shot, all I could think about was coming home."

Her heartbeat accelerated. "You got shot? When? Does it have anything to do with the cocaine scandal?"

He held up his large hand. "Hold up. Yes, I was

shot in Houston. I was a detective with the HPD for about eight years. I was on the SWAT team. I was shot a few years ago. After I was released from the hospital, I told my wife of my decision to come back home to live and she told me of her decision to take a position with the FDIC in Dallas."

Kyra knew the end of the story, since he was here with her now. "I'm sorry, Kevin." To her surprise, she actually meant it. "It's sad when couples break up over something like location."

He shrugged. "Hey, I didn't say it for pity. The marriage was falling apart anyway. We're still pretty good friends. She's actually getting married in a few months on Valentine's Day. She sent me an invitation to the wedding."

Kyra thought of the men in her past and knew the unlikelihood of them sending her invites. Out of the three times she was engaged, none of endings were amicable. "It's good you guys are such good friends. Are you going to the wedding?"

"Haven't made up my mind yet. Would you?"

"I don't know." She ate a few spoonfuls of the sundae as she thought carefully. "I guess if we were on good terms and if I wanted to make an appearance, I would go."

"So it would be like a revenge kind of thing. Not to wish him well."

"Kinda," Kyra mumbled, not wanting to admit the truth.

"So you're not on good terms with any of your high-profile ex-lovers?"

"Not exactly." Maybe if she stuffed her mouth full of ice cream, Kevin wouldn't ask her any more questions. She was wrong.

"What exactly?" He reached across the table and took the spoon out of her nervous hands. "Kyra, look me in the face and tell me what happened."

She did as he asked and gazed into those dreamy eyes. "Well, I'm sure you already know the gory details from when you ran a background check on me. My last relationship ended with my usual flair for trouble. His better half somehow gained entrance into my very secure townhouse and pulled a gun on us."

Kevin held up his hand. "Don't tell me. He was married."

Kyra shook her head, not wanting to relive that horrible day, but she knew she had to. "He was living a double life, so to speak."

"And?"

"He was courting me, but he had a significant other on the other side of Austin. I guess I must have suspected something was wrong. I always insisted he wore a condom. Thank goodness I listened to my instincts."

"Gay?"

"Yep."

"Damn."

CHAPTER 10

Kevin knew the night was going to take a turn he wasn't ready for when Kyra admitted that her last lover was a homosexual. He could only imagine how hard it was for her to admit that, and doubly hard to admit it to him.

She held it together pretty well until they were in the solitude of his truck. She cried. Not a few tears of love gone, but gut-wrenching sobs that told him she'd been holding those tears back a long time.

Tossing caution to the wind, Kevin took Kyra in his arms and comforted her. That was his first mistake. His second was inhaling the clean scent of her hair, and his third one was kissing her.

He just wanted her to stop crying, but as his lips tasted the salt in her tears, they took over. He found himself kissing away her tears, grazing her soft lips with his, and wanting to comfort her in any way possible.

Her lips felt like a hot Texas day. He felt her arms creep around his neck, drawing him close until only air was between them. If only they weren't in his truck. What was he thinking? He'd put those kinds of ideas away with his divorce decree. Slowly, he ended the kiss. "Kyra, I'm not trying to take advantage of you."

She looked at him, her brown eyes darting wildly from side to side. She shifted back to her seat. "You didn't." She took an extraordinary long time straightening her blouse. "We both wanted it, Kevin, or we wouldn't have gotten carried away."

He wanted to refute her words, but it was true. It had probably been building up since he first met her and, to his dismay, that frustration had found an outlet. "Kyra, I can't do this."

"What?"

"Be with you like this. It's not right. You deserve so much more."

She took a deep breath, a long sigh that only meant she was going to say something to ruin the moment. "Okay, Kevin. Are you saying this because we got carried away in your truck and everyone in town can see us, or you just aren't attracted to me?"

She had him. "No. I mean, yes. Hell, I don't know what I mean." He exhaled his frustration with the situation. "Yes, Kyra, I'm attracted to you. I'm just a small-town sheriff, and I know you've dated millionaires. Your father is worth millions. I can't give you that kind of lifestyle. I'm not apologizing for my job, because I love it, but we're oil and water."

"Let me see if I've got this right," Kyra said, facing him with an unrelenting gaze. "You're attracted to me, but since I'm from a big city and have had a few high-profile relationships, and because of what my father does for a living, you figure it can't work out." She sighed. "Kevin, I'm not looking for anything past my time in Wright City. I don't judge a man by his income. I judge a man by what's in his heart."

"Kyra, I didn't mean to hurt your feelings."

"You didn't. You're just doing a lot of supposing without consulting me. You have some insane image of me because my father is who he is. I can't change who or what my father is."

He felt like that space under a snake's belly. "Kyra, I'm not asking you to change anything. I'm just telling you that I won't take advantage of a situation. You're upset. Yes, I'm attracted to you and, yes, I want you, but this is not the right time or place."

She stared at him for what seemed like forever. "Well, I guess that's something. Either you need to take me home or we're going to have to make out again, because we're attracting attention."

He'd been so intent on comforting Kyra, he hadn't given much thought to the crowd gathering at the front window of the Dairy Queen. Now, however, that crowd was very much on his mind. He didn't want Kyra's reputation to be sullied because he couldn't control his hormones. And he was always in control.

He started the truck and drove Kyra back to the hotel. He walked her to her room, thankful Jemma wasn't at the front desk. As was his custom, he unlocked her door and opened the door for her, then handed her the key.

She couldn't hide the shocked look on her face. "Don't you want to come in?" She had the nerve to try to look innocent.

He wanted nothing more, but knew there would be a price for unbridled, unplanned sex, and he wasn't ready to pay. "I'd better say good night here, Kyra. I'll talk to you later."

Kyra studied him and shrugged. "If that's what you want." She opened her door, but didn't venture inside.

Kevin nodded. *Thank goodness, a sensible woman.* He could go home, take an ice cold shower, and fall asleep in his lonely bed. "Yes, it's what I want. Good night."

Before he could take one step, Kyra grabbed his hand and pulled him inside her room. She closed and locked the door before Kevin could realize what was actually going on. "Kyra?"

She stood directly in front of him, barring his escape. "Leaving might have been on your agenda, but it's not on mine. I want you to stay, Kevin."

Kevin knew his fate the minute she dragged him over the threshold. There was no turning back for him or her. "Kyra," he whispered, "I don't want you regretting this in the morning."

She grabbed his hand, led him to her unmade bed, and pushed him down on it. "Kevin, as you can see, I'm a big girl. I can handle my decisions. I know what I want, and right now that's you. Any questions?" She peered down at him with her hands on her hips. "Because tomorrow at the diner, I don't want to hear how I seduced you. This is a mutual decision."

Kevin nodded. He wanted her so much he couldn't think straight. "Kyra, I can't give you what you need."

She stepped closer to him, forcing him further onto the bed. "Kevin, you're what I need. End of story."

He'd been divorced for over two years. Foolishly, he'd thought he had those pesky hormones under control when his marriage ended. He was wrong. He also decided for once in his life to go with the moment. With that thought, he reached for Kyra and she easily went into his arms. He kissed her slowly and gently, wanting to savor the moment.

Kyra must have noticed his readiness. She straddled his lap so they were facing each other. "Well, I'm glad you're finally in the game." She wrapped her arms around him and kissed him so hard he fell back on the bed, taking her with him.

He wanted to memorize every inch of her body. His hands traveled the valley, of her curves before sliding under her blouse. She felt good laying against him. As their kiss became more passionate and breathing became less of a necessity, Kevin rolled her over so that he was on top of her.

Kevin helped her out of her blouse and she helped him off with his shirt. Kyra couldn't keep her mind on her task of getting Kevin's jeans off because she couldn't stop looking at his chest. There should have been a law against looking that good. His upper body was tight skin covering buffed muscles. She couldn't help herself, she had to touch him. She caressed his biceps, his well-developed chest, loving the feel of his very toned body. When her hands passed over his tight nipples, he moaned, fueling both their desires.

Her hands glided over his flat stomach and stopped at the belt buckle on his jeans. But he halted her actions. "Baby, slow down."

"Easier said than done," Kyra said, unfastening the belt and unzipping his jeans.

"Tennis shoes," Kevin whispered against her lips. "I need to take off my tennis shoes."

"Let me." She gently pushed him off her. She kneeled beside him and made quick work of it. "Now, for the prize." She slid the jeans down his legs, leaving his boxer briefs in place.

"Your turn." He pulled her up beside him and kissed her. She felt his sure hands caress her waist and unzip her pants in one quick motion. He also freed her of her underwear and bra in the process. He stared at her nude body. "Beautiful. I knew you'd be beautiful and you are."

Kyra shifted from one foot to another. Kevin's unrelenting gaze would make the most confident woman doubt herself. She wanted to jump under the covers. She felt his eyes assessing her attributes and slowly her uneasiness faded away. When he pulled her closer and began caressing her, Kyra felt comfortable. She trusted this man with her heart.

She watched as he slid off the last remaining piece of clothing between them: his boxer briefs. Kevin's very erect penis sprang free and Kyra's heart starting racing. He was definitely a large man. She was about to doubt the logistics when he chuckled, pulling her into his arms. "Don't worry, Kyra."

She was feeling too content to worry about anything but the way he felt against her. She wanted more. So much more. And she was ready to get the show on the road. She reached for him and kissed him hard and long. Kevin moved until he was on top of her. His kisses left a heated path as he inched his way down her body.

Kyra thought she was going out of her mind as he paid homage to her breasts and rounded belly, and he didn't stop until he parted her legs. Kyra felt his hot breath against her inner thigh and that was almost her undoing. He tasted her gently and she felt her world go out of focus. As his fingers and tongue got intimately acquainted with her, Kyra grabbed her bedsheets and held on for the ride of her life.

"Oh, Kevin," Kyra whimpered as the unfamiliar sensations coursed through her. She wanted to tell him she'd never had an orgasm like that, but somehow words escaped her. "That was awesome," was all she could manage. She panted, still trying to catch her breath.

He kissed her. "Just wait. It'll get much better."

Then it hit her. Condoms. Should she admit she'd been anticipating this moment for days and had bought a box for the event? "Kevin," she started. "I don't take birth-control pills."

He reached under her pillow and retrieved a foil package. "I know. I wouldn't have taken one step in this room if I couldn't protect you. When my brother smuggled this to me earlier at the Dairy Queen, I thought he was crazy, but thank goodness for him." He opened the package with his straight teeth and quickly slid it on his engorged flesh. He moved above her, positioning himself between her legs. Kyra's body was on full alert, waiting for Kevin to take her to paradise.

She didn't have to wait long. He eased into her body with a gentleness that brought Kyra to tears. No lover had ever been that considerate of her needs. Kevin moved against her until he was finally seated all the way home. He kissed her as he started moving in and out of her body. Kyra held on to his trim hips, not knowing if she could take one more powerful thrust, but begging him not to stop.

She heard him curse, wanting to delay the sensation barreling through his body, but it was useless. He screamed her name, touching off her release. When their bodies were finally still again, Kyra caressed Kevin's back while listening to his erratic heartbeat settle down.

She'd never realized she was a cuddler, but she was. She had only been in this town less than a week and she'd become a card-carrying romantic. Normally, she'd be running for a shower and to put on clothes, but tonight she was lying nude in bed, with a nude man. Laughing, she snuggled closer to Kevin.

He wrapped his arms around her and kissed her sweaty forehead. "What's so funny?"

She ran her hands down his arms. "Me."

"Huh?"

Kyra sat up, covering her form with the sheet. She looked down at him. He lay there looking like a sexy ad made just for her. "I always thought I was too inhibited to be this open with anyone."

He pulled her back down beside him. "You're one of those get-dressed-right-after women?"

She nodded, resting her head on his chest. "Yeah, I was. I'd take a shower then dress."

Kevin's hand rested on her stomach. "What changed?"

She wished she knew. "I don't know. I think this place has some kind of spell on me. I feel like a different person. Actually, I think it's you, Kevin Johnson."

"Good answer." He leaned and kissed her as his hands roamed her nakedness. "How about round two?"

CHAPTER 11

Tuesday morning Kyra didn't want to get up.
Her body was absolutely exhausted, but her
cell phone was ringing somewhere in the room.
She forced her eyes open and glanced at the disaster. Clothes were scattered everywhere and someone was in her shower. She attempted to sit up, but
her body protested the movement.

She flopped back on the bed, and let out a tired
breath. She was worn out. What was she thinking
having sex with Kevin last night? He was the
enemy and she let him win the battle. As the memories of the evening's escapades took over her
heart, Kyra thought Kevin was very worth losing to.

The bathroom door opened and Kevin
emerged, smiling and dressed in his clothes. He
walked to the bed and sat down. Kyra thought he
looked very sexy. She tugged the sheet up to cover
her body. She tried to think of something to say
other than, "I had a real nice time," but words
again failed her.

Kevin leaned down and kissed her long and soft. "Kyra, words can't express what I'm feeling right now. I have to get to work. I'll call you later. Stay out of trouble." He kissed her forehead and left the room.

As she watched him close the door, Kyra realized she had turned into one of those romantic freaks. And she decided she didn't care, and drifted back into a much needed sleep.

Nick knew the day was only going to get better. He'd been at work for over an hour and his boss still hadn't arrived. Kevin was never late; he was usually the first person there and waiting anxiously for the other deputies to arrive.

He looked at the clock and decided that Kevin would have a good reason for being over an hour late for work. Nick called the four deputies into his office for the morning meeting.

After assigning duties, the deputies left without another word. Nick started surfing the Net. Kevin had had a good idea the other day about Kyra's dad. Nick decided a little investigation couldn't hurt. And if his boss was where he thought he was, Kevin was going to need all the help he could get.

As Nick read Austin's daily paper online, the phone rang. He picked it up on the second ring, hoping it was Kevin. It was not. "Sheriff's office. Deputy Sheriff Nick Fraser speaking." Kevin was a stickler for proper phone etiquette.

"Nick, what the hell are you doing in Podunk, Texas?"

He laughed at the question. It was his former

boss, Andrew Sanger. Andy had been chief of police in Houston. "Relaxing, Andy. What's up?"

"I could ask you the same," Andy drawled. "I got some fella calling, asking for Kevin's credentials. I was calling to warn him. I knew you'd left Houston after the thing with your wife, but I didn't know you ran to Mayberry," Andy laughed.

Nick chuckled. "Yeah, I always thought I'd be the last person to live in a small town, but here I am. I like it here. Kevin is great to work for. So who's looking for him?"

"Not sure. I had a company rep from Austin call me. They were checking out Kevin's background and wouldn't say for who. Of course, they didn't find anything. I got a hunch who it could be."

Nick had a bad idea of who it could be as well. "Who?"

"That company is pretty pricey. If Pierce Investigations is looking into your background they're only two people who would have requested it."

"And that's who?" Nick already knew, but wanted verification.

"Chandler Chase or the governor. If Chase has Kevin on his radar, there's going to be hell to pay. How does he even know Kevin?"

"Long story. Thanks for the heads-up." Nick hung up and pondered the next move. Why was Kyra's dad having Kevin checked out? Was this a CMA move or was he concerned about his daughter?

Kevin walked through the door with a bottle of water in his hand. Nick had expected a harried-looking Kevin since he detested tardiness, but the Kevin who eased into the room was relaxed, contented, and ready to face whatever the world could throw at him. In short, Kevin Johnson had gotten laid.

Kevin didn't like the grin on his friend's face. "What?" He opened the plastic bottle and took a long drink of water.

Nick shrugged. "Nothing, man. Just got some info from Andy I thought you might want to know about." He shuffled some papers atop his desk, muttering, "Now, where did I put that important information?"

Kevin sighed. Nick was in a mood. Apparently, he had some vital information but was going to make Kevin beg for it. "Okay, Nick, what's up?"

Nick snickered. "I could ask you the same thing. I haven't seen you this calm in years. As a matter of fact, you used to come in to work with a smile like that whenever you and Vena had one of those nights."

"Don't go there, Nick."

Nick searched his face. "Kevin, you know we go way back. We were partners in Houston, and you convinced me to move here. If you and Kyra had . . . you know . . . it's all good. I'm glad you're getting to know her."

Kevin could hear the "but" at the end of that sentence. Nick wouldn't have stuck his neck out this far if it weren't important. "Okay, Nick, spill it."

Nick closed the door and took a seat. "Well, Andy did call this morning wanting to let you know that someone was investigating you."

"Why would anyone want to dig up my information? My law enforcement record is spotless."

Nick cleared his throat. "Andy said only two people use this certain investigation firm 'cause they're so expensive. They look for everything. You know like your first pet, first kiss, first time you failed a test."

This was so not going well. "Who?"

"Chandler Chase and the governor. Since we can rule out you having any contact with the governor and him having you investigated, we can assume that it's Chase."

"Yes, that's my guess too. I think we need to take a closer look at Mr. Chase and find out why he's investigating me."

"Smart. What about his very determined daughter? What are you going to do about her when she finds out you're digging up her daddy's dirt?"

"Please, Nick. One disaster at a time. First thing I need to do is talk to Chase face to face and see what exactly is going on."

"Today?"

"Yes. What's the problem?"

"Look, man," Nick said in that tone, " if you just up and jet to Austin without a word to Kyra it's not going to look right. She'll think you were just using her. It wouldn't be good for business."

Kevin reached for the phone. "You think she'll tell her daddy that I seduced her or something? She's too old for that."

"If you say so. In my experience a woman is a woman. I put nothing past one. So just be careful."

Kevin knew that Nick meant no harm in his

warning. "Don't worry, I'll be careful. And for now, investigating Chase is between us."

"What if she calls?"

Kevin knew that wouldn't happen. "As you said, she's a woman. She wouldn't dare make the first move."

Nick rose and opened the door. "Who made the first move last night?" He left the room.

Kevin shook his head, replaying the night in his head. At first it had seemed like he'd made the first move, but when it came right down to it, Kyra was the victor.

He was in so much trouble. With the knowledge of impending doom, he thought he might as well make it worth his while. He opened his desk, retrieved Chase's office number, and dialed.

"Chandler Chase, attorney," a female voice said. "How may I direct your call?"

Kevin thought this was a one-man show, but apparently not. "Chandler Chase."

"Is he expecting your call?"

"No."

"Sir, Mr. Chase is very busy. You must have an appointment to speak with him."

Kevin sighed. He should have known it wouldn't be as simple as picking up the phone and speaking with the multi millionaire. "Can I leave my name and number?"

"Yes," she said in a clipped voice. "Whom may I say is calling?"

"Sheriff Kevin Johnson, and my number is—"

"Why didn't you say so? Just a minute, please."

Before Kevin could think of anything sharp and cutting to say, Chandler was on the line.

"Chase."

Kevin cleared his throat. "Yes, Mr. Chase, this is Sheriff Johnson."

"Yes."

No pleasantries, no generic greeting. *Two can play this game*, Kevin thought. "I'll be in your office this afternoon." He hung up the phone and drank the last of his water. He needed a Coke.

The next time Kyra opened her eyes it was noon. What had happened to the morning? She struggled to sit up and glanced around the room. It was still a mess, but now it was missing one sexy lawman. Her cell phone rang as she attempted to sit upright. "Hello?"

"Kyra?"

"Kory?" *Oh no, now what's happened?*

"Yeah, you sound like you're still in bed. Girl, you know you don't sleep this late."

Kyra laughed, snuggled against the pillows, and inhaled. Kevin's cologne was still on the pillows, bringing back memories of their intense lovemaking sessions. She had quite a different view of Kevin and she liked it. "I had a busy night."

"I hope it was productive," Kory said.

"Most definitely," Kyra said on a yawn. "It was so good. I'm going to take another nap."

"Sounds like a man was involved."

"He was a lot more than just a man. He was the love god."

Kory roared with laughter. "Is this same woman who said there wasn't a man alive who could satisfy her?"

"Oh, I was so wrong."

"You know I gotta have some details. Is he cute? Is he stable? Does he have any baggage?"

Kyra didn't have to think for one second. "Yes, he's cute, has wonderful manners, and is very stable."

"And, apparently, he's very good in bed."

"That goes without saying."

"Well, where is Mr. Wonderful? Am I going to have to drive to wherever you are to see this fine specimen of male perfection?"

"Who knows? I'm still working on my assignment, you know. I'm sure I'll be back in Austin soon."

"You can't miss Black Friday. It's in two weeks. Who will I go shopping with if you're not back?"

Kyra smiled. She wished she could reveal her whereabouts to her friend, but knew that with two dead hit men, she'd only endanger Kory's life. "I'll be back. I'm sure I'll need some getting-over-a-man therapy, so keep that MasterCard clear." Even as she said the words, Kyra knew her heart wasn't in it. Kevin had replaced her love for shopping.

CHAPTER 12

Through the wonder of electronics, Kevin arrived at the building that housed Chandler Chase Enterprises with the aid his navigational system. He wasn't expecting a five-story glass building in downtown Austin. Busy downtown Austin.

Since moving back to Wright City, Kevin had almost forgotten how much he disliked the big city with all the noises and people. After finding a parking lot, he entered the building and was amazed again. He was expecting Chandler's office to be on the first floor, but he was wrong. Outside of the receptionist and the security guard, no one else was on the floor.

Kevin walked to the counter. "I'm here to see Mr. Chase."

The middle-aged woman smiled, looking at her computer monitor. "Yes, Mr. Johnson, Mr. Chase is expecting you. He's on the fourth floor, suite 415."

Kevin nodded, heading to the bank of elevators. After he pressed the up button, Kevin was beginning to wonder about this man. How did the secretary know his name? Granted, Chase could have alerted her, but how would she know him from any other man?

The doors opened and he stepped inside. He pressed the button for the fourth floor and waited. He barely had time to catch his breath when the doors opened and a young African American woman who looked barely legal to drink greeted him.

"Good afternoon, Mr. Johnson. I hope your journey from Wright City was pleasant." She extended a slender hand to him. "Did you park in one of the nearby parking lots?"

He nodded.

"I'll give you a parking voucher when you leave. Did you have time for lunch?" She started walking down the hall. "I can have something brought in. I order Mr. Chase's lunch about this time. I can make it for two."

Kevin nodded. "Sure, that'll be fine."

"Good. Should be about thirty minutes." She stopped at a set of double oak doors and opened them. She motioned him inside, and the young woman walked down a long corridor and out of his sight.

This office looked every bit as impressive as the Web site. He'd expected some young thing to greet him, but a mature, plump African American woman smiled as he took a seat.

"Sheriff Johnson, Mr. Chase is just finishing up a conference call. He'll be just a few minutes. Would you care for some bottled water? We have Fiji."

Kevin nodded. How did they know? Fiji water

was his brand of choice. Why didn't she offer him coffee, or tea, or even soda? Chase's information was good. He knew that Kevin drank water religiously.

A minute barely ticked by before Kevin had an ice-cold bottled water in his hand. Another minute went by before Chandler made his appearance in the doorway and beckoned him inside his office. "No calls, Carletta."

She nodded at his instructions. "I'll let you know when lunch arrives."

Kevin wondered at this woman. She had to be a receptionist extradonaire to work for a man like Chandler Chase. He walked inside the large office, not sure what to expect. He half expected to see a government official waiting to arrest him, but there was no one. Except a multimillionaire with a problem.

He extended a hand to Kevin and looked him square in the eyes. "Glad to finally meet you, Johnson. My daughter says you don't want her in your town." In the dark suit, he was a force.

He didn't deny it. "She's a reporter. Wright City has had a horrible last few months, and the town needs to heal. The town can't do that if reporters keep swarming around, digging up the past." That seemed like such a long time ago. Now he wanted Kyra in his town for as long as she was willing to stay.

Chase chuckled. "Well, she has an assignment to fulfill and Chase, reporters always finish the job with their dying breath if the case calls for it."

"That's what I'm afraid of. I don't want another

unnecessary death in my town, and I didn't drive all this way to make nice. I came to get some answers."

Chase sat in his leather chair. "I know why you came down here. You're keeping my baby girl alive. She's the most important thing in my life. I'd be crushed if something happened to her."

Kevin took a deep breath. Rich idiots made him sick. "Your daughter is not a thing. She's a person, not an acquisition, not a stock, or part of a portfolio."

"Well, I guess you told me, huh? And that also tells me that my report of you keeping time with her is true."

Did this man have spies everywhere? "We've been comparing notes on the case. She swears she didn't know either of the men sent to kill her."

"That's correct. They're professional hitters. She would have never known those kinds of men."

Kevin took out his handy notepad. "About that. How did you know?"

Chase leaned back in his seat and took a deep breath. "Because I got a call telling me who it was. It's their idea of torturing me. They figure if I know who it is and can't do anything to save her, they win."

Kevin felt like he had starting watching a movie in the middle. Chase's statements only opened up a whole new can of questions. "Why don't you start from the beginning?"

"That would be about five years ago."

Kevin sighed. More questions. "Okay."

"Ever heard of the Ditano family?"

Even living in Houston, Kevin had heard of the

Austin crime family. The Ditanos owned several restaurants around Austin, but rumor had it that the family was connected in every sense of the word. "Yes."

"The rumors are true. The old man came to me when I was just starting my business and I helped him get his business off the ground all those years ago. I was young then, I had a wife and baby and my practice was struggling. I know that isn't an excuse."

"True," Kevin said.

"I didn't know what they were really into until quite a few years later, but then the money was good, and they had brought me more business. I'm sure you've investigated me, just like I have returned the favor to you. As my client list grew, I pulled back on Ditano's business. One of his sons had taken over the legal end of the business anyway."

Kevin knew this would go on forever if he didn't stop it. "You were saying something about five years ago."

"You don't want to know exactly when my foot slipped?"

"I'm sure that will come in time, sir."

Before Chandler could speak, a timid knock interrupted them. "Come in."

The slender woman from earlier entered with a rolling tray. She placed the covered dishes on the solid oak table and quietly left the room.

Chase rose and walked to the table. "Why don't we table that for now and grab some lunch?" He took the gold dome lids off the dishes.

Kevin inhaled the aroma of roast beef. It smelled

almost as good as Jay's. "Sounds like a plan." He joined Chase at the table. After he took the first bite, Kevin knew this food was better than Jay's.

They were both silent as they devoured the lunch. Over a slice of sweet potato pie, Chase resumed the story.

"About five years ago, the youngest Ditano, Julian, was charged with murdering a UT student. The old man asked me to help his son defend Julian. Initially, I agreed."

"What changed your mind?" Kevin took the last bite of pie.

"A little investigating. I found that Julian had been quite a hell-raiser while attending UT the previous year. At first, he kept saying that it was a crime of passion and he hadn't meant to kill her."

"But?"

"It's not a crime of passion if you shoot her three times, and stab her five, then try to dismember and burn her body. The Ditanos tried to cover up her cause of death, paying off the medical examiner. When that didn't work, they staged a mix-up and had her body cremated before her family could view it."

"What?"

"You'd be surprised what a million dollars will do in this city."

Kevin shook his head. "Not really."

"It wasn't always like this. I didn't want to be involved with that kind of case. That's when all the trouble started."

Kevin stared at a very different Chandler. "They started with threats and then escalated?"

"No, they started with a gun to my head when

Julian was given a death sentence last year. The older son, Miguel, said it was my fault and that I should give my life, since Julian had to give his. The only thing that saved me was the old man. He told them not to kill me."

Then everything became clear. "But that safety net didn't extend to Kyra."

Chandler bowed his head. "I never meant for her to get hurt. She's all I have left, since her mother died last year. After Julian received his execution date a few weeks ago, they put a price on her head."

"And you somehow had her boss assign her a story that would send her away," Kevin reasoned. This man was a piece of work. Kevin almost felt sorry for him.

"Yeah, I'm pretty good friends with her boss's boss and he assigned her the story in Wright City at my request. I knew she'd be safe somewhere remote until I could work something out with Miguel. I never dreamed they would know where she went or send hit men there to kill her."

"And you have no idea how many men they're sending? There've already been two deaths; when are they going to give up?"

"When she's dead."

Kevin saw the problem and had no idea how to solve it. He needed to keep Kyra safe, but he also had to protect his town. Could he do both effectively? "Look, I want to protect Kyra, but she's pretty determined to finish her assignment. I can't shadow her and she wouldn't let me anyway. Maybe you could talk to her?"

Chandler laughed, but it was hollow and full of

hurt. "We don't have the typical father-daughter relationship. In fact, I guess you could say it is pretty dysfunctional. All through her formative years I was working, so her mother raised her. Then in her later years I tried to make her into what I wanted. She fought me every step of the way. That's why she is a journalist instead of an attorney. We disagree on just about everything. I love my daughter, don't get me wrong, but she's pigheaded. Especially about something she wants or believes in."

So much of Kyra made sense. She was used to fighting for what she wanted and not stopping until she got it. His mind floated back to the night before, when he saw her cry. For all the toughness she displayed, her soft side won his heart. "You don't think she'd take your advice?"

"Oh, she'll take it, but will she act on it would be a better question. If Kyra ever gives in without a fight, then my child is sick or someone has taken her brain."

Kevin laughed. "Now that's the Kyra Chase I met." He stood and shook Chandler's hand. "Thank you for meeting me, sir. If you get any more messages let me know." He handed Chandler a card. "That has all my contact numbers. Call anytime. The quicker we can catch them, the better it is for everyone involved."

"Thank you, Kevin. This is all my doing, but when this is all over, I'll have to thank you properly. Right now, you take care of my baby girl and keep her alive."

"I'll do my best," Kevin promised and walked

out of the plush office, digesting the information he'd received. He was going to have to call his brother and get some information on the Ditano case.

After he retrieved his truck, he headed back to Wright City and Kyra. He'd once thought a conversation with Chase would give him all the answers he needed. Instead, he got more questions, more problems, and possibly more killings.

"This is the last load, Ms. Chase," the burly furniture deliveryman said. "Will there be anything else?" He stood in the doorway of the small house, his pale face red from the exertion of manual labor. "We hooked up the washer and dryer for you too. Don't tell the boss, he hates when we do that."

Kyra smiled. The two men not only set up her bed, but they put her computer desk and bookcase together for her as well. "Thank you, so much." She glanced at his name stitched on his blue shirt. "Charles. I really appreciate it." She dug into her purse and pulled out two one-hundred-dollar bills and handed them to Charles.

But he shook his head. "Oh, no, ma'am. That's not necessary. Just part of the delivery service and you've already been charged for it."

Would she ever get used to this? Back home the deliverymen would refuse to assemble any of her furniture, let alone hook up the washer or dryer, and still expect a tip. "You guys did so much." She wanted to do something for them.

"It does my heart good to see someone finally renting this house. Mr. Cotton was a nice man and I'm glad to see someone just as nice as you living here."

"Thank you. You're very kind."

He nodded. "I live just down the road a piece. If you have any problems just give me a holler." He tipped his hat and went to truck, where his partner waited.

Kyra watched the men leave, but she didn't go directly inside. She noticed a car parked across the street. It didn't quite fit in with the rest of the old neighborhood. *Kyra, stop it,* she told herself. If someone saw her car they would think it didn't belong there either. She watched the car drive off and then went inside her house.

She sat on the small fabric couch and exhaled. Moving day was uneventful and was missing one sexy lawman. Kevin had known she was moving today. Why hadn't he come by to offer his delicious manners? She reached for her purse, which stood on a bedside table, grabbed her cell phone and dialed. Kevin picked up on the second ring.

"Hey, Kyra."

"You're not going to ask how I got your number?"

"Not important. What's up?"

"I was hoping you were," she giggled. "Not really. I was calling to see if you wanted to have dinner at the diner later to celebrate my new residence." She hoped he wanted to break in her bed later, too.

"Dinner sounds good. I should be back by then.

We need to talk when I get to town." He ended the call.

The man with the good manners apparently left Wright City and is sending a jerk back in his place, Kyra mused. Where had Kevin gone, and why didn't he say anything about leaving town when he was making sweet love to her last night or this morning?

If she'd had time to dwell on it, she would have, but her cell phone rang. It was Auggie. *Might as well get this over with*. Kyra answered the phone, plastering her smile on her face, hoping against hope it would come across in her voice. "Hi, boss."

"Don't you 'hi boss' me," Auggie said. "What's this I hear about you talking to Kory? I told you not to tell anyone where you were."

"I didn't tell her where I was. I told her I was on assignment per your instructions. What's the big deal?"

"The big deal is that there are people looking for you and they want to kill you. If Kory calls again, do not answer the phone. She's having your signal tracked."

If she wasn't already sitting down, she would have fallen flat on her face. Kory was her best friend. This was so not happening. "Surely the chancellor hasn't lost his mind and wants revenge."

Auggie sighed. "It's not the chancellor. You need to be very careful about any contact with people in Austin and that includes your father. Buy a prepaid cell and turn your regular cell off. Do not turn it back on until you're on your way back to Austin."

She'd never known her boss to talk to her condescendingly before. When Auggie had used that harsh tone it meant they were on terror alert red and it was damn serious. Who wanted to kill her? Were those two hit men really in town to kill her? How did they know where she was?

CHAPTER 13

Kyra, in her own wisdom, decided not to wait for Kevin to have dinner at the diner. She sat in a nice corner booth, observing the customers. There was something about eating in this place that made her feel at home.

It was early evening, so Jay wasn't working, but her very efficient staff was keeping everything going smoothly in her absence. Kyra smiled as she noticed the young woman approaching her table.

"Hello, Ms. Chase." She placed a large glass of sweetened iced tea on the table. "The special for this evening is smothered pork chops with onion gravy, mashed potatoes, and corn on the cob with pecan pie."

Kyra's mouth watered at the thought of dessert. "Sold. When I leave this place I'm going to have to work out every day just to fit into my clothes. Jay doesn't believe in calorie-friendly meals, does she?"

"No, ma'am. Jay always says food should be enjoyed and not everyone is supposed to be skinny."

Kyra sighed. "That's why she runs every morning. I'm not doing that. The day you see me out there running, you'd better hope there's a major sale somewhere."

"I know that's right." The young woman walked away.

Kevin slid into the seat opposite her. "I guess you couldn't wait, huh?" He let out a tired breath. "You know, I'm beat."

Kyra shrugged. "And? What am I supposed to do? You just left without any word this morning."

He reached his large hands across the table and grabbed hers, caressing it gently. "It was unavoidable, Kyra. I needed to talk to a possible suspect in the case."

His touch was doing crazy things to her. It was heating her blood like an inferno. "So who did you talk to, or is that privileged information?"

"You know I can't reveal information in an ongoing investigation, Kyra. Unless you're going to try to seduce it out of me later. Then I might be willing to share."

At least that is something, she thought. "Maybe I'll try to wring it out of you later."

Kevin smiled. "Yes, please."

Kyra tried to keep the giggle down in her throat. But the thought of the sheriff, who she once thought was uptight, begging for sex was just too much. The giggle escaped and tumbled out of her mouth into laughter.

"You know you will pay for this," Kevin mumbled. "Many times."

Kyra didn't have a retort to his sexual threat. She hoped he lived up to his promise. She was about to tell him so when the waitress approached the table with her meal.

Kyra's attention was momentarily diverted from Kevin to her delicious meal. As usual, the food smelled delicious, and the portions were huge. She could feel the pounds attaching themselves to her waist.

"Women worry too much about food," Kevin told the young waitress. "I'll have the same."

"Yes, Sheriff." She smiled at Kevin as she left the table.

"I think you have a fan club," Kyra said, taking a bite of her dinner. "She didn't smile at me like that when she took my order."

Kevin didn't refute her. "You're not the sheriff either. I uphold the law, what do you do?"

Well, she had him there. "I report what you do."

He looked at her with those light brown eyes and leaned closer so that only her ears could hear, "Well, you will have a lot to report when I get through with you."

She had to think of something, anything, to get her mind off his mouth. "Where did you say you went today?"

"Uh-uh. You know the rules. Are you and your millionaire father close?"

Kyra wasn't surprised at the question. She'd been waiting for it for over a week. "Close enough."

"Which means not close at all," Kevin said. "I'm very close to my parents. I see them almost every day."

"That's nice, Kevin. I'd like to meet them before I leave Wright City. What are they like?"

The waitress brought Kevin his food and a glass

of water, then quickly departed. He took a bite of food, closed his eyes, and moaned. "This is delicious."

"Kevin, tell me about your parents," Kyra persisted.

"All right. They're just parents. David Sr. and Dorrie. My dad was one of three surgeons at the hospital until about three years ago when he retired. Mom was a high school counselor, and she retired last year. They're very supportive. When my marriage went bust, they didn't blame me, they didn't blame my ex. Mom is all about healing. You know, getting over the bad parts of your life. When I came back here, Mom started me reading again. I'd forgotten how much I loved it over the years. I owe the person I am now to my parents."

Kyra wiped her eyes. She'd had that kind of relationship with her mother, but that ended when her mom died a year ago. Her father was merely a shadow in her life. Only there to dispense his logic for her life and what she needed. What career she should choose? Whom should she date? Boy was that a wrong call, she remembered of her last romantic fiasco. Taking her father's advice was always a gamble and usually she lost.

"Kyra?"

She blinked, realizing that she was staring at the handsome sheriff, but not seeing him. "I'm sorry, Kevin. Were you saying something?"

"I was offering you a napkin. You're crying."

Kevin watched as Kyra dried her eyes and regained her composure. How could one question cause a waterfall? He'd already guessed there was a rift between father and daughter, and they'd recently started to rebuild their relationship, but there was something else. Had Kyra known of her father's involvement in the Ditano case and the repercussions of not defending the youngest Ditano?

"How about we get the dessert to go?" Kevin suggested. "You can show me how the Cotton place looks."

Kyra grinned. "Is that anything like come and show me your drawings?"

At least it was a little smile. "Possibly. Like I said earlier, we do need to talk in private."

"This sounds serious."

Kevin couldn't hide the truth. He could skate around with little problems, but he couldn't lie to her about her father. "It is quite serious and it's a conversation best kept between us and no one else."

"Okay. I'm going to the ladies' room. I'll be right back." She rose and hurried away.

While she was away, Kevin took care of the bill and persuaded the waitress to pack their desserts in a bag, and now he waited for Kyra. He knew she was probably in the bathroom either crying or splashing water on her face after she cried.

"Okay, Sheriff. I'm ready." Kyra stood next to him. "I'd ask where my ticket is but I see your credit card receipt on the table. Quite a big tip."

Kevin rose, grabbed the paper bag with their desserts inside, and shrugged. "Everything about me is big." He watched her turn a shade of red he didn't think was possible. "I was referring to my spirit, my heart, and my love for the town and its people, Ms. Dirty Mind."

She looked at him with those big brown eyes that told him she didn't believe one word of it. "Well, Kevin, where are we going?"

He grabbed her hand and led her out of the diner. "I thought we'd already discussed that."

"You mean you were serious?"

He had a lot of questions, and the only way to get some answers was to spend some time with her. "Of course I was serious."

Kyra hugged him. "Thank you." She took the sack from his hand and walked to her car.

Kevin watched her slide into the small car and laughed as she peeled off down the street. *She is challenging, if nothing else,* he thought as he ambled to his truck.

It took him five minutes to get to Kyra's rental house. In that time, Kyra had warmed up the pie in the microwave and had placed it on the coffee table along with bottled water for Kevin and a glass of wine for her.

She let him inside and he was blown away with what Kyra had done to the place in one afternoon. He'd expected the small house to be cluttered with unnecessary pieces, but it was very roomy. The living room had a small sofa and a love seat, both made of the same denim fabric. A tall lamp stood proudly in the corner, lighting the room. One would have never thought two murders occurred in the house just months before.

"It looks great, Kyra." He took a seat on the couch.

"Yeah, I like it. It's the first place I've decorated

all by myself." She sat next to him, kicked off her shoes, and tucked her feet under her.

"You didn't decorate your house? I mean, wasn't it in *Texas Monthly* last year?"

That brought a brand new stream of tears. "Two years ago. My mom was a furniture nut. She decorated my place. It was the last thing we did together. After she died, I didn't have the heart to change it. She knew exactly what went with what. I didn't think it was possible, but I think I miss her more each day that I'm in Wright City. She would have loved this town."

Kevin glanced around the room, looking for a tissue or paper towel. He noticed the napkin next to the pie and handed it to her.

"Thank you. I don't know what is going on with me today. I haven't thought about Mom this much since she died."

Kevin moved closer to Kyra and drew her into his arms. "Maybe it was something that triggered an old memory."

Kyra rested her head on his chest. "I think it's you. Mom would have taken one look at you and would insist I marry you on the spot. She had a thing for Southern gentlemen."

"So you're saying I remind you of your mother?" Kevin inhaled the fresh scent of her hair.

Kyra sat up. "No, silly. I'm saying you make me think about a happier time. My mom was such a romantic. Dad is anything but. I used to wonder how they stayed married. I know he loved her in his way. To Daddy, it's business first, family second." She had new tears.

"Kyra, how did your mother die?" He hoped the Ditanos had nothing to do with it.

"She died suddenly of a stroke. The day it happened, I tried to call Daddy, but he wasn't taking calls. He was in some meeting and couldn't be disturbed. By the time he reached the hospital, Mom had been dead for two hours."

She cried again and he comforted her. "He feels really guilty about it," she continued. "At first, I was very angry at him for letting her die. Over time, I came to forgive him. Since I've been here, I've noticed that people take family first, job second. That's the way it should be."

Kyra sat up, took a sip of her white zinfandel, and faced Kevin. "I don't want to end up like my father. Yes, my father is a millionaire, but he doesn't have anyone proclaiming undying love for him like the people of this town have for Mr. Cotton, including me. I can't seem to turn around without someone saying how great he was and how he would give you the shirt off his back if that's what you needed. I want people to remember me for the good I've done, not for the money I had. Yeah, I had a cushy life growing up. I'd much rather have had a father who loved me for me."

Kevin was at a loss. He wanted to question her more about her father's business, but he had got ten times more information than he bargained for. Chandler Chase had a lot to answer for and Kevin was going to make sure he did.

CHAPTER 14

After they'd consumed the pies, and made out like teenagers, Kyra snuggled closer to Kevin, not believing how fast her agenda for the evening had changed. She'd intended for him to beg for it, but instead she was the one purging her soul. Oddly enough, she felt better for having done so.

Kevin's muscular chest heaved up and down before he finally spoke. "Kyra, I saw your father today."

She sat up, looking him directly in his eyes. "What did you say, Kevin?"

"I spoke to your father today. I drove to Austin, went to his office, and we had a conversation," he said.

Kyra wondered what these two men had to talk about. "Is that why you asked about him earlier?"

"Yes. Kyra, there are some crazy things going on right now and I have to protect the town. Two men have come to town to kill you and someone has killed them. There has to be a connection and I'd like to find it before someone else turns up dead in my town."

"I would like to know who has it in for me." She glanced at Kevin's sincere face. "I can't imagine the chancellor being this upset about me doing that story. Besides, he's going to prison, and there's not a thing anyone can do about it."

Kevin wrapped his arms around her. "There is such a thing called revenge. People kill for a lot less."

Kyra read between Kevin's words. "You think this has something to do with Daddy?"

Kevin cleared his throat. "I'm not following you."

Kyra laughed at the stupidity of men. "Come on, in the last few weeks strange things started happening to me. Strangers approach me and already know my name. My boss hands me a story that lands me in a small, isolated town and tells me not to contact anyone, and my dad tells me not to call him. I know something is going on around me. I just don't know what."

"True, but what makes you think it has anything to do with your father?"

"Because of the guy."

"What guy?"

"About a month ago, I was in the parking garage of the newspaper. It was really late and this guy came out of nowhere and asked me if Chandler Chase was my father."

"Why would he ask you that?"

"Kevin, it's not an uncommon question. I grew up in the Austin limelight. Everything I've done has been reported in the society pages since my first kiss. People always ask me stuff like that."

"I can't imagine having a life like that," Kevin said. "Even when I lived in Houston, my life was pretty quiet. I couldn't imagine the press following me around."

Kyra couldn't imagine him in that setting either. "That would explain why you're here, wouldn't it? Well except for why you're here?" She wanted to know as much as she possibly could about the person who'd stolen her heart.

"Does this qualify as an interview?"

"No, this is the talk we didn't have last night, or this morning since you ran out on me," she teased.

"Kyra, I didn't do it on purpose. I was late for work. I'm never late for work. I didn't mean any disrespect to you."

Kyra placed a finger on his lips. "Kevin, I was kidding. I know you love your job. You're a very dedicated sheriff and this town is your heart. I wouldn't have it any other way."

He kissed her finger and playfully bit it. He laughed when she quickly moved her hand. "I didn't leave because I wanted to. If I had had my way, we'd still be there right now. As you said, I do love my job, and I had to check out a lead."

This was the bad feeling about the investigation she'd been having. He drove all the way to Austin to see her father. It had been there the whole time, but she ignored it because it was her father. "You do think Daddy has something to do with someone trying to kill me?"

As if he could tell where her mind had gone, he said in soothing voice, "No, Kyra, your father doesn't have a contract out on you. He does love you."

Kyra heard the undertones in that statement. She moved closer to Kevin wanting to shut her father out of the room and their conversation, but there was something that had to be said. "I know he does, Kevin. In his way and on his terms."

"But?"

He knew her so well already. "But strange things have always surrounded my father. Yes, he's a brilliant attorney and has made most of his money legally. In my younger days, when I was attending college, he always knew my every move before I could say anything."

Kevin moved closer to her, so close that there wasn't any room for air between them. He started caressing her face. "Such as?"

She took a deep breath and tried to focus on anything but the gentle strokes Kevin applied to her face. "Such as, say I ran into someone with maybe not so great a history. Minutes later, my dad would call me and tell me I was there to study, not chase men."

"Okay, that's scary."

Kyra nodded. "Tell me about it. It was like he had some kind of psychic connection to me or something. Then I found out differently."

"He was having your movements shadowed," Kevin said quietly.

"You know, Kevin, you could have let me say it. But you're correct. Mom found out and, for the first time, she was angry at Daddy. My shadow was one of my closest friends at the time, who was immediately fired and dropped out of school the next semester."

"So he was paying for her to go to UT along with you?"

"I know. UT isn't a cheap school. Later, he said it was worth it and would do it again."

"I totally agree with him."

"Kevin!"

He sat up to explain his point. "Look, baby, if I had an endless supply of money and it was my only child, hell yeah, I'd hire someone, but it would be a guy. Someone who could really protect my child."

She had two options. She could take the "women are just as good as men" argument, or she could cuddle up next to Kevin and just forget about it. She decided on a compromise. "Remind me to kick you about the man-woman thing later. But for now, I guess I can see your point and Daddy's for that matter. So is my dear Daddy protecting me now?"

He sighed. "Kyra, you're treading into some dangerous territory. You might find out things about him you don't want to know."

"But at least I'd know what I'm up against. Even though I have the best security guard right here." She patted Kevin's leg.

"True," he admitted, "but even I can't deflect bullets."

That was a sobering thought and reminder. "I can't either, but together we could."

Kevin stared at her. "I appreciate your enthusiasm, Kyra. I agree if we work together things would go much easier, but are you ready to follow my rules?"

Kyra mulled the thought over for about ten seconds. "No, are you ready to follow mine?"

Kevin smiled at her. She saw the wheels of his brain turning, thinking of a master plan. Kyra had a master plan of her own and it had nothing to do with her father. She moved to sit on his lap.

"Kyra, what are you doing?"

"Agreeing to disagree." She kissed him soundly on his lips. "You know we're not going to resolve this tonight and there are so many more important things we need to discuss." She wiggled her hips to get more comfortable.

A barely audible sigh escaped his mouth. "Oh, baby, if you move again, I won't be responsible for my actions." He caressed her back with one hand while his other hand was just as busy in her lap, playing with the button on her jeans.

Kyra leaned closer to him, giving him all the incentive to keep going. "I hope so, Sheriff." She lowered her lips to his. "How about a game of chase?"

"How about game of sheriff?"

"You win." Kyra rose from her position, smiling at her handiwork. "Looks like you already started playing without me." She motioned at his very noticeable erection.

He rose slowly and stood next to her, wrapping his arms around her, pulling her body snug against his. "Yes, I did, and you're going to put me out of my misery."

It was nice to know that he wanted it as bad as she did. Kyra grabbed his hand and led him down the hall to the master bedroom. She was going to break in her bed the right way.

Parked on the darkened street in his Mercedes, he waited patiently for the sheriff to leave. He'd taken this job as a favor to Miguel Ditano, but this supposedly super-easy job had been anything but.

He realized he had been standing out like a sore thumb since he arrived in Wright City a few hours ago. After making a few inquiries, he located the house easy enough. Kyra's BMW stood out just as bad in a place where trucks, SUVs, and practical cars were the norm. Her sporty car was like a beacon in a storm.

He glanced at his watch. It was almost ten. Shouldn't the good sheriff be leaving by now? What on earth was he waiting for?

His plan was simple. Wait until she was alone, preferably fast asleep, and take her out. *One shot to head should do it*, he reasoned. Two shots would alarm the neighborhood and the sheriff. He could be back in Austin collecting his million-dollar fee by the morning before anyone had found her body.

He heard someone walking down the street, taking slow, careful, deliberate steps. He took out his prized possession, a Walther semi-automatic sports pistol, his taut body tensed with anticipation. Had he been outbid for the job? Surely Ditano hadn't double-booked a simple kill. If he had, he'd kill Ditano the minute the payment cleared. The steps neared the car then suddenly crossed the street. The figure was in shadows thanks to him being in a hick town with no street lights. Then he saw it. The figure was alone. The second figure he made out with no problem, and put his gun away. It was a damn dog.

He laughed at himself for being so paranoid. This was Hicksville, for goodness sake. There were no other contract killers within miles of this town. He looked across the street and noticed the living room was darkened which meant only one thing: the sheriff and Chase had taken their party to the bedroom. It would be at least thirty minutes before he left, or it could be the morning. He settled down in the front seat of his car for a nap. Because of his occupation, he was a light sleeper and would hear the sheriff's truck the minute it started.

He heard more footsteps, but ignored them. *Just another hick resident walking their mutt*, he thought. He picked up his cell phone to text his wife his nightly goodnight message.

The last thing he heard was the glass in the passenger window shattering and his last thought was of his wife.

When Kevin walked into the room, all he could think about was getting Kyra naked and in bed as soon as possible. Kyra, on the other hand, had other ideas. She wanted to do the undressing and he would have to let her.

He sat on the bed, waiting for her to get the show on the road. She stood before him in a lime green bra and panty number that did crazy things to his already hard manhood. The bra had just enough lace not to leave anything to his warped imagination. She'd taken off his shirt and was now working on his boots.

When she finally freed both of his feet, she unbuckled his belt and unzipped his pants. His erection popped free as she slid the pants and underwear down his legs. "Now, I believe you said something about being seduced," she said as she stood. She slid off her panties and unsnapped the front hooks on her bra, and stood before him naked as the day she was born.

Gently, she pushed him back on the bed, settling on top of him. She kissed him on the mouth, cheek, neck, and chest. Kevin thought he was going to lose his momentum, but in Kyra style, she surprised him by heading south.

He pulled her back to his mouth just before she took him to paradise. He rolled her on her back and returned the favor. He kissed her ears, cheek, lips, and nuzzled her neck. She smelled like a dream laced with something naughty and it only fueled what he felt for her. He kissed her lips again, then moved lower to her breasts, paying them homage one at a time. He was delighted when he heard her moan and beg for more.

"Please, Kevin. I don't know how much more I can take," she whispered as she flailed her arms wildly.

He realized she wasn't in the throes of passion as he'd hoped, but was reaching for something under her pillow. Smiling, she handed him a condom.

She'd outfoxed him again. "Always prepared," he said, taking the plastic package from her hands. He opened the package with his teeth and hurriedly sheathed his manhood. "I guess that makes two of us." He moved over her and entered her in one smooth stroke. "Now that's what I call a homecoming."

Kyra wrapped her long legs around him and pulled him down for a kiss that made any other thoughts flee his brain. He released the last bit of control and made love to the woman in his arms.

He wanted to slow down, but he couldn't. Something about Kyra made him want to stay inside of her for as long as possible. He'd never felt that way about any woman in his life. Not even his ex-wife. What was so different about the woman writhing beneath him?

"Kevin," she moaned against his lips.

He immediately stopped. "Am I hurting you? Want me to stop?" He prayed not, but if he had to, he would.

"Not unless you want me to kill you," she laughed. "I thought I heard a noise. Like someone walking."

"Kyra, you're worried about that now? Clearly, I'm not taking care of business. I should be the only thing on your mind."

"You are." She raised her hips to get his attention to get the show back on the road.

Kevin moved against her and lowered his lips to her. "I got this." And he let his body do the rest of his talking for him. And he did a lot of talking.

CHAPTER 15

Kyra turned over in bed as the sun peeked through the wood blinds in her bedroom. She wanted to shut out the day as much as possible. She snuggled closer to the muscular chest behind her. Something about having a strong man in bed just made anything else pale in comparison.

She sighed as she leaned back on the pillow to get a better look at Kevin as he slept. Her hand gently caressed his face. Giving in to the morning after, she kissed his forehead. His eyes fluttered opened and he smiled at her. "Good morning. You were fantastic."

"You weren't so bad yourself." Kyra sat up, pulling the sheet with her to cover her naked body. "My body feels like it ran several marathons."

"Same here." He pulled her down next to him, ripping the sheet from her hands. "Got time for another race?"

She reached into the nightstand and retrieved a condom for him. "For you, always."

Kevin laughed. "You're becoming a habit, Kyra.

For the second night since I moved back here two years ago, I haven't slept in my own bed. People are going to start to talk."

Kyra didn't care. She was used to being the subject of conversation, but Kevin, on the other hand, wasn't used to that kind of lifestyle. She didn't want him feeling bad about their time together. "Do you care?"

He looked at her with those luscious brown eyes that melted her heart. "I care about you. I'm used to people wondering about me and my family. I don't want people whispering about you and scarring your reputation."

Kyra wasn't expecting such an honest answer. She kissed him and moved on top of him. "If we weren't about to have sex, we definitely would be after hearing you say that. That's just about the sweetest thing I've ever heard." She kissed him again and she settled against him.

Kevin closed his eyes and wrapped his arms around her, as he adjusted her body to his. Then he stopped. Just like that. "Wait, I haven't put on the . . ."

It was too late. Kyra threw caution to the wind and slid onto Kevin's most rigid body part, while she kissed the rest of his sentence away. After three engagements gone bad, she was seldom adventurous these days; that was Kory's department. Kyra knew there was always a price to pay for indulgence, and this time she hoped with all her heart she would pay. "Are you mad?"

He grinned up at her. "Hell no. I normally don't take chances like this, but there's something about you that has my mind in a time warp. Probably next week, I'll be freaking out about this."

"Well, that's good to know, stud." She leaned down and kissed him.

"You'll pay for that." He rolled her over so that she was on her back.

Kyra didn't mind the power play; in fact, she welcomed it. She could wake up like this for the rest of her life. She caressed his back as he moved deeper inside her body. Each time, Kyra wasn't sure if she could take one more delicious stroke, but she was going to try. Between his heated kisses, a moan of pure enjoyment escaped her lips.

"You okay, baby?" he said against her lips.

"The best."

"Good, 'cause I don't think I'll be able to stop." He continued loving her senseless.

Kyra wanted to prolong the orgasm barreling through her body for as long as possible. Kevin seemed intent on quite the opposite, and increased the tempo of his surefire strokes, driving Kyra closer to the edge. She could no more stop it than the feelings she had for the small-town sheriff. She wrapped her arms and legs around him and hung on for the ride. "Oh, my God, Kevin," she said in wonder. Then she let out the loudest scream of her life, and Kevin joined her.

Both were too sated to move, talk, or do much of anything else. He eased off her body and pulled her close to him. She heard the rapid beat of his heart as she drifted to sleep.

"Okay, Bitsy, you can go out in just in a minute," Gladys Turner told her canine companion. "I don't know why you're so antsy this morning. You went out twice last night." She looked around her small living room for Bitsy's leather leash.

Bitsy stood at the front door, barking continuously. Bitsy's chubby body was anxious to go chase the neighbor's cat, most likely.

Gladys was tempted to forgo the leash, but she had earlier noticed the sheriff's truck parked in front of the Cotton house. She walked outside and glanced down the street to check the probability of letting Bitsy walk without a leash. She spotted the truck easily, still parked in front of the reporter's house. She marched back inside and faced Bitsy. "Sorry, honey. The sheriff is still there. We'll have to find your leash."

Bitsy barked and took off for the back of the house.

Gladys followed her friend to the kitchen. Maybe, just maybe, that blonde child knew where her leash was. She walked into the kitchen and laughed. "Bitsy! You're a mess."

Bitsy stood next to her food bowl with her leather leash in her mouth, looking at Gladys with those big brown eyes that did no wrong.

"All right, I forgive you. I know you hate the leash, but it's the law." She attached the leash to Bitsy's gold-plated collar, a present from Gladys's grandson.

They started on their daily journey of touring the neighborhood. Bitsy was a present from her oldest son ten years ago when her husband passed away. Gladys, not being a dog lover, was reluctant to take the dog in the beginning, but Bitsy had a way of growing on her.

Since Gladys retired from being a registered

nurse a few years ago, she was glad Bitsy was there to keep her company. She filled a void she hadn't known was there. Bitsy was an excellent listener. Bitsy was also nosy.

Like this morning. Bitsy was pulling Gladys by the leash down the street. Third Street wasn't busy for that time of the morning; it was barely nine. Most people had gone to work or school already. She noticed the car from last night. *Seems like the sheriff wasn't the only overnight visitor on the block*, she thought. She'd noticed the car when Bitsy was taking her nightly walk, and was surprised it was still there. It was parked in front of Callie Jenkins's house. *Lord knows that woman wouldn't have a gentleman caller and he sure wouldn't be driving a Mercedes.* Callie's only son lived in town and drove a restored 1979 Ford F-150.

Bitsy continued her quest to get closer to the strange vehicle. As they neared the parked car, she noticed a man slumped over in the driver's seat. Maybe he was spying on the sheriff and fell asleep on the job?

Gladys was going to tap on the window, just so the sheriff didn't catch this idiot and throw him in jail. The closer she got to the car, the more unease she felt. The man's eyes were closed, but she couldn't mistake the stream of dried blood that had trickled down the side of his pale face. Having been a nurse for thirty years, she knew he was no longer with the living. "Oh, my God, this man is dead!"

For the first time in a long time, Kevin considered taking the day off and staying in bed with

Kyra. He was letting a woman come between him and the job. He watched her sleep next to him with a satisfied smile on her pretty face without a care in the world. She was oblivious to the fact that she'd upset his perfect life.

After his divorce, Kevin thought he'd never feel any kind of emotion for another woman. His ex-wife, Ravena, had betrayed him by taking a job in Dallas without consulting him first. Granted, the marriage was troubled and he'd been shot in the line of duty as a Houston police officer for the second time. And there was no way Ravena would have moved to Wright City. Divorce was the only option. It took him a year to get over his failed marriage and he had no plans of embarking on anything, romantic or otherwise.

Up until a few weeks ago, Kevin had a peaceful life and no one questioned anything he did. At least, not anymore. Kevin liked order and predictability. He had a feeling that Kyra had blocked those words out of her vocabulary. Kyra was a reporter and therefore questioned everything, much like her millionaire father. That was where Kevin's problems started.

He sat up in bed with his mind buzzing with thoughts. First and foremost, he had to prevent another killing in Wright City. Then Kyra could be on her way back to Austin and out of his life. *Okay, Kev, you know the last thing you want is Kyra out of your life. Take it slow, brother.* He took a deep breath and looked down at Kyra. She was staring back up at him with those sexy eyes.

He laughed at his prior thoughts. If he had two

more minutes, two days, two weeks, two months, two whatever, he'd gladly take the time he had left to be with Kyra.

She moved closer to him. Her long fingers slid under the covers heading straight for the most erect part of his body. She closed her hand around him, squeezing softly, not enough to hurt, but just enough to make his eyes roll to the back of his head in delight.

She pulled back the sheet and Kevin knew exactly what was about to happen. He was going straight to paradise. Or, at least, he hoped so. Kyra's eyes met his for his approval or disapproval.

He nodded, took a deep breath, and braced himself for her next move.

She took him in her mouth. Her hot breath was doing crazy things to his body. All the blood was rushing to the one organ Kyra was servicing. His brain was on autopilot. His hands caressed her silky hair as it fanned his waist. His head lolled against the pillows in reckless abandon. As her tongue worked its magic, Kevin tried to help by raising his hips, but she pushed him back.

"Let me show you how much you mean to me."

And he did. Kevin slid his fingers through her hair. When he knew he couldn't take one more ounce of pressure from her mouth, he exploded.

He stared at the ceiling as his body calmed down. "Damn, baby," he panted. "You're amazing."

"Really?" Kyra moved next to him. "I haven't done it often, but I thought you were worth it." She held his hands against her heart.

Now they were heading into some mighty dangerous territory. What on earth was he supposed to say to a loaded statement like that?

"Kevin, you don't have to do the 'baby, you're the best' thing. I don't expect it. I do believe in voicing my opinion."

He had to say something, but every word was caught in his throat and determined not to leave his mouth. He wanted to tell her how he felt. How could he? He had no idea of his feelings. Kyra would expect some kind of response.

"Kevin, you're thinking too much," she said simply. She rose and put on her bathrobe. "How about a shower?" She walked into the bathroom.

He waited for her to close the door but she didn't. She started the water, dropped her robe, beckoned him to join her, and stepped inside the stall.

Kevin laughed as he hurried to the bathroom. He might be going down for the last time, but at least he would enjoy it.

After the best shower of his life, Kevin sat at the small kitchen table watching Kyra as she fixed breakfast! Talk about a woman full of surprises.

He glanced around the small kitchen. Memories from the previous summer clouded his happy thoughts. So much had happened in the house since then.

"Kevin, you have a strange look on your face," Kyra said, bringing him a cup of coffee. "I know. I don't have water. Sorry, baby." She kissed him on the forehead. "You have to quit doing so much thinking."

He took the hot liquid, and even though he didn't drink much caffeine, he made an exception. "Thanks, honey. I was just thinking about Mr. Cotton and everything that happened here this summer, ending with Regan getting shot."

Kyra set a plate of pancakes, bacon and eggs in front of him. "From what I've heard, it was an awful time. People can't stop saying good things about Mr. Cotton. That's the story I'm going to write about. How he helped everyone in town and wouldn't turn anyone away. I've heard Regan call him 'uncle.' How is she related to him?"

He inhaled the aroma of the food. If the pancakes tasted as good as they looked or smelled, she was an amazing cook. "She's not."

"Why did she call him uncle? The information I found stated he left everything to Regan."

Kevin cut up his food and took a bite. "He was a family friend. He was like her mentor. I hate to think what would have become of Regan if Mr. Cotton wasn't there in her formative years."

She sat at the table with her plate piled as high as his. "I know there's a story there, but this is our time. There'll be plenty of time to get the real story. This morning, I want to learn more about you."

Kevin shrugged. "Not much to tell."

"Oh, come on, Kevin. Tell me about being a sheriff in a small town after living in Houston." Kyra doctored her coffee. "I know you're health conscious. Why?"

"Heart attacks and strokes are rampant among African Americans. My family is pretty healthy and I want to keep my body in top working order. I've seen too many people take handfuls of pills every day just to stay alive. I don't want that."

"I'm always afraid Daddy is going to drop dead of a heart attack or something. I know my relationship with Daddy is strained and I'm working on that, but I'm not ready to lose him."

From his conversation with Chandler the previous day, Kevin could only imagine how distant Kyra and her father were. *He is a piece of work,* Kevin thought. "I can't even imagine what I'd do if something happened to my parents. It was bad enough earlier this year when my brother had gotten injured on the job. When they brought him home from the hospital, he was helpless. We had to do everything for him. He needed total care, but Mom was determined to keep him at home while he recouped. It was hard seeing him like that, but we all pitched in. My dad fed and shaved him, Mom cooked, I kept his spirits up and helped him exercise. Elias bounced back quickly. It took eight weeks, but he got well and then fell in love with the girl he should have married years ago."

"I know that smile," Kyra teased. "You're proud of your brother."

He couldn't deny it. The crisis had brought his family even closer together. "I'm also proud of my parents. Not every parent is strong enough for that. Then, later, when Regan was injured, we went through it again. I mean, she has her family, and they're very helpful, but you still go through it."

"I know. Every time I've talked to Regan, her mom was at her side. She said the wedding is the day after Christmas. How nerve-racking is that?"

Kevin didn't think so. "It's a symbol. She always

celebrated Christmas with Mr. Cotton the day after Christmas. They're getting married at the Safe Haven on Columbus Street."

"I've seen the house. It's being remodeled. I would have figured a big church wedding. Why the Haven?"

"It's another long story."

Nick walked down the hall to Kevin's office, concerned that his friend hadn't been in his office to give him the details of his trip to Austin to visit Kyra's father. In fact, Kevin hadn't checked in when he returned to town.

That could only mean one thing: Kevin talked to Kyra instead. Nick could only imagine how that conversation went. The phone on Kevin's desk rang. Nick answered it before it rang a second time. He assumed it was Kevin, but he was wrong.

"Sheriff Johnson's office, Deputy Fraser speaking," Nick said.

"Deputy who?" an older woman asked.

"Fraser," Nick repeated slowly. "The sheriff isn't in. Can I help you?"

"I know where the sheriff is. He's at the reporter's house on Third Street."

"Are you calling to report that?"

"No, this is Gladys Turner and there's a dead man on my street."

That got his attention. "Mrs. Turner, are you certain he's dead? Maybe he's asleep." The burning feeling in his stomach told him otherwise.

"Young man, I was a nurse when you were still a seed rolling around in your daddy. I know what a corpse looks like. He has dried blood on the side of his face."

"Okay, Mrs. Turner, we'll be there in a few minutes. Are you going to be okay until a unit gets there?"

"Who do you think you're talking to? I know a unit refers to Derek getting here. As I said, I've seen a dead body before and looks like he's been dead awhile. I'd say at least twelve hours."

"Yes, Mrs. Turner. Go back to your house and Derek will come get your statement. Do you know the victim?"

"He's a stranger. He looks like one of those guys on television."

Nick listened as the dial tone hummed in his ear. Apparently, Mrs. Turner had finished her conversation. Nick called Derek's cell phone and explained the situation. "Check it out for me and call me back."

Ten minutes later, Derek reported in. "Nick, Mrs. Turner was absolutely correct. There's a dead body. You know, the sheriff's truck is parked across the street at the Cotton house. Should I tell him?"

"No," Nick said. "I'll tell him." The day was certainly looking up. He couldn't wait to see the look on Kevin's face.

CHAPTER 16

Kyra watched Kevin as he washed their break-fast dishes and decided that yes, she was in love with this man. He had not only volunteered to make the bed, but also to clean up the kitchen. Yep, she was going to fall hard when this was over.

The doorbell sounded, alarming both of them. Kyra jumped out of her seat. "I wonder who would be knocking on my door." She walked to the door and laughed. "Baby, it's Nick. Should I let him in or give you chance to sneak out the back door?"

Kevin dried his hands on a kitchen towel and hurried to her. "You can open the door, smart ass." He lightly tapped her on her bottom. "That's for being so sassy."

Kyra had never been so turned on from a repri-mand before. She took a deep breath and opened the front door. Nick grinned at her. "Good morn-ing, Kyra, could I speak with Kevin? Or is he just too tired to talk?"

Kevin stepped into view and Nick's chuckles

ceased. "Very funny. How did you know I was here?"

Kyra also wanted to know. Not that she was hiding anything, but it would be nice to know who ratted her out. "Yeah, who's telling my business before I can?"

Nick laughed, stepped further inside her house, and closed the door. With both the men being over six feet, Kyra noticed how small the room actually was. "Please, sit down, Nick and tell us why you're here."

He glanced from Kyra to Kevin, then shrugged. "Mrs. Turner ratted you out. She said Kevin's truck has been here since about seven last night. Living room light went out about ten. That time line sound correct?"

Kevin cleared his throat. "Why is this so important?"

A look passed between the men that told Kyra's reporter sense that something big had happened, but her sense as a woman wanted to let her man take care of it. "I have some calls to make." She kissed Kevin and stood. "I'll be right back."

Kevin watched Kyra as she left the room. Then his eyes focused on Nick, who was smiling. "All right, let's get this over with. What's so important?"

Nick rose. "Let's walk across the street and I'll show you."

Kevin figured this was something big and apparently not for Kyra's reporter ears. "All right." He had to tell her something. "I'll meet you outside."

"Reporting to the little woman? It's so sad when a brother falls in love. Now you'll be telling her when you go to the bathroom," Nick teased.

Kevin wasn't going to let Nick bait him. "Just wait outside," he said, walking to the bedroom. When he opened the bedroom door, Kyra was on her laptop, surfing the Internet.

She looked up from her computer. "What's wrong?"

"I don't know." He walked toward her and sat on the bed. "Words can't express what I felt last night, and this morning, Kyra. I wanted to have more time to discuss it."

"Kevin, don't worry. Go do your job. I totally understand. If I had a hot lead, I'd be doing the same thing."

That was definitely true. She'd drop him like a hot potato in her quest for a story. "Okay, I'll call you when I can." He kissed her softly on the lips and left the room.

He met Nick on the porch. "Now, what's so important that Mrs. Turner is telling everyone where I slept last night?"

Nick nodded. "Across the street."

Kevin looked to the black Mercedes parked across the street. There were two police cars, the medical examiner's car, and Henry Jenkins's truck parked in front of Mrs. Jenkins's house. "Okay, what happen to Mrs. Jenkins?"

"Nothing. What happen last night with you and Kyra? Looks pretty hot and heavy if you guys are playing house already. You didn't cook breakfast, did you?"

"No and no. I cleaned up the kitchen." Kevin

smiled, remembering all that he and Kyra had shared in the last twenty-four hours. "Who died?"

Nick motioned for Kevin to walk to the crime scene. "You're going to hate this, especially with you getting closer to Kyra and all, but he was a stranger in town. Two shots to the temple. Doc here says the first one did the job, don't know why a second shot was fired."

Kevin muttered a curse. This was all he needed—another body. "Any ID?"

"Yes. His name is Anthony Talbot. His ID says he's from Travis City, Texas. Yes, it's a suburb of Austin. His wife says he texted her about ten-thirty last night. Doc says he was killed shortly after that."

Kevin shook his head. "How could I not have heard two shots? Why didn't Mrs. Turner hear shots?"

"Silencer," Nick said. "No one in the neighborhood heard any kind of noises except for the racket you and Kyra were keeping up."

He almost had Kevin until the last bit. "Right. Make sure you go over the car. There has to be something we're not seeing. Three professional hits in less than two weeks, yeah, there's something we're not seeing."

"What did Chase have to say about all this? Is he involved?"

Kevin shook his head. "Ever heard of the Ditano family?"

"Texas's answer to the Gambino family. Hell yeah. What does a crime family have to do with all this?"

"Contract on Chase, and the elder Ditano over-rode that, but it doesn't apply to Kyra."

Nick stopped walking and stood directly in front of Kevin. "Please tell me that Ditano didn't order a hit on Kyra. We're going to be overrun with contract killers. You know they're not going to stop until the deed is done."

Kevin noted the serious look in his friend's dark eyes. "Don't you think I know that? I don't know who's killing the contractors before they can get anywhere near Kyra. Chase said they only call and tell him who they've hired. He wouldn't have enough time to hire someone to come after the killers." He took a deep breath. This morning had such possibilities and now it was headed straight for the crapper.

"And they were all shot in the same fashion. The wound is always clean with very little blood. They get close enough for it to be a small wound."

Kevin's cell chirped to life. He looked down at the display. EJ. "Hey, man, what's up?"

His brother laughed. "I could ask you the same thing. Regan said your truck was parked in front of the rental house all night."

"Why is everyone in my business? Yes, I stayed over. The rest is none of your business. I'm in the middle of something right now, can I hit you back?"

"Okay, brother, I get it. You gotta let this woman catch her breath," Elias joked.

Kevin wanted to tell his DEA agent of a brother to mind his own business, but he didn't. "If you must know, there's been a murder. Third one, actually," Kevin admitted.

"Wow, bro. Anyone I know?"

"Maybe in your professional capacity, other than

that, I doubt it very seriously. It's no one from Wright City. All three hail from the Austin area and are contract killers."

"You know I'll be down in a few hours. Why don't you fill me in on what's going on? I could give you a hand. I'm spending a few days with Regan. She said something about registering for bridal stuff."

With all the commotion going on in his life, Kevin had completely forgotten about his best man duties for his brother's wedding. "I thought she couldn't travel until the wedding. Even traveling thirty miles to Waco might be too taxing for her. She's still healing from some serious injuries, EJ. You don't want her back in the hospital before the wedding."

"There's such a thing called the computer," he joked. "She just wants me to help pick out colors and stuff. Besides, I haven't seen her in almost a week. I could give you a hand with this murder business. I'll run the names through the computer and see if any flags pop up."

"Thanks, man, let me know when you get to town." He ended the call. "EJ is coming down later today," he told Nick. "He's going to run the victims' names through the computer and see what comes back."

Nick nodded. "Good. So, we're done here?"

Kevin looked at the scene before him. He could have stayed, but it wouldn't have served any purpose. He glanced across the street to Kyra's place. She was the biggest part of the puzzle, but for some reason someone was keeping her safe from the contractors.

"Kevin?" Nick nudged his friend. "You know you can't offer her protection, because she's not going to take it. And, right now, someone wants her alive. Maybe it's a rival family."

"Please tell me you're not thinking it's a war between crime families in Wright City over a reporter from Austin?" Kevin rubbed his head. This was so not a good day. And when he glanced back across the street, Kyra was standing on the front steps. To Nick, he said, "Meet you back at the office."

Nick smiled. "Later, man. Go handle your woman. If you're not in the office by lunch time, I'll send Derek to get you." He left before Kevin could answer.

Kevin shook his head and walked across the street.

Kyra knew something huge was going on and every sense in her body told her she should be there getting the scoop. Still, she didn't move. She was rooted to a spot on her front porch waiting for Kevin to return. As she realized what she was doing, she knew she'd crossed over to the other side. She'd gone totally female.

He approached with a slow smile. "Another assassin from Austin."

Kyra already knew the other part of that sentence he'd left out. "Dead." It wasn't a question.

Kevin didn't take it as one, either. He switched to his sheriff mode flawlessly. "Kyra, someone wants you dead in the worst way. Any idea who?"

"You'd have to ask Daddy." She sat down on the steps. "I think he has an idea. I should have gone with my instincts earlier and refused this assignment, and this mess wouldn't have followed me here."

He sat beside her. "And I'd never have met you," he said softly. "Baby, it would have followed you anywhere." He took a deep breath. "Kyra, I'm going to say something you probably don't want to hear, but it has to be said."

Oh, she didn't like where this conversation was going. "What is it, Kevin? I'm not some fragile woman, I can take it." She gathered up her dignity and faced him with a forced smile.

"Kyra, I never said you weren't strong. You're a strong, independent woman and I know you can handle yourself accordingly." He moved closer to her. "I'm telling you this for your own safety. There's a price on your head. A very high price. It doesn't matter how many attempts it takes, it won't stop until you're stopped or I can stop them."

"You said you didn't think Daddy put a price on my head. Who did?"

"I said he's involved, but that's not important right now. What's important is that we need to be proactive in your safety. I can have someone guard you."

She shook her head at the absurdity of having a bodyguard. It reminded her too much of her past. "No, Kevin. Then the whole town will know I brought all this trouble with me. I prefer everyone only speculating about me. As you said, someone is killing the men before they get to me. Don't waste your manpower." No matter how sexy and concerned Kevin looked, Kyra wasn't giving in this time. She was tired of people thinking they had to watch out for her.

"I appreciate your concern about my budget. We do have the manpower to protect you. It wouldn't look good if the daughter of one of the richest men in Texas was killed in our town."

"I don't want a bodyguard, Kevin." She hoped the tone in her voice was convincing.

"What about a compromise?"

"What kind of compromise did you have in mind?"

"We spend the evenings together. You can interview me for your story and I'll know you're protected."

Kyra had little or no options. "Where are we doing these interviews?"

"We can do them here or we can do them at my place. Where did you have in mind?"

"I want to do more than just sit around my place or yours. I want to learn more about Wright City." And she wanted to learn more about Kevin.

"I think I can handle that. You leave that to me," he said with a sly grin. "You'll see places only the locals know about. I've lived here most of my life."

"I look forward to it," Kyra said. She could only imagine the places Kevin was referring to.

He chuckled. "I can't believe it. We actually compromised on something without World War Three breaking out." He cleared his throat. "Baby, I gotta get to work. My brother, Elias, is coming down today to visit Regan and is going to help me with the case." He stood in front of her, pulling her up with him. "I'll call you later." He kissed her gently on the lips.

Kyra licked her lips and nodded. "I have some research to do at the newspaper office," she said.

By the time Kevin arrived at the office, Nick had everything in full swing. Derek and the other deputies had also returned to the office and were in Nick's office discussing their options about the third body.

"Do we know for sure they're after Ms. Chase?" Derek asked, leaning against the counter and sipping a Coke. "Maybe it's just a strange coincidence."

"Derek, that's what I like about you. The glass is always half full. Unfortunately, I have proof to refute your theory." Kevin closed the door to Nick's office so they could have privacy. "Now, gentlemen, this is for our ears only, but yesterday I went to Austin and interviewed Chandler Chase, Kyra's father." He looked at the stunned faces. Only Nick knew of his trip. "Because of some past business connections with the Ditano family, a hit was placed on the elder Chase. Because of his ties with the grandfather, the hit on Chase was cancelled." He wondered if any of the deputies would read between lines.

Derek gasped. "But according to my cousin, when a hit is issued, and is cancelled by someone in the family, it's not really cancelled. It's merely transferred to a more expendable member of the family."

"That's correct, Derek. The hit transferred to Kyra. The Ditanos aren't going to call off the hit just because three men have gotten killed. So we need to cut this off at the source."

The deputies looked at one another, then to Kevin. "How? They'll just keep sending them."

"I'm open to any ideas. Although this is our priority, don't forget we still have a town to protect. Don't let your other duties go to the wayside looking for the next contractor."

"So, does Ms. Chase need a security guard?"

Kevin smiled, remembering the morning conversation with Kyra. "Yes, she needs protection, but Ms. Chase denied it and since someone is killing the men before they get anywhere near her, we can shift out attention elsewhere. But I don't like her being unguarded during the day, so Derek, you get Kyra duty. I want you to follow her movements and report back to me."

Derek nodded. "Yes, Sheriff. How long do I stay on duty?"

He hated that his social life would now be a very public matter. "Until I pick her up."

"Why are you picking her up?" Derek had the nerve to have an innocent look on his tanned face.

"If you guys must know, I'm letting Kyra interview me for her story. Derek, you'll need to do this in plain clothes. A uniform will really stick out to Kyra. Let me know the minute any new information comes in about any of the deaths." Kevin rose and left the room.

In the privacy of his office, Kevin mulled over the deaths. They all had same MOD: method of death. Two clean shots to the head. It was like searching for a needle in a haystack. He was going to have to go over each death with a detailed eye and maybe, just maybe, something would jump out at him.

He pulled files out of his top desk drawer, where he kept all his open cases, which right now were the two hit men. He thought about dialing Chandler and reporting the death, but decided against it. All he would do was curse himself. Besides, there wasn't much he could have done anyway. The last thing he needed was Chandler Chase in Wright City.

An hour later, Kyra didn't drive to the newspaper office. She drove to her landlord's house. Brenda opened the front door before she could ring the doorbell.

"Kyra, it's nice to see you. Is there a problem at the house?" She motioned Kyra inside.

Kyra entered the house, taking in its homey décor. The room was immaculate, not a thing out of place. Pictures of all sizes adorned the walls. Pictures hung proudly of Regan and a young man. A gorgeous black-and-white Corgi sat on the fabric couch. Apparently, the dog was used to strangers, and didn't even bother to bark to announce Kyra's presence. Kyra sat in a love seat across from the silent dog.

"That's Mopsy," Brenda explained as she took a seat on the couch. "She's so used to people coming in and out of the house since Regan's accident, she doesn't even bother to bark anymore."

Kyra wasn't sure how to broach the subject and knew this was delicate ground. "That's kind of why

I'm here. As you know, Brenda, I'm a reporter, and I was assigned a story about the cocaine scandal of last summer."

Brenda studied her with dark eyes. "Yes, I know."

Kyra pressed on before she lost her nerve. "I want to do a story about Mr. Cotton instead. It seems like he helped just about everyone in town in one way or another. I think it would be a wonderful human interest story."

Brenda nodded, but didn't say much else. It was almost as if she was weighing something very heavy in her brain. "Well, Regan would be the person you should talk to. She knew Donald better than anyone. He was like a father to her. He left everything to her."

Kyra kept getting the feeling that there was something very dark lurking behind Brenda's comments. She almost sounded jealous of the relationship Regan had with Mr. Cotton. Hopefully, she'd find out soon.

CHAPTER 17

Kyra walked into Regan's bedroom. Regan was dressed in a blue silk nightshirt sitting up in her queen-sized bed and talking on her cell phone to her fiancé, if the lovey-dovey talk was any indication. Her bed was littered with bridal magazines, invitations, and her laptop computer.

"I'll see you soon, honey. We have lot of work to do on the wedding," she said, noticing Kyra in the room. "Kyra is here. I'll talk to you later."

Regan ran her hand over her short hair. "Is there something wrong at the house?" She waved her hand at the chair next to her bed. "Please sit down."

Kyra took the seat. "Thank you, Regan. It's not about the house. Well, maybe in a roundabout way."

Regan smiled. "Kyra, I'm not as weak as I look. I can take bad news. Kevin and Elias are a little over-protective. They are about as bad as my family and everyone else in town."

That gave Kyra the incentive to push on.

"Regan, I want to do a story about Mr. Cotton. From what I've heard, everyone in town loved him, and I'd like to show what a good man he was."

A lone tear cascaded down Regan's face. "He *was* a good man and he loved helping people. Unfortunately, that's what got him killed." She took a deep breath, trying to hold back more tears, and losing the battle. She reached for a tissue and wiped her face. "I'm sorry, Kyra. It's still hits me hard sometimes. I think it's a wonderful idea. When he died last summer, I had to know what happened to him. He didn't deserve a scandal linked to his name after all the good he was trying to do for this town. That's how Elias and I reconnected last summer. He helped me piece together what really happened and we ended up breaking up a major cocaine operation that killed so many innocent teenagers. Unfortunately, that's when I was injured. He proposed a few weeks later."

Kyra wanted a love like that. Regan and Elias might not have dated long, but they had real love. "That sounds wonderful. I'd really like to meet him before I leave Wright City."

"He's on his way down here from Dallas. We need to register for the wedding, since it's just about a month away. We're getting married on Boxing Day, as the Brits call it."

"The day after Christmas," Kyra said. "That sounds romantic. You know, starting the New Year off right."

Regan smiled. "I don't know about all that. It used to be the day I spent with Uncle Potbelly, I mean, Mr. Cotton."

"Was that your name for Mr. Cotton?"

"How did you know?"

"I'm a reporter. I notice things. Everyone in town referred to him as Mr. Cotton. So far you're the only one calling him that."

"Guilty. I'm the only one who called him that."

Kyra knew from the contented look on her face that Mr. Cotton was a positive force in Regan's life. "When can I interview you?"

Regan thought for a minute. "How about today? We can have lunch at Jay's. I haven't had her food in a while and it would be fun to get out of the house."

"What about your mom?"

"Oh, she's busy looking for the perfect mother-of-the-bride dress," she said casually. "You can interview me and I can grill you about Kevin. It's nice to see him focused on more than work. For the record, I think you guys are good for each other. The women here drool over Kevin, just because he's a Johnson, but you give him a run for his money."

It was so smooth, Kyra hadn't seen it coming. "You're good."

Regan smiled back at her, throwing back the covers. "Just give me a few minutes to get dressed." She rose gingerly. "I know what you're thinking, but I'm feeling pretty good."

Kyra observed Regan, and she did look better than the first time they met. "Okay, Regan, I'll wait downstairs."

"Thank you, Kyra. It's nice to be treated like an adult again."

Kyra nodded and went downstairs. Brenda was

sitting on the couch, several bridal magazines spread out before her and Mopsy by her side. "Is Regan asleep?"

"No, she was getting dressed."

"Dressed?"

"Yes, she's going to let me interview her over lunch at Jay's." She noted the concerned look on Brenda's brown face. "If you're, worried about her health, you're more than welcome to come along."

"No," Brenda said a little too quickly. "I'm sure she just wants to get out of the house. The doctor says she needs to build her strength back up anyway. I know I'm overprotective, but I'm in the health profession. I know what can go wrong." She wiped away a tear. "I won't bother you with the horrid details, but I almost lost my baby twice last summer and I'm not going to allow a third time."

"I understand," Kyra said. "I'm sure she just wants to get out of the house for a while." Kyra really didn't understand what exactly Brenda meant. *Regan and her mother seem close,* she mused. But things were seldom what they seemed.

Regan came downstairs dressed in a DEA sweatshirt, and jeans that seemed to swallow her slender frame. "Mom, I'm going to have lunch with Kyra."

"I know, baby. You be careful." To Kyra, she said, "I only ask that you take my car or Regan's. I've seen that little sardine can you drive. Much too fast, I might add."

"Mom," Regan pleaded. "Not now. I'm sure Kyra's car is perfectly safe."

"My SUV has more room," Brenda pointed out.

Regan sighed. "We'll take my Trailblazer."

Her mother nodded and went back to looking

through the bridal magazines. "Have a nice lunch. What time is Elias coming by?"

Regan grabbed a set of keys, and handed them to Kyra. "He didn't say. He's going to see Kevin first."

"Okay. I'll make something special for him for dinner tonight."

Regan kissed her mother on the cheek and they left.

"Okay, tell me about Mr. Cotton." They were settled in a corner booth at Jay's. Kyra took out her mini tape recorder, set it on the table between them, and turned it on. "Don't worry, I'm not going to use everything you say, just the good parts."

Regan nodded, and grabbed a menu. "Why don't we play twenty questions? You know, you ask a question and I'll ask a question."

Kyra saw the harm in that instantly. But could she deny this woman who had been through so much? "Deal. Can I go first?"

"As soon as we order," Regan said, waving at a young man to take their order.

With their orders placed and sweet tea before them, Kyra started her questions. "I knew Mr. Cotton was in your life. What do you remember most about him?"

Regan took a sip of tea. "I guess his unconditional love for me. I'm sure you don't know this, but I used to weigh well over two hundred pounds. Growing up, food was my comfort for everything. My mother and I didn't have the best relationship.

Mom has always been thin. Naturally, she wanted me to be thin too. Don't get me wrong, Mom loves me, but she would never show it. She'd call me fat, and just about every other name that went with being an overweight child and teenager. I'd run to Uncle Potbelly for solace. He told me I was beautiful no matter what size I was."

Kyra thought of Regan as a chubby child and her heart wept for all the hurt she must have endured from her mother, of all people. "I'm sorry, Regan."

"Don't be sorry, Kyra. It made me stronger. I had Uncle Potbelly. He encouraged me to go to college, get my master's degree, and so many other things. I guess you could say he brought me and Elias together. And I'll always be thankful for that."

Kyra heard the love in Regan's soft voice. She had dearly loved her uncle. Could Kyra have confessed that kind of love for her biological father? Most likely not.

"Okay, it's my turn," Regan said.

For a brief moment, Kyra had forgotten about Regan's part of the deal. She wanted to know about Kevin. But so had Kyra. "Okay, hit me." Kyra took a sip of tea, hoping Regan didn't detect the nervousness in her voice.

"Do you like Kevin?"

Okay, it wasn't what she was expecting. *Maybe this is a trick*, she thought. "Sure, I like Kevin, when he's not being a stick in the mud."

"Don't play, Kyra. You know what I mean. Is he just a dalliance while you're in town or do you really care for him? I'm asking not only for me, but for my fiancé. Elias and Kevin are close and I'm very fond of Kevin. He's been through too much these last few years to let me sit idly by and let you crush him like a rotten tomato."

"I know where you're coming from, Regan, and I wish I could answer your question, but I can't. Not and be completely honest with you."

"So what is it?"

"I don't know. I like being around him. He's brutally honest, which is kind of refreshing for me, but he loves his job. So I'm taking it one day at a time."

Regan nodded. "I guess I should be happy with your answer, but I'm not. I like you Kyra. I think you're exactly what Kevin needs. I don't know if he has another heartbreak in him."

"You know, my heart can get broken as well. Kevin thinks I'm going to leave Wright City the minute my story is done."

"Well, are you?"

It is time to confess it someone, she mused. Time to lighten her heavy burden and tell another human soul. "Actually, I've been thinking . . ."

Regan smiled. "I knew it. You're in love with him, aren't you?"

"Does it show?"

"A woman can tell these things. Have you told him?"

Kyra realized that for the first time in her journalism career, she'd lost control of the interview, but she didn't care. "Of course not."

Regan reached across the table and touched Kyra's hand. "It's okay to be in love, Kyra. There's no shame in admitting that you care about someone else. I always thought I wasn't missing anything not having a special person in my life. The moment Elias burst into my life, I realized I was lonely and wanted someone to love me."

"And Elias is that man?"

Regan leaned back in her chair and nodded smugly. "Yes, he is. He's worth everything to me."

"How so?"

"If I'm having a bad day with therapy, it's like he senses it. Just hearing him on the phone brightens my day. We talk every day, and so far we haven't run out of things to say to each other."

"That's amazing, Regan. Maybe that love was there all along."

She laughed. "Possibly. But when we were in high school, Elias was Mr. Popularity. I didn't think he'd look twice at a chubby girl who was always buried in her studies when he had all those cheerleaders running behind him. But, truth is, we both had a crush on each other and were too stupid to say anything back then. I guess that was why it so easy for us to pick up where we left off all those years ago."

Kyra pondered her situation with Kevin. He was so unlike any man she'd ever met in her life. He hadn't backed down from her father when he had to ask the tough questions, yet he did have a soft side as well. "Well, Kevin and I hadn't known each other that long, but it feels different."

Regan leaned toward Kyra. "I also know Kevin is a stickler about reputation. In fact, all the Johnson boys are. He'd never do anything to sully your rep. If the chatter around town is true, he's spent the night with you twice. He might not say he loves you, but I know he's feeling it. Hey, look, our food is coming."

For once, the conversation, not the delicious food had Kyra's attention. She watched the waiter as he deposited their food on the table, made sure they had everything they needed, and left.

"Do you think he'll say it to me?"

Regan placed her napkin in her lap, then looked at Kyra. "Do you want him to? I know you're in a sticky place right now, so do you really want him to declare his feelings for you?"

"At least once. It would be nice to know."

"He could say the same."

"I knew you'd be practical. I've been burned so many times with men claiming they loved me and didn't. They loved me to get close to either my father or his money." She reflected on the select number of lovers she'd had over the years. High profile or not, they'd all been dogs.

"Well, Kevin, much like Elias, is his own man. I bet he doesn't care one bit that your father is a millionaire and has the power to buy and sell him."

"I know that's what keeps drawing me closer to him. I think I'm more confused than before."

Regan laughed. "Yeah, I know that feeling. But in the end it will be worth it."

CHAPTER 18

Later that afternoon, Elias walked into the sheriff's office expecting to see his younger brother frazzled and drinking bottle after bottle of soda. He wasn't expecting the picture of his brother taking a nap with a smile on his face!

He knocked on the open door, waking Kevin. He opened his eyes, yawned, and stretched. "Hey, man. About time you got here. It's almost five. Dallas is only two hours away."

Elias sat down in the chair facing the desk. "Sorry, I left later than I had anticipated. I was getting the report I promised you." He gazed at his brother's wistful expression.

"Well?"

Elias placed the three-page report on Kevin's desk. "Before we get started on that, I have to ask."

"What?" Kevin didn't hide his skepticism. "Have you been talking to Mom?"

"Better. Regan."

Kevin sighed. "Yeah, they had lunch today. Five people called and told me, so it's not news, EJ."

Kevin's life had become so predictable in the last few years. It was nice when things got shaken up, even if Kevin was totally against it. "No, I was referring to Kyra Chase, the millionaire's only child. Rumor has it you've been keeping company with her for two nights straight."

Again, Kevin surprised him. Instead of Kevin getting all crazy, and demanding that everyone stay out of his business, he smiled. "There's no point in denying it. Yeah, we've been talking."

"By talking, you mean . . ."

"Don't be crude, EJ."

Elias stared at his brother. For Kevin to spend the night with Kyra was one thing, but for him to have a murderous look in his eyes was quite another. "So do you care for this woman? Regan says she's really nice, super smart, and has a sassy spirit."

Kevin stood, walked to his office door, and closed it. "That's just it, EJ. All these deaths are connected to her. Not only is my job on the line, so is my heart. I'm in a tight spot, and there's really no solution."

EJ knew that spot well. He had been in the same spot earlier that summer with his fiancée. It was a hard fight, but he won her hand in the end. "Kevin, that just means she's worth it. If it were easy, everyone would be in love."

"I hope you're right, Elias."

Kevin let his brother's information about the contract killers sink in slowly before totally exploding. "EJ, what the hell do you mean, their files were inaccessible?"

"Just what I said. Even with the security clearance I have, I could only get a partial report on them."

"So you're telling me these killers for hire work for the government? My government? I'm paying for killers?" He already knew that, but it was just the idea of it all.

"Kev, calm down. Yes, the government does have a department of contractors. Unfortunately, the name of that department isn't known to the rest of the intelligence community. Most of what I know is hearsay. So take what I'm about to tell you with a grain of salt."

Kevin leaned back in his chair. It seemed like such a good idea this morning when EJ suggested running the names through the government database. Kevin had hoped for some kind of clue, but now with one roadblock after another, he had begun to give up hope.

"Kev? You want the upside or not?"

"Hit me."

Elias smiled. "Now that's my pigheaded brother. Okay, there's a group of contractors assigned to the states. You know, to keep things level. If there's some nut in a clocktower somewhere picking off students, or whatever, they go in and take him out with as little fuss as possible. All your victims are with the government. So beyond the basic information, little else is known. I did find out why they were getting dispatched here."

"Why?"

"You're really not going to like this," Elias said.

"What else is new? I have to know what I'm up against. I don't even know if I can stop this mess."

"True. This is going all the way up the chain, brother. The Ditanos have a lot of juice. Not enough to save Julian from prison and a death sentence, but enough to get the best contractors in the United States. As soon as Ditano finds out about the last guy, another contractor will be on his way."

Kevin lowered his head in his hands. How was he going to stop an army? He was going to need a serious miracle.

"Kev, I know this looks pretty hopeless right now."

"You're damn right! I got three murders, a woman with a price on her head, and someone is killing the killers before they can kill her. I'm so tired of this. I'm tired of people dying in my town and being helpless to stop it."

"There is a way," EJ said after Kevin finished his tirade.

"I'm listening."

Elias opened his mouth to speak, but his cell phone rang. After a few seconds, Kevin knew it was his future sister-in-law. "Oh, baby, I'll be there in about fifteen minutes." He ended his call and rose. "Wedding plans. We'll talk about this in the morning. I got a plan marinating in my head, but I need to work out some details. Call Chase and get some info on the next one."

Kevin nodded, dreading the call already. "Got it. Kyra's interviewing me tonight, so call my cell."

Elias looked at his brother.

Kevin laughed. "I know what you're thinking. She denied protection, but I have someone watching her. She interviews me and I show her around the town. I have to let her think she's in control."

Elias shrugged, knowing bull when he heard it. "Meet me at Mom's in the morning."

Kevin nodded and waved his brother out the door. "Will do. Tell Regan hello for me."

"Okay."

Miguel Ditano slammed his fist against the wall, shaking the house to its core. Another man killed. And he thought it would be easy avenging his brother's imprisonment.

Now he had to explain to his father why a sum of $3 million dollars was missing from the accounts and why Kyra Chase was still alive. He also had to explain why they needed yet another million to hire another contractor to terminate the asset.

He walked through the fifteen-room mansion to his father's master bedroom. Mario Ditano sat at his oversized desk, looking at a spreadsheet on his desktop computer. The years had been very kind to his father. His dark hair, streaked with gray; his brown eyes still bright with activity. Nothing went on in the Ditano family without him knowing about it.

Miguel cleared his throat. "Dad, I just got news that Talbot was killed."

"Yes, I know. I also know that against my wishes, you have been trying to make good on the Chase hit."

"Yes."

Mario nodded. "And we're down three million dollars. And you're here to tell me that you want to hire yet another assassin."

"Yes."

"Why?"

"How can you ask that with Julian in prison? If Chase would have kept his word and defended Julian, he wouldn't be in jail right now."

"You're letting your love for your brother cloud your judgment, Miguel. Julian did commit a horrible crime and he must pay."

Miguel couldn't believe his ears. This was the man who killed people for looking at him wrong, and now he was spouting ridiculous dribble! "What are you saying, Dad?"

"I'm saying we've shelled out three million dollars and she's still alive. When do we just give up?"

Miguel didn't know the answer to that. "One more try."

Kyra was sitting on the couch in her rented house, assembling her notes on Donald Cotton. Regan had been very helpful with her information, when she wasn't crying. Regan loved her uncle and missed him terribly. It seemed Donald didn't know a stranger. He sounded like a very sweet man that she would have been proud to have known.

She'd made a plan of attack on paper. Setting out to interview people in Wright City to get other angles was a good start. She'd also have to go back to the *Wright City Record* to do more research on Donald. She made a list of the people she needed to see, with his attorney at the top of the list.

This was the kind of story she'd always wanted to write. Not just about a man in the wrong place at the wrong time, but a man with a heart as big as Texas. Although Regan and Elias had cleared Cotton's name, Kyra wanted to do something bigger.

She heard footsteps on her front porch. Her heart skipped a beat, and instantly she knew it was Kevin. She walked to the front door and opened it. There he was, in all his glory, in her doorway, dressed in jeans, starched shirt, and boots.

"Hey, baby," he said, leaning down to kiss her. "How was lunch with Regan?" He walked inside the house.

She closed the door and walked back to the couch. "How do you know who . . .?" She shook her head. "Oh, right. The small town thing. Yes, I had a different idea for my story and I went to talk to Regan. So we had lunch today. She's really sweet."

Kevin moved the stack of papers to the coffee table and sat on the couch. "Yeah, she's had a tough time healing, but she's an angel. Best thing for Elias."

"Seems like everyone in town likes her too. People were constantly interrupting us while we were having lunch at Jay's. They were happy to see her out and about. The funny thing is very few people asked about her mother."

Kevin nodded. "Yeah, her mother was a piece of work until the explosion."

"Explosion?"

"Yeah. Last summer, the people who killed Mr. Cotton wanted to threaten Brenda. They tried to kill Regan by blowing up her car. Regan wasn't in the car, but she was close enough to it to get thrown about fifty feet. She was bruised up, but that's when Brenda changed. Then when those same idiots kidnapped Regan and she ended up getting shot last summer, Brenda turned into Super Mom. I'm surprised she let Regan out of her sight."

"She called twice."

Kevin laughed. "That's Brenda. She overcompensating. She's driving Regan nuts. Like she can make up for thirty-six years of being a bad mother in a few months time. Don't get me wrong, the new Brenda is a hundred times better than the old Brenda, but it has taken some getting used to."

Kyra's mind raced with all the possible scenarios according to Kevin's blanket statements. "Well, hopefully, I'll never meet the old Brenda. She did seem to harbor some kind of resentment toward Mr. Cotton, but I'm sure that's a long story."

"About thirty years long."

Kyra wanted to lighten the somber mood in the room. "So, when do I start my interview with you?"

"I thought you shifted the focus of the interview."

"I did. I still need some good, solid quotes from the new, honest sheriff." She moved closer to him. "How about dinner?"

"Sounds good. How about barbeque? Marvin's is the best in the state."

"You're trying to tell me that one of the best barbeque places in this giant state of Texas is here in Wright City? I must have missed that article in *Texas Monthly*," she said sarcastically.

But Kevin wasn't to be outdone. "When you get

there, you can read Marvin's copy of the article. It's on the wall by the cashier."

"You're kidding!"

Kevin shook his head. "I don't kid." He grinned. "Okay, that's a lie. I don't kid often."

"What are we doing after dinner?"

The slow smile on Kevin's face spoke volumes. "Oh, let's just play that part by ear." He stood and offered his hand to her. "I have a few surprises for you tonight."

Kyra took his hand and rose. She kissed him quickly. "I hope so, Sheriff." She walked to her bedroom, grabbed her purse and her keys, and they were out the door.

Kyra shook her keys at him. "Want me to drive?"

He took her keys and locked her front door. "No. That car is too small. Once was more than enough." He handed them to her. "We'll go in my nice, roomy truck." He grabbed her hand and led her to his truck.

Walking into Marvin's Homestyle Barbeque wasn't anything like Kyra had imagined a small town barbeque place would be. She kept imagining a small building with a pit outside. Yes, Marvin's was like that on the outside, but on the inside it felt like home.

The small building held four twelve-foot-long picnic tables topped with red and white plastic tablecloths. The counter was in the back of the room. On this certain evening, Marvin's was packed.

When she and Kevin entered the room, the boisterous crowd became very quiet. He put his arm around her and whispered, "Normally, they're not this nosy. They just have to get used to you."

Kyra's heart swelled at his words. Was he implying there was a reason for the town to get used to her? "You know, the same thing happened at Dairy Queen. I think it's you," she teased him.

He guided her to the back of the room and pointed to a blackboard used as a menu. "What do you like? Please don't say chicken."

"I was going to say you, but I think I'd like some ribs. I haven't had them in a while."

Kevin smiled at her. "Don't make me have to take you outside."

"I'd rather you just take me." Where was this sassy talk coming from?

"Good evening, Sheriff. Haven't seen you in a while," a large black man greeted them. "This must be that lady reporter I been hearing about. She's just as pretty as everybody says." He nodded at Kyra. "What can I get for you?"

Kevin nodded at her. "Ladies first."

Kyra gave her order of ribs and a loaded baked potato. She looked at Kevin before he gave his order. "How's that, Sheriff? I don't think there's a low-calorie item on the menu."

"Very good, Kyra." To the gentleman behind the counter, he said, "I'll have what she's having."

"Okay, Sheriff. Name's Marvin," he told Kyra in that Southern drawl that dripped like molasses. "I'm the owner of this place. Anything wrong with the food, let me know. Anything wrong with the sheriff, let his momma know. She's sitting right over there." He nodded to his left.

Kyra laughed. "Oh, you know where we're sitting."

After Kevin paid for their meal, Kyra dragged him over to his parents' table. To make matters worse, Chris was also in attendance. "Hi, Mom, Dad, Chris. This is Kyra Chase." He tried to nudge Kyra to keep walking. "We don't want to interrupt your meal. See you later."

"Kevin Johnson," his mother said in that tone. "Don't you dare try to run away with this pretty woman. There's plenty of room for two more."

He sighed. He was as trapped as a turkey the day before Thanksgiving. "Fine." He guided Kyra to the empty seat next to his mother. He sat next to Kyra.

"It's very nice meeting you, Mr. and Mrs. Johnson," Kyra said as she spread a cloth napkin over her lap. "Wright City is a lovely place."

"Please, it's Dorrie and David. Yes, we love it here. It's a good place to raise a family."

"Mom?" Surely, his momma didn't just go there in front of everybody.

"I was just saying," his mother explained. "You act like I'm trying to sell her on what a good husband you'd make. I'm sure she already knows that."

Chris coughed indiscreetly.

If he could have left without making a bigger scene than his mother, he would have. But Kevin had to take it like a man.

As if she could sense how embarrassed he was, Kyra grabbed his hand under the table and caressed it. She winked at him, which filled him with impending doom.

"You don't have to tell me, Dorrie," Kyra said. "He's all man." She leaned and kissed him quickly on the mouth, taking the sting out of her barb.

"Oh, isn't that sweet," Dorrie said. "You know, Kevin isn't much for those public displays of affection, but I see he doesn't seem to mind now."

"You're right, Mom. What a difference a couple of days make." Then he said for Kyra's ears only, "And nights."

Now it was her turn to blush.

CHAPTER 19

"Where are we going, Kevin?" Kyra asked after they'd left the main highway and were headed down a road with no lights. *How do people in the country do this stuff?* They only light they had was the illumination from his electronic dashboard. The navigation system announced that they'd left the city limits. And she didn't have her prepaid cell phone with her. "I was just teasing at dinner. There's no reason to take me down to the river and drown me," she said, half teasing.

"I should let you simmer in your own overactive imagination juices, but I won't."

"Where are you taking me, Kevin?"

"Now, you just told my momma that I was all man. What would I look like if I told you?"

Kyra knew she sounded like a hypocrite, but there were no lights on the road. It reminded her of so many stories she'd heard in the news about young girls following their boyfriends to some deserted place and getting chopped into a million pieces. She also knew Kevin would never do anything like that. *Isn't that what those people always say after the murder spree?*

The truck stopped. She turned to Kevin. "Okay, buster, what's going on?"

He pushed a button to let the windows down. "Wait for it."

Kyra couldn't mistake the amusement in his voice. "Wait for what?"

He glanced at the clock. "That." He gazed straight ahead.

Then she saw it. More lights than she could imagine. It was a river boat. A crowded riverboat, apparently; she heard music, horns blaring, and yells coming from the opposite direction. Then it was gone.

She looked at him. "Sorry."

"Nothing to be sorry about. You're in a strange place and I guess you could say I'm stranger."

"Hardly," Kyra said. "I do trust you and I appreciate what you did. It was kind of shocking being in a place with no lights. But it was gorgeous seeing the boat go by. What is it, anyway?"

"Esmeralda's Riverboat floats by here twice a week. It's en route to Austin. It's a three-day cruise from Houston to Austin by way of the Rio Grande. You know, this is part of it. We just call it Wright City Falls."

She nodded, taking in her view. If she were a silly romantic, which she was not, she'd love this. The reflection of the full moon was bouncing off the still water. Not another sound could be heard. Kevin turned on his CD player and Robin Thicke's sexy voice filled the interior of the truck. That was not fair. Robin was one of her favorite singers and she didn't know how Kevin knew, but somehow he did. "You're playing dirty, Sheriff." She smiled at him.

"Is there any other way to play with you?"

Kyra's mouth hung open, not knowing exactly how to respond. "Touché."

"Wow! I can't believe it. No comeback," Kevin said laughing. "This has to be some sort of world record.

Kyra took it like a woman. "You'd better enjoy the moment, 'cause it won't happen often."

"Don't I know it." Kevin leaned his seat back into the reclining position and gazed up at the sky. "Isn't it a nice night? Even if we did have to eat with my parents."

"I think your parents are great. When my mom was alive I don't think she and Dad ever relaxed like that over dinner."

"Mom doesn't eat out much, but every now and then Dad will convince her she doesn't have to cook every night. I guess it's a hard habit to break after almost forty years of marriage and raising four boys."

Kyra couldn't imagine such a scene. *Chaos*, she thought. *Sheer and utter chaos*. She thought back to her childhood. Dinner was always quiet and tense.

"Kyra, you're thinking again," Kevin said. He moved his seat back further. "You know the best thing about having a four-door truck?"

She couldn't imagine. "No, but I'm sure you're going to tell me, right?"

"I'd rather show you." He reached for her and guided her onto his lap, facing him. He kissed her softly. "You taste like barbeque."

She had been told many things before, but never, never, had she been told she had barbeque breath. She'd never been asked to make out in a truck, either. The day just couldn't get any better.

Kevin's hands wandered over her body. "You know, you're the first woman I've brought out here. Mom would be proud."

"Why?"

"Isn't this romantic? Mom is big on romance," he said, his hands settling on her backside. He kissed her again, this time longer and softer. "You know, the river, the moonlight, Robin Thicke on the stereo."

"How did you know?" Her lips hovered above his, waiting to make contact.

"The first murder. Remember, I searched your tiny car. I saw the CD. I didn't see any others, so I naturally surmised he was the flavor of the month."

"You're awful." She kissed him with all the emotions she felt for the evening. "Just awful."

"You like it."

"Yeah, I do."

Early the next morning, the doorbell rang.

Kevin's eyes popped open at the sound.

"Who is that?" Kyra purred, moving closer to him. "You sure know how to show a girl a good time, Kevin."

Last night was a dream. He'd only brought Kyra to his house to show off his pride and joy of restoring his home. But once they entered his house, the only room Kyra saw was his bedroom.

The bell sounded again before he could answer.

He glanced at the bedside clock. It was barely nine in the morning. Who on earth would be knocking on his door? Nick would have called before just showing up on his doorstep.

Kevin didn't want to get out of bed. Kyra's nude body felt too good snuggled next to him. Then he heard it.

"Kev, get your butt out of bed. I know you're in there," Elias called out.

"Damn, it's EJ." Kevin looked at Kyra. Did she have any idea of how sensual she looked against his pillows? "Sorry, babe, it's my brother. I forgot I was supposed to meet him at Mom's this morning." He rose out of bed, struggling into his boxer shorts. He looked around the room for his jeans, but couldn't find them. "They're in the living room," Kyra said, laughing. "Remember, you were stripping for me last night?"

Kevin grinned at the memory. "I seem to remember you undressing me the minute we got into the house."

"You say tomato," she quipped, obviously remembering the exact same thing.

Life would never be boring, he thought. "I'll try to get rid of him," he promised as he left the room.

He spotted his jeans on the back of the couch. "Man, we must have been nuts last night." He pulled on his jeans and opened the door.

Elias's hand stopped mid-knock. "I thought I was going to have to break down the door. I didn't bring my key with me." He walked inside the house. "What's with you, Kevin? You were supposed to meet me an hour ago. I figured you overslept, and you look like you just rolled out of bed."

Kevin yawned. He might have just opened his eyes, but he hadn't gotten much sleep. Not with Kyra Chase in his bed. They were busy most of the night. "I did. Can we do this a little later?"

Elias sat down on the couch, studying his brother. "Now, my cop senses tell me something is going on that you don't want me to know about."

Kevin knew that if he didn't get his brother out of there fast, Kyra was going to make an appearance and Elias wouldn't have to suppose anything. Kyra would definitely set him straight. "I don't know what you're talking about."

"Let's see. My health nut of a brother, who usually runs five miles a day, hasn't been on his morning run for two days, according to the town gossip. And you didn't run this morning. Your usually predictable routine has been askew. Plus, I see a woman's designer handbag under the coffee table. So that leads me to believe that there's a lady about."

Kevin shoulders sagged in defeat. He wanted EJ to meet Kyra. But not like this. "You're right as rain. But why don't you give us about an hour?"

"You'd better make that two," Kyra announced as she entered the room in her clothes from the previous night. Her hair was still disheveled, but it made her look sexy as hell. "I'm Kyra Chase," she said, sitting next to Elias and shaking his hand. "I'm renting the house from Regan."

"Elias Johnson."

"Glad to meet you. I'm sure you can give me all the dirt on Kevin." She rose and faced Elias. "As you can see, we're just getting up and he has to take me home."

Kevin had been so transfixed by her presence, he'd only caught the last of her conversation. "Why am I taking you home?"

She walked to his side, wrapping him in a hug. "I need new clothes. My work is at home, so that's where I need to be." She rose up on her tiptoes and kissed him.

Kevin was getting lost in her heated morning kiss, when he remembered they had an audience. He had to snap out of this. Elias would probably run straight home and tell their parents the news that Kevin had a woman spend the night. "Have you changed your mind about police protection?"

"We agreed on night protection. I'd say you got that one locked."

Elias laughed, rising from the couch. "Okay, guys, I'll give you some morning-after time. Kev, I'll be at the courthouse later." He left without another word.

"See what you did," Kevin said, not feeling the strength of his words. "You made EJ leave."

Kyra ignored his words. "I did not. He could have stayed if he wanted to. He probably felt like the odd man out." She took his hand, leading him back to his bedroom. "Now, Kevin, first show me your house. Then you can feed me breakfast."

Kyra sat at Kevin's small kitchen table slack-jawed, as her father called it. He'd shown her around his home, room by room, and described all the work he'd put into the house.

He wasn't the man she thought he was. Not in the least. His house was probably twice the size of her townhouse, and the house was full of love. He'd installed the hardwood floors himself. His mother helped with blinds, his father with the major remodeling, and even his brothers had assisted him with the house. Kevin had a house that love built. Kyra couldn't imagine her father doing anything so manual.

Now she watched Kevin prepare her breakfast. She'd originally thought he'd go to McDonald's or even Jay's for breakfast, but he surprised her by insisting on making it himself.

"I'm not as good as Mom, but I can scramble some eggs and cook some bacon," he told her as he placed some bacon on a baking sheet and put it in the oven. "Mom's speciality is omelets."

"You're not cooking with those fake eggs, are you? Jay would have my hide if I ate something healthy like that. You know she detests any healthy cooking." Kyra inhaled the aroma of coffee brewing. Hazelnut. Her favorite flavored coffee: the only thing that kept her from running to Starbucks in nearby Waco.

"No, I don't use fake anything. I don't have to," he said honestly. "Normally, I jog every morning, with the exception of the last few days, so I usually eat a healthy breakfast." He looked back at her.

"Well, that wasn't my fault. You could have gotten up and done a quick run this morning."

"And miss waking up next to the sexiest woman in Wright City? I don't think so."

Kyra shook her head at his remarks. He had that compliment thing down to a science. No wonder all the women in town were so enamored of Kevin.

"Oh, Kevin, you're making my head swell with all this sweet talk."

"You making a certain part of me swell too."

Kyra's mind spun with the possibilities. "Oh, Kevin," she said, her voice thick with emotion.

"Not this morning, Kyra. We have too much to do," he said in the old Kevin voice. "I have to find a murderer before he strikes again."

"Well, that certainly puts a damper on the morning's festivities."

"So you don't want breakfast?" Kevin asked, putting some eggs on a platter. "I guess I'll have to eat all these eggs by myself." He opened the oven door and pulled the bacon out.

"Catch me letting you eat all that by yourself," Kyra said, eyeing the bacon. She'd have to try that. Never in her years would she have put bacon in the oven to cook. But Kevin had and it came out nice and straight, just like at a restaurant.

Kevin laughed, but continued to cook. When he presented her with a breakfast that would do any woman proud, she sighed in satisfaction. "This looks great, baby." She eyed the fluffy scrambled eggs, bacon, potatoes, toast, and all the trimmings.

"Well, I'm glad you approve," Kevin said, handing her a plate. "Remember, save some for the cook." He sat at the table and stared at Kyra, mesmerized. In his seven-year marriage to Ravena, he'd never felt this relaxed at breakfast. Not even in the early years of their often stormy marriage.

Meals together seemed to be an afterthought, just like most of the other things in their life.

With Kyra, however, everything was different, including meals. They were cooking for each other. Although Kyra was a much better cook than he was, it wasn't about that. It was about the effort.

"Kevin, you have this look on your face," Kyra said, concerned. "Is everything okay?"

He gazed at her. How could he fall in love with her in just a week's time? It took him a year with Ravena. "Yeah, it's just about perfect."

She smiled at him. "Well, that's good to know."

CHAPTER 20

After Kevin dropped her back at her place with specific instructions to check in with him every hour on the hour, Kyra changed into fresh clothes and figured out her plan of attack. There was little she could do about the assassins. It was hard to pick out the stranger in town, when she herself was a stranger in Wright City.

So she focused on her assignment. She wanted to speak with Mr. Cotton's attorney to get a better fix on the man himself. Town appreciation of Mr. Cotton was high, but Kyra needed some facts. It was almost lunchtime, she realized. *Might as well start the day with lunch at the diner.*

She arrived at Jay's a little after noon and, as usual, it was crowded. Jay met her at the entrance. "Hello, Jay," Kyra said. After glancing around the room, Kyra didn't see one spare chair. "Looks like standing room only."

Jay nodded. "Yeah, it's usually like this on Thursdays for the lunch special. If you have some time to spare, why don't you come back in an hour? It will have cleared out a little."

"Sure. I do need to see Mr. Hinton. You think he's in his office at lunchtime?"

"Yes, he eats dinner here. Usually lunch is in his office. He'd be the perfect person to interview for a story on Donald. He's probably known him the longest."

"Thanks, Jay. I'll see you in about an hour." She walked out of the diner and started to walk the few storefronts down to the attorney's office.

Her cell phone rang before she took another step. A cold chill crept up her spine, immediately alerting her to danger. It was a prepaid cell, according to Auggie's instructions. *No one should have this number.* So who was calling? She answered the phone with trepidation. "Hello?"

"You didn't call," Kevin said. "Where are you?"

After her heart started beating again, she answered him. "I'm on Main Street. Jay's was super crowded, so I'm going to interview Mr. Hinton. Hey, maybe I can interview your folks, too?"

"Why?"

"Duh, they knew Mr. Cotton."

"Oh, I thought you were trying to dig up info on me as a child or something like that," Kevin said. "Mom and Dad knew Mr. Cotton since they were young. Just about anybody in town can give you some insight on him."

"Don't you try to get me off the fact that you have my cell phone number and I didn't give it to you."

"So?"

"So?" Kyra started walking down the street again.

At least he kept her on her toes. "How did you get this number?"

"Does it really matter how I got your number? The bigger question I should be asking is why would you have a prepaid cell phone when I know you have one through a national carrier."

Okay, he had her there. "I have my reasons."

"I just bet you do. I don't want those reasons to get you killed. I don't know what I'd do if something happened to you."

"Thank you, Kevin. I'll be careful." Kyra wanted to say that she could take care of her own business, but in this case, she was clueless. "My boss didn't want me to use my phone and told me to get a prepaid cell."

"That didn't raise a flag? You didn't question his logic?"

She sighed. "No, Auggie is my boss and he knows what he's doing. He sent me here on a story that has already been done a million times from every possible angle. So, no, I didn't question his logic. If Auggie says so, there's usually a good reason."

"Since I don't know Auggie personally, I'll have to go with your instincts."

It didn't sound like he trusted Auggie or her. "Thank you, Kevin. Now, I really need to go see Mr. Hinton."

He actually laughed. "Okay, I get it. You do have a job to do. Wild-goose chase or not. How about dinner tonight?"

"Sure. Where are we eating?"

He cleared his throat. "Well, my mom was so taken with you the other night. She wants me to bring you to dinner. EJ is bringing Regan, so I'm guessing there be some wedding talk."

The next week was Thanksgiving and the much anticipated wedding between Elias and Regan was four weeks after that. Kyra had been privy to many society weddings in her lifetime while living in Austin. She'd never experienced a small-town wedding. But since the date and the place of the wedding had so much to do with Mr. Cotton, Kyra felt she really needed to be there. "Oh, that sounds fun. Regan looks so happy when she talks about your brother. I can see why she's so taken with him. He's so handsome and those biceps, women just don't stand a chance."

Kevin was quiet for longer than Kyra thought necessary. "See you at five." He ended the call.

She turned the phone off and placed it back in her purse, thinking about Kevin's odd response. She stopped in front of the small storefront of the attorney and walked inside.

"You know you're losing it," Elias said.

"Tell me something I don't know, big brother," Kevin said. They were sitting in Kevin's office discussing the next move. "She thinks you're hot."

"And you're jealous! In case you hadn't noticed, I'm engaged, and she's sleeping with you."

Kevin darted a glance in Elias's direction. "True. I don't know what it is about her, but she has me seeing red most of the time. I told her to call me every hour to check in. I had to call her!"

"I thought Derek was shadowing her."

"He is. He'd already reported where she was

and what she was doing. I just would love it if she followed my directive just once."

Elias grinned. "This is bad how?"

"Well, for one, she's using a prepaid cell. Then she wanted to know how I found her number."

"You know, in some circles that's called stalking," Elias said. "How did you get her number?"

"I noticed the phone wasn't the same one she was using when she first came to town. Curiosity got the best of me, so while she was sleeping, I dialed my cell with her cell."

"Ahh," Elias said.

Kevin knew he'd stepped over the line, but there was little he could do. With three murders on his plate, he felt justified in his actions. "I'm within my sheriff rights. There was just cause."

"Hey, you don't have to explain it to me," Elias said. "I've been there. I think you should tell Kyra what you're feeling."

"No point. She's going back to Austin when her story is done. And that will be the end of that."

"How do you know that?"

"Because I do," Kevin said flatly. "She's a city girl. Worse yet, she's a high-society city girl."

"So why invite her to Mom's?"

"Have you ever said no to Mom?"

"Well, no. Regan would kill me."

"Exactly. Now let's figure out how to stop all the killing going on in my town." Kevin reached for the reports. "There has to be something I'm missing. Who in Wright City would be able to kill professional assassins and not leave a trace?"

Elias sat back in his seat. "Another assassin."

Kevin shook his head. He'd thought about that,

but still the question arose. "Who and how or why would they hide in Wright City?"

Elias opened his mouth to speak, but his cell began to play classical music. "Regan," he explained unnecessarily to Kevin. He answered his phone with a smile. "Hey, honey."

Kevin took that time to walk down the hall to get an update with Nick. Unfortunately, Nick didn't have any news. Kevin told him Elias's idea. "I can't think of any new residents in town, but nose around and see what you can find."

"Sure, Kev. How about we run it through the FBI database, too? I'm sure EJ can do that."

Nick prepared to leave his office and Kevin walked back to his office. Maybe with his brother's help, something would happen soon.

James Hinton met Kyra as she entered the office. "Well, hello, Ms. Chase. What can I do for you?" He motioned her toward a chair. "Please, sit down."

After she was seated, Kyra took out her trusty notepad and told him of her quest. "Mr. Hinton, as you know, I'm a reporter and my original assignment was to cover the cocaine scandal of the summer that resulted in the death of Mr. Cotton."

Hinton nodded. "Yes. That was an awful time for this town. I've been here most of my life and I've never seen so much devastation in one summer. Reminded me of when the lads were going off to Vietnam."

"How so?"

"So many deaths." He shook his head as if that

alone could erase the memories of just a few months ago. "You were saying?"

"Oh, yes, since I've been in Wright City, I keep hearing about what a good citizen Mr. Cotton was to the town and I want to reflect that in my story. Like a memoir kind of thing."

"Oh," Hinton said. "I'm sure there'll be plenty of people in town singing Donald's praises."

Kyra detected a ripple of something in Hinton's baritone voice. Was it jealousy? "Would you be included in that singing?"

"Of course. I was his attorney for over thirty years. He was one of my closest friends. I miss him every day. It was all her fault."

"I'm sure he was. He seemed like a wonderful man. I wish I'd met him," Kyra said proudly. "There are so few true black male role models."

Hinton looked at her. "You might have a different opinion if you knew the true story."

"Why don't you enlighten me? I need the truth about him. And I'm sure if it's something Regan or her mother doesn't know, they'd like to know as well." She reached in her purse and pulled out her miniature tape recorder. "I hope you don't mind." She turned the recorder on and set it on the desk.

"No, I don't mind," Hinton said. "I have nothing to hide. I was Donald's friend for almost forty years. He's always been one to help. I always thought he was doing penance for something he'd done in his younger days."

"Because he wanted to help people?"

"In a sense, yes. He came to town barely twenty years old, no family, no relatives, nothing. The first thing he did was join the church. He volunteered for just about everything at church. He mowed the lawn, cleaned the church, and he volunteered to take the kids on field trips and such."

Kyra thoughts matched Hinton's, was Cotton trying to make up for some horrible deed? "Was he married?"

"No. He'd finally found love at the age of sixty-five and then he was killed. Pitiful, isn't it? All that time he helped people, putting love on the back-burner, then he finds love and is killed before he can propose."

"Talk about karma."

"I don't think I know her. Is she new in town?"

Kyra didn't bother to explain to the aging attorney about the New Age term. "Never mind. Is his former love still in town?"

"At the courthouse in the records department. She's been there over twenty years. Rose Calles will be happy to talk to you about Donald."

"What was the one thing you remember most about him?" Kyra hoped his answer wouldn't bring her to tears like Regan's did.

Hinton leaned back in his chair, a smile plastered on his weathered brown face. "Safe Haven. He didn't like the youngsters not having a place to go after school. Although he didn't attend college himself, he was an advocate of education. Safe Haven was his vision, more or less. It was going to have computers and books and tutors for kids who needed help with their homework. Regan is just like him. She's got a big heart, even with that no-account mother of hers. She's going ahead with plans for the Haven and has put in some of her own money to make sure everything is done. Once that news story hit the papers, donations poured in and that place had more money than Regan could shake a stick at. She's doing good things for the town and for Donald with the Haven. When it opens in January, the kids will have a place to go after school and parents won't have to worry about their kids getting into mischief in their absence. I don't think Donald would have wanted his name in the title. But I think he'd be pleased."

"I do too," Kyra said quietly. "I think it's wonderful that his dream will be realized. No wonder Regan and Elias are getting married there. It will bring closure to so many things."

Kyra wiped away a tear. Hinton's answer might not have been as emotional as Regan's answer, but it was quite the same. She wasn't going to be able to handle many more interviews like this.

CHAPTER 21

Miguel knew what he had to do.

Since three paid assassins had returned from the Chase assignment in body bags, and once the news was out about the deaths, few other contractors were willing to chance a visit to the small town, and even increasing the money for the job to $3 million hadn't helped. Apparently money couldn't buy him a kill.

He sat in his home office, mapping out his plan. He'd do it this weekend. Zipping out of Austin on the pretext of visiting his brother at the state prison would mask it perfectly. His father wouldn't ask too many questions and never wanted to visit Julian in prison. He didn't want to see his youngest son behind bars, and worse yet, now on death row. His father always said it was too long a ride to only visit with Julian for two hours a day.

Miguel knew it was all up to him. And this would be the last attempt to kill Kyra Chase. If he didn't succeed, the contract would be terminated and his father would have been right. He should have left well enough alone. But he couldn't desert his brother. In one way or another, Chandler Chase would pay for his crimes of betrayal against the Ditano family. He should have defended Julian as he promised and all of this could have been avoided.

Thursday evening, Kyra prepared for a night with the Johnson family. After such an emotionally draining day, she needed something relaxing to focus on. Plus, she kept having the uneasy feeling that she was being watched.

She knew interviewing people in Wright City about Cotton was going to be a task, but she hadn't dreamed that each interviewee would have her crying. Donald was truly a great man and loved people. Kyra still had at least ten more people to talk to tomorrow. She could only imagine what that was going to be like.

She dressed in black slacks, a coordinating black-and-white silk blouse with a V-shaped neckline, her mother's favorite pearl necklace, and modest heels. She was brushing her hair when the doorbell rang.

She opened the door and smiled. "You clean up nice, Sheriff." She kissed him and then ushered him inside.

Kevin was dressed in dark slacks, a fitted shirt that did his body good, and leather shoes. "You look beautiful. You're going to make Skip's tongue hang out of his mouth." Kevin walked to the couch and took a seat.

"Skip?" Kyra sat next to him, wanting to hear more about Kevin's life.

"Yeah, my oldest brother. He came back to Wright City with his three sons a few months ago after his divorce. He's staying at Mom's right now until he can get his bearings."

"Oh, Kevin, why didn't you say something?" Kyra felt bad for him and didn't know why. "I'm sorry."

"It's not your fault, Kyra. Although Skip's divorce was the second casualty in our family, it's been a good experience for him. When he decided to return to Wright City, one of the surgeons retired and he got the job as head surgeon at Wright City Memorial."

"He's a doctor?"

"Yeah, just like Dad. His speciality was neurology in Houston, but here he does a little of everything." Another fact Kyra hadn't known.

Oh, she really had to do some serious information gathering at dinner tonight. "Wow. Amazing. How old are the boys?"

"Trey, Kyle, and Jason, ages eight, seven, and four, respectively."

Kyra jumped up from the couch. "We need to go to the store," Kyra said. Kevin looked at quizzically. "I can't show up at your parents' without something for them."

"Baby, that's not necessary." He stood beside her.

Kyra shot him a look. "My mother would come back and haunt me if I didn't go bearing gifts. I'll just be a minute." She ran to her bedroom and grabbed her purse. Kevin was standing by the door waiting for her. "Someone trained you well."

Instead of him rising to the occasion, Kevin shrugged off her comment. "Thank my mother."

"I will."

After a not-so-quick stop at Wal-Mart, Kyra and Kevin arrived at his parents' house. He parked behind a black Tahoe. "See, EJ and Regan are already here." He helped Kyra out of the truck.

"Kevin, I'm sure they will understand." Kyra had wanted to wrap the gifts, but due to the constraints of time, Kevin convinced her to forgo it.

"The boys will love you after they see the gifts. I can't believe you just spent this much money." He retrieved the bags.

Kyra hadn't thought about the amount of money she had spent. "You picked out the gifts. It's partly your fault." They walked toward the large two-story house.

"Not," Kevin said. "I merely gave suggestions." They stopped at the front door. "Now, the Johnson household can get a bit rowdy, especially since everyone is home. So if it gets to be too much just let me know."

Kyra waved away his remark. "This coming from the same man who told me that Austin was that-away? I think I can handle a little noise. I've dealt with politicians and lobbyists when they've been drinking, so I think I can handle three energetic boys."

"Okay. Remember, I told you so." He opened the front door and ushered her inside.

Kyra's heart filled with something she couldn't

identify. As soon as she and Kevin walked inside the house they were engulfed in a sea of hugs before introductions could be made. "Baby, this is my brother, David Jr. We call him Skip."

Kyra shook hands with an almost identical version of Kevin. As the men stood next to each other, Kyra could see subtle differences between them. Skip was a little taller than the others. Elias was more muscular, while Kevin had a runner's build. They all had light brown eyes, wavy hair, and a smile that would be the death of her.

"It's a pleasure to meet you, Skip." The boys ran into the living room at a breakneck speed. "This must be Trey, Kyle, and Jason." The boys were identical to their father. Kyra presented each boy with a bag. "This is for you. Your Uncle Kevin said you guys were still getting settled." She bent down in front of them and said, "If you don't like it, it's your uncle's fault." The room erupted in laughter.

Each boy opened his present and then looked to their father. Skip peered in the bags and then at Kyra.

Kevin whispered in her ear, "Told you."

Okay, maybe she went a little overboard on the computer games. But there was no sense in buying just one Nintendo DS, when there were three boys. She could easily imagine them fighting at every turn, driving Dorrie crazy. "Skip, please let them keep them."

Skip looked at Kevin. When Kevin nodded, Skip relented. "Okay, guys. What do you tell Ms. Chase?"

"Thank you!" They all but shouted, then ascended upon Kyra with hugs, nearly knocking her over.

"You're welcome." Kyra had given many gifts in her lifetime that cost way more that what she spent on the boys, but never ones that made her heart swell with joy. This was more exciting than her first, second, and third marriage proposals.

Kyra noticed Regan sitting on the couch next to Kevin's mother. She smiled at Kyra and attempted to stand but Kevin's mother stopped her.

"No, dear, you need to relax. Brenda would hurt me if I didn't take care of you," Dorrie said. "You need to save your strength for the wedding."

Regan sighed. "Mom, I'm fine. I promise."

Kyra took a seat on the other side of Regan. "Hello, Regan. How are you feeling?"

She smiled. "Pretty good. Had a hard day of therapy. I'm so glad you could make it. Mom was wondering if Kevin had forgotten to ask you."

"No, he didn't. I couldn't meet three boys without a gift in hand. I love get-togethers. I didn't know Kevin had another brother, let alone nephews, until an hour ago."

Kevin's mother laughed. "Sounds like my son. He plays it pretty close to the vest. Drives me nuts."

Kyra giggled. "Me too."

Dorrie rose. "Okay, time for dinner," she announced.

Kyra watched in amazement as the boys took off running for the stairs. She looked at Kevin for clarification.

"Wash their hands."

"Oh." Kyra had a feeling she was going to learn a lot about the Johnson family that night.

*   *   *

"Okay, Kevin. So what's up with Kyra?" Skip asked his brother as the men were in the kitchen clearing away the dishes while the women talked about the wedding.

"Yeah, Kev," Elias chimed in. "We can make it a double wedding."

"Oh, that was not funny. You know she's going back to Austin when the story ends and all this assassin mess is over." Kevin carried another load of dishes to the counter. "Man, I'd forgotten how many dishes it takes to feed our family."

Skip loaded the dishwasher. "Don't evade the issue. She dropped some serious green on those games for the boys. She must be rolling in it."

Elias cleared his throat. "Skip, Kyra's dad is Chandler Chase, the attorney to the rich and powerful."

"Whoa, what the hell is she doing in Wright City?"

Kevin sighed. "It's a long story."

Skip nodded, understanding. "Well, my brother is in love with an heiress. I can't see her settling here and I can't see you settling there."

Kevin couldn't either. "Give that man a cigar."

"It's going to work out, Kev, you'll see," Elias said.

"If you start spouting nonsense about stars and karma, I'm going to put you in jail, EJ."

"Then I wouldn't have my security clearance anymore. Who would run all those reports for you?"

Kevin raised his hands in the air. "Okay, you got me."

CHAPTER 22

Kyra and Regan sat at the dining room table with bridal magazines, catering menus, and floral lists scattered between them. Dorrie was preparing tea in the kitchen. Kyra took the time to carefully inspect Regan's physical appearance. She looked healthy. Tired, but healthy. Or about as healthy as a person could recouping from a serious bullet wound injury.

"Regan, I have to ask. You called Dorrie, 'Mom?' "

Regan smiled. "Yes, I did. She's been like a mom to me for a lot of years. I always thought she was the coolest mom, so when Elias and I got engaged, I asked her if I could call her mom and she said of course."

"How did Brenda take that?"

Regan shrugged. "I don't know. Haven't told her." She glanced in the direction of the kitchen. "Besides, there are no other women in the Johnson household. And Mom loves to do the tea thing, and Dad just gives in to her, but doesn't really enjoy it. I think we're good for each other."

Kyra wiped away a tear. "You know, every time I talk to you, I start crying, Regan."

Regan walked to the coffee table and retrieved some tissues for Kyra. "It's okay, Kyra. Everyone takes a journey. You're on a journey right now."

Kyra dried her tears. Regan also seemed so down-to-earth; why was she suddenly talking gibberish? "I'm sorry, what?"

She laughed. "Mom says every person goes through this. The craziest things make you cry. You're on an emotional journey, and you'll find clarity. When you find that clarity, you'll understand."

"What kind of journey is this?"

"You can laugh, Kyra. I did the exact same thing last summer. I think I grew more emotionally in less than a month than I had all my life."

Kyra reflected on Regan's claims. She knew Regan had been through more in one summer than Kyra had endured in her lifetime. Maybe there was something to this journey thing.

"Okay, are we ready to discuss a wedding?" Dorrie asked, entering the room with a silver tray. She sat the elaborate tray in the center of the dining room table.

Kyra couldn't believe the looks of the tea service. It could rival any European tearoom. Dorrie had the Royal Doulton tea service, complete with the tiny porcelain coffee cups with matching floral saucers. A three-tiered tray held scones, cakes, and cookies. "I'll pour the tea," Kyra said.

Dorrie nodded and sat down opposite Regan. "Now, dear, while Kyra is pouring our tea, tell me what you and Elias want at the wedding."

"Mom, we don't want you guys spending your money. Elias and I can afford to pay for it ourselves."

Dorrie looked hurt. "Oh, honey, we want to. Please let us do something for you and Elias."

"Mom, we can afford it. Don't worry."

"You've made Elias so happy. And us."

Regan sighed. It was a losing battle. Dorrie was on the verge of tears because she so desperately wanted to contribute to the wedding. Kyra had an idea that could solve all their problems and keep the harmony of the wedding.

Kyra cleared her throat. "I have a suggestion."

Both women looked at her. "Well?"

"A bridal tea. Dorrie could host a bridal tea for you, Regan. We could have cute little sandwiches, salads, cookies, scones. You know it would be fun."

Dorrie smiled. "I like it. You know we'll have to invite the people from church. Just give me your list of friends from Fort Worth you want me to invite."

Regan grinned at her. Then to Dorrie, she said, "That will be great, Mom. I'll get my list together. I know it's going to be an awesome event."

Dorrie beamed under Regan's encouragement. "Yes, it will be. Now, what about your dress? How many bridesmaids are you going to have?"

Kyra wanted to ask why Brenda wasn't in attendance at this planning party, but knew better of it. "Regan, how big is the Haven?"

"Oh, that's right. You haven't seen it," Regan said. "Why don't we go there tomorrow? It won't officially open until Janaury when school resumes. You can have a sneak peak."

"That sounds great." Kyra's mind began to race with all the possibilities. She could take pictures of the Haven. It would add intrigue to her human interest story and give readers a visual. "We could eat lunch at Jay's afterward."

"Deal," Regan said.

"About your dress?" Kyra reminded her. "I've been engaged three times, so I know a little bit about that. What kind of dress? You know, we can look on the Internet for some. Vera Wang's dresses are gorgeous."

"You've really been engaged that many times?" Regan whispered. "What happened?"

Dorrie took the role of mother seriously. "Regan, that's not polite. Kyra might not want to share such personal events with us, being that she's only known us for a short time."

"Oh, I don't mind sharing." It seemed like a lifetime ago. "The first one was when I graduated from college. Brian Clifford was a law student at UT and worked at my father's firm. I was twenty-two and he was thirty. A week before the wedding, his past came to my apartment." She looked into confused faces. "He already had a family."

Regan gasped. "How awful. What did you do?"

"Wasn't much to do. Called off the wedding, went to Europe for a month, came back and went to grad school."

"Wow, I don't know if I could have done that," Regan mumbled. "Did you see him again?"

"Oh, yeah. About five years ago, I ran into him at the capitol building. He's on wife number three now."

Regan shook her head.

"It's okay, Regan. The next time was Harry Benson, and I'm sure you guys know who he is."

"Heck yeah, he's one of the owners of the San Antonio Spurs. He's gorgeous."

"Yes, he still is very gorgeous. This time it was all me. I met Harry right about ten years ago at a basketball game. He swept me off my feet. It happened so fast, the next thing I knew I had a five-carat diamond ring on my finger and was shopping for another wedding dress."

"What happened?" Regan's brown eyes were fixed on Kyra.

"All the glitz finally wore off. I didn't love Harry, I loved being in the limelight. I called it off two weeks before the big event."

"Do you still see him?" Regan asked.

"Yes, he gives me season tickets every year."

"I'm almost afraid to ask about number three," Regan said.

"Now that one was kind of tragic. Three years ago, I found myself engaged again. Daddy said he was tired of laying out all that money for weddings and I didn't come through. This time, I had everything. I was blissfully happy. Bryce Hillcort was sensitive, caring, very into the arts. He encouraged me about my writing, and I encourage him to paint professionally. He was an artist. As we were making plans for our small, intimate wedding, his significant other barged into my townhouse wielding a gun."

"What?"

"Yeap. The ultimate down-low brother. He totally had me fooled. It took me a long time to get over him."

This time Regan and Dorrie both had tears in their eyes. "When did you finally get over him?"

"This week." Kyra wiped her eyes and noticed the man responsible for easing that hurt away staring at her.

CHAPTER 23

Kevin stood in the doorway of the kitchen, quietly listening to Kyra's recounting of her failed engagements. So many things about her made sense now. Being hurt so many times made her outspoken, distrusting of men, and eager to cut one up in a hundred pieces. But there was an inkling of still wanting to believe in love. He saw it every time she talked about Elias and Regan.

He smiled at her. He wanted to do something romantic, but knew that was impossible. He had to remember she was going to leave town and his own heart was going to be at stake. But was it already too late? His gut told him it was. And he always listened to his gut. He was already in love and there wasn't a damn thing he could do about it.

Skip patted him on the back. "You know, you could just go in there with the women and show her how much she means to you. It's not a sin to fall in love quickly, little brother."

Kevin faced his brother and stepped back into

the kitchen, so the women wouldn't hear him. "Who said anything about being in love? Yeah, I'm attracted to her, but love is a strong word after only a week."

Skip threw a dish towel at him. "Man, come on. We all know you're in love, you know you're in love. That's just the man in you talking right now. Kevin, you took her to Wal-Mart, and you hate shopping. My gosh, you buy almost everything on-line if you can."

Kevin knew it was useless to deny anything at this point. His brothers knew him better than anyone. "I know. This is just different and there the whole murder business, too."

"You still have no idea who it could be?" Skip opened the dishwasher and took out the clean dishes. "I just can't imagine an assassin walking the streets of our sleepy little town."

Kevin laughed. "As you recall, last summer this town wasn't so sleepy. I don't think there're many towns like Mayberry left in this country anymore. Drugs and senseless killings are the way of the world nowadays. Even here in Wright City. And from what I've been able to glean from the Internet about Miguel Ditano, this is far from over." His cell phone chirped to life. Kevin looked down and noticed Nick's number on the display. "It's Nick," he told the men.

He answered it on the second chirp. "Please tell me you have some good news."

"I wish, boss," Nick said. "I ran across something and it looked kind of strange, and I thought I'd check it out with you. Not only did I hear you guys were shopping in Wal-Mart like a married couple, but I also had a message from the last murder victim's wife."

Kevin's heart started to race. A clue. "What? Did she find something?"

"It's more like what she didn't find."

"Speak English," Kevin said, letting his temper get the best of him.

Nick chuckled. "All right, man. I would have thought you getting some on the regular would have helped your disposition."

"Nick!"

"Okay, okay. The widow claims her husband was missing a necklace and a gold pin. It's a thin gold chain with some kind of crest on it. Apparently, he wore it everywhere. The gold pin had the same crest on it."

"How much is the stuff worth?"

"That's just it. It's worth crap. She thought it was odd, since it wasn't a robbery."

"Was there some kind of insignia on it? You know, maybe the assassin's union?"

"Close, but no cigar," replied Nick ruefully. "The insignia denotes the organization."

Kevin could see the pieces sliding into place. "So the items taken were only of value to an associate member. See if the widow can fax a picture of the missing items. If she doesn't have a picture, asked her to describe it."

"Already on it," Nick said. "She's looking through old photos as we speak. Should have something by morning. I just wanted to run it by you officially. Should I call your place or Kyra's when I get something?"

"I'm hanging up," Kevin announced, trying not

to smile. He placed the phone back into its holder on his belt.

"Good news?" Elias asked, sitting at the table.

Kevin nodded. "Could be. I think it might help us find out who the killer is. Some items are missing from the corpse."

"It's something," Elias said, encouraging his brother.

"I know it's a straw, but at least it's a good straw."

Kyra stared at Kevin as they drove to his house. She had so many emotions running through her mind at one time, she couldn't give any one of them her complete focus. With all the resources she'd had at her disposal in Austin, there was nothing that could compare to the evening she'd shared with the Johnsons.

She felt a part of their large family with just one dinner. Something she hadn't felt with her own biological father until after her mother died. She never felt an emotional bond with her father. Yes, he was a great provider, but a nurturer he was not. Chandler Chase kept everyone important in his life at arm's length. In all her years, she never saw her parents even share a kiss, let alone hold hands or hug. Dorrie and David Johnson hugged, kissed, and were very much in love. They loved their children, grandchildren, and future daughter-in-law unconditionally. Dorrie treated Regan like a daughter and loved her with all her heart. The way it should be between a parent and a child.

"Okay, baby, you've been quiet since we left

Mom's," Kevin chided. "What's going on in that stubborn head of yours?"

Kyra sighed. She didn't want to rehash the events of her three fiancés, but thought Kevin might want to talk about them.

"Nothing. I know you heard my story of my three engagements and thought maybe you wanted to talk about it." She turned in the seat so she was facing him. "I know that's probably a lot of times to get engaged, but . . ."

"Kyra, I don't care about that," he stopped her mid-confession. "That's in the past. I told you two weeks ago, I had checked you out."

She remembered that little detail, now. "I didn't think it would have relayed the fact that I was engaged three times."

"Society column."

"Oh." Kyra cringed at the memory of the last time she appeared in the infamous column. "Sorry you had to read about 'the girl who cried wedding.' That columnist had it in for me by then. She wanted my job as lead investigative reporter."

"I could tell she had it in for you when I read that piece. I'm surprised she's still at the paper."

"She got demoted to the records department after that little episode. She's still there and has been trying to work her way back up."

"Is it working?" Kevin parked in front of his house.

"Not really. She's tried to make it up to me a few times, but I'm not falling for it. She can't go to another paper because of what happened."

"So, in a sense, you're the reason she's stuck in a nowhere job at the newspaper."

"Forget it, Kevin. Denisha Sprague doesn't have enough money to buy a designer purse, let alone pay for a professional hit."

He got out of the truck and walked around to help her out. "I know. I was just putting pieces of the puzzle together."

Kyra didn't want to talk about work. She wanted the wonderful evening to continue. "How are you coming with the bachelor party? Are you going to order strippers?"

"Good evening, Kevin." A kindly woman called from the house next door. "It's so nice to see you entertaining." She walked to the truck, inspecting Kyra under the illumination of the street light. "My, you are as pretty as they say. I see you're enjoying the town."

She pushed her small hand at Kyra. "I'm Martha Hughes. I've known Kevin since he was a baby." She grinned at him.

Kyra smiled. Martha was about sixty if Kyra was any judge of age. She was a tall, lean woman and was dressed for exercising. "Then we'll have to have a talk real soon." Kyra grabbed Kevin's hand.

Martha nodded. "I usually walk about seven in the morning and at night. I'm going for my nightly walk now."

"Have a good walk, Martha," Kevin said, leading Kyra to the house.

"I was young once too, Kevin." Martha started toward the street. "I know you want to get your groove on, as my grandson calls it." She waved and started walking down the sidewalk.

Kyra hugged him. "Is she going to be all right? I mean, she doesn't even have a dog to protect her."

Kevin laughed. "Are you kidding? Martha has a black belt in karate." He unlocked the front door. "She teaches a class at the senior center. Mom says she might take the next class."

Kyra was about to step inside the dark house, but Kevin stopped her.

"I need to check out the place first." He pulled his gun out of the holster. "Stay here until I say all clear." He entered the house without another word.

She watched him, deliberating the possibilities. She decided that if she had to die, she'd rather do it with Kevin, than standing on the porch alone. She followed him inside the house.

"Can't you follow just one of my directives?" He flipped on the living room light.

"I thought I heard you say 'all clear,'" Kyra whispered.

"Liar." He continued walking through the house with his gun drawn.

They checked all the rooms, including the garage, and found no sign of intruders. He holstered his gun. "Okay, everything is good. You can relax."

"How about you take that gun off first," Kyra said. "I can't relax the way I want if that thing is poking me in my hip."

He laughed, but took off his gun holster. "Better?"

"Much." She sat on the couch and turned on the television. "Want to watch a movie?"

He sat by her, took the remote out of her hand, and turned off the television. "Actually, I would like to talk."

Oh, this did not bode well with Kyra. Men only wanted to talk when it was curb-kicking time. Things were going so well between them, but it looked like her bad luck with men was holding strong. "So talk."

"I wanted to talk about tonight. I know my mom can be persuasive when it's something she really wants. I heard you suggest the bridal tea and I thought it was a great idea. She and Dad are so happy that Regan and Elias are finally together and getting married, they want to pay for something, but neither will hear of it. It's kind of been a thing since they announced the engagement. I wanted to tell you how much that meant to me that you were able to keep the peace."

"That's what you wanted to talk about?" She couldn't keep the incredulousness out of her voice. "I thought you were giving me the shove."

He laughed. Then he leaned toward her and kissed her gently. "You'll never hear those words exit my mouth." He kissed her again. "That's for giving the boys the computer games. After dinner, you wouldn't have realized they were in the house." He kissed her again, pulling her onto his lap.

Kyra was thinking how good he tasted when a thought bulldozed its way to the front of her brain. "I thought Regan and Elias just dated this summer. Why would your parents be so happy?"

"Because way back in high school, Regan and Elias were study friends, and Mom wanted him to ask her out. He had a thing for her then, but he was too scared of rejection. So when they reconnected this summer, it was like all the pieces just came together. Mom was so happy, because she always liked Regan. She says she finally got a daughter." He wiped her tears. "Why are you crying?"

"I think it's must be this town." Kyra rested against Kevin's chest. "It seems every time I hear a story in this place, I start to cry. Your mom is so sweet and she deserves a daughter. I must be going through some kind of a brain-sucking moment. Normally, I don't do this weeping."

He wrapped his strong arms around her. "That just means you care about the people you're hearing about. You're starting to like it here, aren't you?" He kissed her forehead.

"Yes, I am. Even without a Starbucks or a mall. Can you believe that?"

"Yes."

Kyra looked at him. She wanted to say it, but the words caught in her throat. He looked adorable with that slow, sexy smile that promised her a night of pleasure. He was worse than any drug on the market. She was hooked on Kevin and there was nothing she could do about it, even if she wanted to.

CHAPTER 24

The next morning, Kyra heard a phone ringing. She shifted her position in Kevin's bed and moved closer to him. The phone rang again. Kevin put his arms around her naked body. She could wake up like this for the rest of her days. There was something about snuggling next to a muscular man in bed that made her forget about her job as a reporter.

Almost.

With a sigh she opened her eyes and glanced around the room. Kevin was reaching for the ringing phone and grumbled something that sounded like hello. Within a few minutes, Kyra could tell it was Regan.

"Sure, Regan. She's right here." Kevin pushed the phone at her.

Kyra took the phone, pulled the sheet up to her neck, and cleared her throat. "Good morning, Regan." She punched Kevin in the stomach for laughing at her.

"Hi, Kyra. I hope I didn't catch you guys at a bad time. Elias said most likely you'd be at Kev's. I'm very pleased."

Kyra was very pleased as well, but for quite a different reason. "Oh, no, Regan. It's fine. Is something wrong?"

"You said you wanted to see the Safe Haven and I wanted to know what time."

Kyra's mind raced over the events of the previous night. Then the light bulb went on. "How about noon? We can eat lunch at Jay's and then go by the house. I need to check on a few things at the newspaper and interview a few more people for my story."

"That sounds great. Mom still won't let me drive and I don't feel up to it either. Do you mind picking me up?"

"Of course not. See you at noon."

Regan laughed. "Tell Kevin he's invited too."

Kyra laughed and pushed the end button. She handed the phone to Kevin. "Regan invited you to lunch with us today."

He smiled. "I wish I could, just to see the look on your face, but Elias has some leads to follow up on. What else are you doing today?" He pulled her closer to him.

Kyra inhaled, not wanting to move one inch. She would love to spend the day in bed with Kevin and block out all that was wrong in her life, but that wasn't a possibility. Auggie would be expecting a story. He might not like the one she handed in, but he could never say she didn't do her job.

She felt Kevin's hands moving over her naked

body. He leaned and kissed her softly. "What are you doing today? Or is this going to turn into a hard interrogation?"

"Kevin Johnson, was that a double entendre?" She hoped with all her heart that it was.

His lips did all his talking. He kiss her hungrily, as if they hadn't sated each other many times during the night. Kyra returned his kisses with the same intensity. She was like a wanton teenager in his arms. Her body twisted out of control, feeling two of his fingers enter her.

Kyra didn't think she had an orgasm left in her pliant body after the night they'd had, but she wrong. Oh, so wrong.

Before she could recover from that burst of pleasure, Kevin replaced his fingers with his most rigid body part. He slid inside easily and they moaned in concert. He moved against her slowly, gently increasing speed and pressure until they both saw paradise.

He rolled off her body, but held her close. "Baby, I don't know what you're doing to me, but I like it."

Kyra wanted to tell him that he was doing the same thing to her, but that took too much energy. She snuggled closer to Kevin and fell asleep.

"Sorry, I'm late," Kyra said as Regan let her inside the house.

Regan smiled knowingly at her. "Don't worry about it. I know how amorous those Johnson men are."

Kyra glanced around the house. No Brenda. "Where's your mom?"

Regan was dressed in jeans, a sweatshirt, and tennis shoes. She shrugged as she grabbed her purse. "She took Mopsy for a walk. She might meet us at the house later." Regan handed her a set of keys. "I think your car is cute, but do you mind driving my SUV?"

How could Kyra deny Regan anything? "No, I don't mind." They left the house after Regan locked the front door. "I got a late start this morning. I didn't make it to the newspaper office."

"We can go by there after you see the house. The *Wright City Record* did a huge story on the remodeling of the Safe Haven. You can get some background on that too while you're researching Uncle Potbelly."

"You want to go to the paper?" Kyra couldn't keep the surprise out of her voice. They got into Regan's SUV with Kyra behind the wheel. She liked her little sports car, but she also liked the roominess of Regan's SUV.

"Yeah, I need to order some pictures of Uncle Potbelly for the wedding anyway."

"Okay. It'll be nice to have company at the newspaper. The owner gives me the willies. The last few times I've been there, he's always watching me." After making sure Regan was secure in her seat, Kyra started the SUV and they headed to the diner.

Regan nodded. "Yeah, that's Carter. He's a little older than us. I think mid-forties. He kind of does his own thing. He left Wright City right after high school and didn't come back until a few years ago when his dad died and he had to take over the newspaper."

"His clothes don't seem to fit. He wears an Armani suit. I don't know many small town editors that are ballin' like that."

"Yes, now that's weird. The paper only comes out once a week, and it's no secret that the paper is struggling, but he just bought a Mercedes. But, on the other hand, he hasn't let anyone go because of the economy. The paper needed some high-dollar upgrades a few years back, and he did them without raising the price of the newspaper."

Kyra's reporter senses were on high alert. "Maybe he's getting subsidized by the government for being a small business. Independent small-town papers are becoming extinct. The larger corporate-owned newspapers are eating them up like candy." Kyra parked across the street from the diner.

Regan refused her help, and got out on her own. "I don't think Carter's getting outside financial help. My friend Natasha's dad used to do the accounting for the older *Record,* and knew they were almost broke because he refused any outside funding."

"Why isn't your friend's father doing the accounting for Carter?"

"He retired after the accident."

"Accident?" Kyra fought the urge to take out her notepad.

They walked across the street, entered the diner, and were soon seated at a table. Regan continued her story.

"Natasha's dad was working on the books one

Saturday, and someone broke into the newspaper office. He was there all alone, and two men beat him up. He had a broken leg, broken ribs, and a concussion. They left him for dead. Carter found him a few hours later."

"Did they ever find out who did it?"

"No. Carter paid all the hospital bills and gave him the equivalent of what he would have made for the next twenty years. So he retired."

"Why?"

Regan shrugged. "Carter said he felt awful about it since he'd just taken over the paper. He's been doing the accounting himself since. Natasha's dad even offered to do the accounting for him on part-time basis to show his thanks after he'd recuperated, but Carter told him no. He said he'd prefer doing everything himself."

The chain of events convinced her of her earlier suspicions. She'd definitely have to give Carter Record a closer look. "What did your friend's father say about all this?"

"Not much. It took about a year for him to heal from all the surgeries, and by then the mystery surrounding it had died. Now, Uncle Potbelly always said there was something wrong with the whole mess. He thought it was too convenient. He said it was too slick and he didn't trust Carter."

"I think your dearly departed uncle was very right."

"This place is wonderful," Kyra said as she walked around the Donald Cotton Safe Haven Center. "Everything looks perfect."

Regan led her from room to room. "Yes, Mom helped me a quite a bit. We put down laminate floors to withstand the kids' traffic throughout the house. I've hired a few retired school teachers as tutors."

"Are you going to have after-school snacks for the kids?" Kyra thought it would be a great idea, but knew it would take a registered dietitian and at least two other people.

"I'd like to, but finding someone with those credentials and willing to relocate here would be a task. But I only want good quality help for the center. I don't want another scandal linked to Uncle Potbelly's name by hiring inferior people."

Kyra read between the lines and knew Regan meant business. "I might actually know someone."

Regan's brown eyes lit up. "With qualified creds?"

Kyra nodded. "From the University of Texas. She's actually a reporter friend, who's never actually used the degree she went to school for."

"Oh, and you'd think she'd want to live here? I probably couldn't pay what she's making at the paper."

"It wouldn't matter. She had a really good divorce settlement. I can call her after the assassin thing is solved, but I'd bet my last pair of Jimmy Choo stilettos she'd be interested."

Regan smiled and hugged her. "Thank you, Kyra! That would be great. I wanted to hire all certified people and the dietician position had me worried."

They entered the kitchen and Kyra shook her head in amazement. The kitchen had all stainless

steel appliances, including a commercial-sized refrigerator. Kyra ran her hand on the stone coun-
tertops. Everything in the room was functional,
and very durable. "Kory would love this."

"Elias picked out most of this. He helped Kevin
redo his house a few years back, so now he thinks
he's ready to go on one of those house makeover
shows."

Kyra looked around the room as if seeing it in a
new light. *This is a good cause,* she thought. "Regan,
I'd like to make a donation."

"No, Kyra, you don't have to. We get donations
all the time. Right after the story broke, the donations poured in. I have enough to keep it running
for at least five years. I don't want to deter you, but
the Haven is doing okay. Are you sure you want to
donate? "

"I'd like to, Regan. Besides, I want to do something for Mr. Cotton."

"But you didn't know him."

Kyra smiled. "I feel like I did."

Regan's brown eyes searched Kyra's face for
what seemed like forever. "All right, I'll let you
make a donation if you do something for me."

Kyra studied Regan's innocent face. Was she setting Kyra up for something she would regret? Kyra
didn't think so, but knew whatever Regan was
going to ask of her was going to be something life-
changing. "Sure."

"Would you be my maid of honor?"

Kyra gasped. Was that it? Why would Regan
choose her? "Regan, are you sure? I'm sure there
are people around here who would love to be in

the wedding party. I mean, I'd be honored, but I'm sure that one of your girlfriends would be crushed if you didn't ask them."

"Nat says it's okay. Besides, you've never treated me like an invalid and I'd consider it a big favor if you would be in the wedding. I really couldn't choose between my friends to be my maid of honor, and this way, everyone is happy being bridesmaids. Besides, I have to have my future brother-in-law's girlfriend in my wedding or tongues will wag."

So sweet, innocent Regan had a master plan? Who knew? "Who's the best man?" She hoped she didn't have to walk down the aisle with some really short guy.

"It'll be so much more fun if I don't tell you. You just have to wait four weeks to find out."

"What about the fitting for the dresses? When I put the story to bed, I'm going back to Austin."

Regan shook her head. "We both know you're not going to be able to put Kevin out of your mind, so I know you'll be here. Besides, Mrs. Miller is going to make the dresses and she just needs to see you once and we can do that today."

"She doesn't need to do more fittings? Most of the weddings I've been in, I've had at least three fittings before the main event."

Regan laughed. "Harriet Miller is one of the best dressmakers I've ever seen. I bet any one of her gowns could rival any New York designer, even Vera Wang."

"Not Vera," Kyra said sarcastically. "No one can hold a candle to her."

"Mrs. Miller can. She's making my wedding dress too."

"Well, if you have that much faith in her, I can too." Kyra hoped the dresses didn't look too homemade.

"I do. When we go to her house, you'll see how many gowns she's made. She's made just about every gown in every wedding in Wright City for the last twenty years. Everyone in town uses her."

"Regan, you had me when you told me she was making your dress. Will she accept a check from Austin?"

"Yes, she would, but there's no charge for the dresses."

Kyra had a sneaking suspicion it was probably due to Regan's dead uncle. If she was wrong, she'd be surprised. "Why? I mean, that's not a lot of time. How many bridesmaids are you having?"

"I'm having four bridesmaids. Elias and I were trying to keep it small, but it's morphed into this large thing. We both have too many friends, family members, and work associates to keep it intimate."

Kyra nodded. "I completely understand. If I ever get married, it definitely will be small."

Regan giggled. "I'll have to keep that in mind."

CHAPTER 25

Kevin was only half listening to his brother as he walked into his office later that morning. His mind was on too many things to focus on just one. His thoughts ran to Kyra, who was trying to kill her, would he catch the next one, and who on earth in Wright City could have been a government assassin in a past life?

"Kev, are you even listening to anything I just said?" Elias took a seat in front of his brother's desk. "You really got your head up your ass. I know there's been a lot going on in town, but I know you can handle anything that happens."

Kevin stared at his brother. "But?"

"Shouldn't someone be shadowing Kyra? Regan's with her."

"Someone is watching her. Derek is shadowing her movements. He either texts or calls me every time they leave a place. Kyra is supposed to call me when they change positions. You see how well that's going."

"Well, that makes me feel better. Where are they now?"

"They just left the Haven."

Elias smiled. "I still can't believe I'll be married in four weeks, but I can't wait."

Kevin laughed. "Yeah, I just bet."

"Make jokes, I know you're next. I've never seen two people fighting love harder than you and Kyra. Someone has to fall first, Kevin."

"Well, it's not going to be me. Nursing a broken heart sucks." He decided now was just as good a time as any to change the subject. "How about helping me solve this mess?"

"You're avoiding the issue, but okay, man. Has the widow faxed in those pictures yet?"

Kevin shrugged, then looked in his in-basket, riffled through the few papers, and didn't find any fax sheets. "I'll check with Nick."

"No need, boss," Nick said, ambling into the room. He nodded at Elias as he placed the photos in front of Kevin. "These were here first thing this morning. Unlike some people," he mumbled.

Kevin shot Nick a hard look. The other deputies would have scurried out of the room without another word, but not Nick.

"Man, it's already all over town that you've had an overnight guest the last few nights. I thought it would have taken the edge off you."

Elias laughed. "Me too."

"You both got jokes this morning," Kevin said, trying not to smile, but it was infectious. "Can we get to work?" He looked at the three photos the widow had faxed them. "Can you get this blown up?"

Nick shook his head. "Been trying all morning, but if I make it larger, I lose the clarity."

Kevin sighed. "Can you make out the letters on the pin?"

"I can make out the last letter, which is an A. I talked to the widow and she's looking through her pictures on her computer. If she finds it, she'll e-mail me the file."

"Damn. I hate all these straws," Kevin said. "I would like just one solid lead on the case."

Harriet Miller was all Regan said and more, Kyra realized. After touring Safe Haven, the women had decided to visit the seamstress to satisfy Kyra's curiosity.

The small house was cozy, reminding Kyra of one of those retro dressmaker's stores in Austin. Harriet was a plump woman of probably fifty. Her salt-and-pepper hair was pulled back into a pony-tail.

"Now, this is the big-city woman everyone is talking about," she said, looking Kyra up and down. "I'm always glad to see a woman who isn't afraid to eat. About size sixteen."

"Yes," Kyra said. "It's all Jay's fault. She doesn't fix diet food." She had to blame someone.

Harriet laughed. "Honey, you can save that one for the sheriff. I'm sure he likes a woman with meat on her bones."

Kyra shook her head. "I'll have to ask him the next time I see him."

"Now, you know, my best friend lives next door to him. So I know all your secrets."

Busted. "Yes, ma'am." Kyra knew when she had been outdone and this was one of those times. "Tell me about your dresses."

"I can show you." Harriet stood and walked into an adjoining room and motioned for Kyra and Regan to follow her. "I've been making dresses for more years than I want to remember. Never had any complaints. Even had a few of my dresses in a national magazine a few years back. I might not be this Vera person I keep hearing about, but you won't look like you jumped off the turnip truck, either.

Kyra forced herself not to smile. "I'm sure your dresses are just fine."

Harriet grunted her response. "The eyes don't lie." She opened a door to another room and it was chock full of formal gowns, evening dresses, and other formal wear.

Kyra was amazed. She was in awe. The dresses were gorgeous and didn't look homemade at all. She touched one of the dresses and pulled it off the rack to better examine it. "Is this silk?"

"Yes, it is. Special ordered from New York. I have a few connections up that way," she explained.

Nothing and no one in this town seemed to be what she thought they were. She was expecting a little old lady dressmaker complete with an old-fashioned sewing machine in the corner of the living room. Harriet was the complete opposite. Her sewing machine looked pretty top-of-the-line, complete with an onboard computer!

Harriet must have been reading Kyra's mind. "I know, it's a high-dollar one, but it runs like a dream."

Kyra caressed the fabric, reveling in the smooth feel. "I understand, but it's still you doing the work. What kind of dress has Regan picked out?"

Regan laughed. "Oh, sorry, I forgot to tell you. Mrs. Miller picks out the dresses. So no one knows what it looks like until the week of the wedding. You'll know the color, which is teal, but that's it."

Apparently, Harriet Miller was also an eccentric artist. Kyra didn't know if she could deal with not knowing what her dress looked like, if it would fit, and how it would look on her voluptuous frame. "Can I have an idea of what the dress will look like?"

Harriet studied her intently. "No."

Kyra was stumped. "How will I know if it's going to look right on me?"

Harriet stared at her as if she had begun to speak a foreign tongue. "You will know because I made it. I'm making the entire wedding party's dresses, except for Brenda's, of course."

Kyra met Harriet's steady gaze. Explanations were unnecessary when it came to Brenda. Kyra looked at Regan and she nodded as well. Kyra didn't want to be included with Regan's mother on any account. "Okay, Mrs. Miller, I believe you, and since Regan has so much trust in you, you got my vote."

Harriet sighed. "Well, thank goodness. I thought I was going to have another Brenda on my hands. I'll see you ladies in three weeks."

Kyra nodded, and Regan rose slowly. Kyra instantly went to her side. "Are you okay? Maybe I should take you home."

She brushed away Kyra's helping hand. "I'm

fine, Kyra. I'm not going to get better if people keep babying me."

"Okay, Regan," Kyra said. "We've been doing a lot of things today and I didn't want you to overexert yourself."

Regan wiped away a tear. "I appreciate your concern, Kyra. But I've been laid up on my back for the last four months. I'm ready to start living again."

"How can I help?"

"By not helping."

"Gotcha."

"Thank you, Kyra."

The more Kyra drove Regan's SUV, the more she liked it. It was roomy and had all the amenities of her little roadster she admired on her way home from the newspaper office with Regina.

Kyra glanced over at Regan. Her eyes were closed and her breathing was slow. Kyra realized Regan had fallen asleep. Today was probably too much exertion for her. If Kyra had been sensible, she would have taken Regan straight home, but Kyra knew Regan wanted her independence back, and Kyra would do her best to give it to her.

She parked in front of her rental house and gently shook Regan awake. "Regan, I need to do a little research on the Internet." Sure it was lie, but a good one.

Regan yawned. "Okay. I need to call Elias anyway." She reached over and patted Kyra's hand. "I know what you're doing, Kyra. Thank you."

Kyra smiled. "I don't know what you're talking

about. I really do have to do some research." She opened the SUV door. She didn't mention that the information she was looking for was a new car.

They walked inside the house. As Kyra helped Regan out of the SUV, she glanced around. There was that feeling again. She could have sworn she'd seen someone while they were at the newspaper, but she was wrong. She shrugged off the feeling. Regan sat on the couch while Kyra went to retrieve her laptop. When she returned, Regan was asleep on the couch. Kyra dialed Kevin's cell number and waited for him to pick up.

"Hey, everything okay? Why are you back at your place?" Concerned was etched in his deep voice, making him sound even sexier, if that were possible.

"Yes, sweetie." Was that her voice? "I wanted you to know that Regan was with me and she's asleep on my couch, just in case Elias is with you."

"Why don't you take her home?"

Kyra looked at Regan's sleeping form. "Long story. I'm doing some research. See you tonight."

"Of course. Why don't you come to my place after you drop Regan off?"

"Sure."

"Something's up."

"Kevin, what are you talking about?"

"Kyra, I know you. You never give in this easily."

"Yes, I do. When there's sex involved, I'd agree to almost anything you say." She thanked the heavens no one else heard their racy conversation. Then she heard the chuckles of both Elias and Nick.

"Kevin Johnson, you have that darn walkie-talkie thing on! I'm going to kill you!"

"Oh, baby, I didn't know you were going to start talking all sexy."

She couldn't stay mad at him, even if it was his fault. That was the exact moment she knew she was in heart-stopping, mushy-talking love with Kevin Johnson.

CHAPTER 26

Kevin had lost his mind. Either that, or he was head-over-heels in love and just hadn't realized it until that very moment. Kevin knew the probability of Kyra saying something he'd regret was high, but still he left the phone in walkie-talkie mode.

"Kevin, I can't believe you put Kyra out there like that." Elias laughed. "Man, you're going to be paying for that for a long time."

He hadn't doubted it for a minute. "I know."

"If I could interrupt the girl talk with some actual sheriff business," Nick said, placing a sheet of paper on Kevin's desk. "Did I say that? How crazy is this?"

Kevin shrugged. "Pretty crazy. Since I'm the one always telling you to do some work." He scanned the paper in front of him. "The widow found more pictures?"

Nick smiled. "Yeah. The symbol is pretty clear." And it was: three arrows connecting, making a circle with the letters NSE. "Derek is making some copies so we can distribute them to the other deputies."

"Good. I don't want this guy getting any idea of what's going on, so no one outside of this department should have these pictures."

"You think we have a chance in hell of finding him?"

"No, but we have to give this a shot. If he took a pin and necklace off a dead body, my guess is he's wearing them." He looked at his brother. "What's NSE?"

"National Security Evaluators. It's a Black Ops group so named because they operate just south of the law if necessary, for the good of our country, of course," Elias explained. Black Operations were usually covert operations that were highly dangerous, just shy of military protocol and outside of the United States. "No one knows much about the organization except the name and there's probably about twenty members, but I can't even be certain about that. That's the last official head count."

Kevin didn't like the sound of that. "So they have like carte blanche to kill."

"Within reason. I mean, they can't just go shooting people down just because they want to; there's has to be a threat to the American way of life. Usually, it's something outside the U.S. If they're stateside, they can take contract work, because they have a high security clearance."

"Can you check if the first two victims were members of this department?"

Elias sighed. "That's the tricky part. If they're members of NSE, I won't be able to verify it. That's a very secret department, even my security clearance won't help. The best bet is to talk to the spouses but usually they have no idea what their mates are doing until after the fact."

Kevin was close. He knew it. If only he could find the one stone that held all the information, he'd be able to save Kyra and prevent any more murders.

Kyra hadn't done anything this impulsive since the last time she got engaged. All the signs were there and it was time. It was time to say good-bye to her little roadster.

After dropping Regan off and getting back behind the wheel of her car, she knew it was time. She drove to Wright City Chevrolet armed with the knowledge of what a new Chevy Trailblazer should cost. And since her car was paid off, the dealership would owe her a little cash.

Which was exactly the case. The dealership owed her a little over ten grand in the deal. Kyra was pleased with her new black SUV, with a sunroof, as she drove to the newspaper office. It was after five, so hopefully the owner wasn't there.

She waved at the receptionist as she headed to the morgue of old newspapers. She entered the room and took a deep breath. She loved the smell of old newspapers. Her office in Austin never smelled liked that. Her office smelled like, well, an office. It hardly reminded her of a newspaper office at all.

"Well, I see your still researching you're story, Ms. Chase." He was standing across the room.

Where the heck did he come from? She had thought she was alone. "Yes, Mr. Record, I've had a change of heart and want to focus more on Mr. Cotton. I was just looking for issues about the Safe Haven."

"I was just checking on some research myself." He walked toward her. "Perhaps I can help you with Mr. Cotton."

Kyra took in his black Armani suit. "That's not necessary, Mr. Record. I'd hate for your suit to get dirty."

"Nonsense, it just looks expensive." He walked to the first row of papers. "Let's see. Cotton was killed in June and I believe work started on the Haven a few weeks after Regan was hurt. I believe the July Fourth edition is your starting point." He grabbed a bundle of papers and carried them to the reading table. "I'd be glad to tell you anything you want to know about Cotton as well. Granted, I was away most of the time, but I can tell you about the last few years."

"Okay, tell me your impressions of Mr. Cotton since your return home." Kyra sat at the table and took out her tape recorder. "You don't mind?" She nodded at the small recorder. "I like my quotes to be consistent."

He smiled at her. "Yes, I'm sure you do. You wouldn't have been able to bring down the chancellor otherwise, right?"

"Correct. I'm glad we're on the same page. Now about Mr. Cotton," she reminded him.

"Of course. I knew Donald while I was growing

up as well. But when I returned home after my father died unexpectedly, I really appreciated knowing him."

It was going to be another one of those crying interviews, Kyra feared. "How so?"

"Well, I'd been living mostly on the East Coast, and small town living had been forgotten. Cotton helped me get reacquainted with Wright City. I realized how important this place is to me. I began to treasure this town again. Not many places you can walk around town and feel safe. I want to keep that. That's what Donald wanted."

"Yes, what do you think about Safe Haven?"

"I think it's a great idea. Regan picked up where Donald left off. I'm glad she has his spirit, unlike that mother of hers. Donald had been nothing but kind to her, and that's how Brenda repaid him, by getting him killed."

"You mean Regan's mother had him killed?"

"No, she didn't hire a hitter if that's what you're asking." He let out a frustrated breath. "I've probably said too much. Let's get back to Cotton. He was a good man and thanks to Regan and Elias, his name wasn't linked to a scandal."

This man still gave her the willies, but she saw him in a different light. "That's a nice lapel pin." Kyra admired the unique pin. "Where did you get it?"

"I can't remember," he said. "Probably on one of my many trips to Europe."

Kyra nodded. "Anything else about Mr. Cotton I should know? I've gotten glowing reports from just about everyone in town. I would have loved to have met him."

Carter agreed. "Yes, he had friends from all walks of life. I can't think of one person in town he hasn't helped."

Kevin paced the length of his living room. Where was she? After checking with Regan, he learned that Kyra had dropped her off hours ago. He hadn't been able to contact Derek, either. Something wasn't right. He tried Kyra's cell phone but she never picked up. Now she was missing.

He dialed Nick's cell and sighed. He hoped he wasn't making a big mistake. "Nick, Kyra is missing. Have the deputies make a pass through town and I'll check out the rental house."

Nick laughed. "Kevin, you're overreacting. Besides, her car has been seen at the Chevrolet dealership since early afternoon. Think she's getting that car serviced? I didn't think they serviced foreign cars."

Kevin didn't either. "Maybe she's interviewing someone there?" He looked around for his truck keys. "I'll check there first. Thanks, man, talk to you later." He set the phone on the table and grabbed his keys.

He heard a knock at the front door. Now what? He grunted as he went to the door. "Just what I need," he grumbled. He swung the door open wide and all bad thoughts fell out of his mouth.

"Well, are you just going to stand there or are you going to kiss me?"

He pulled Kyra into his arms and kissed with all the pent-up frustration she caused him on a daily basis. When he finally tore his lips from hers, he closed the door. "Baby, I've been worried. Where have you been? Why is your car at the dealership? And why are you driving that SUV?"

She had an excited gleam on her pretty face. "If you give me another kiss like that, I'll tell you." She led him to the couch and motioned for him to sit down.

He did as she directed and she sat on his lap. Kevin knew that excited look: something wonderful had happened and she had to tell him. And he had to listen. Right after he kissed her again. He had intended for it to be a kiss that showed how much he missed her today, but it evolved into something he wasn't expecting. His hands crept under her blouse as they were exploring each other until he heard her laughing against his lips.

"You think you're going to get me to shut up that way?" she teased against his lips. "It's not going to work." She moved just far enough away to get his attention.

"Okay, baby, what happened today?"

Her face lit up. "Well, actually, I spent most of the day with Regan and it was really nice. I'd forgotten what it felt like to be with someone who didn't know my father, or anything about my life. It was nice not to have to live up to anyone's expectations."

Kevin cradled her closer to his body. "I'm glad you had such a great time with her. I think she really misses getting out without Brenda watching her every move."

"Well, yeah, there's that. I met Harriet Miller today."

Okay, that one got him. "Why did you meet Harriet? I know she's making the dresses for the wedding, and she doesn't like people taking a peek until she's finished with them. Is she making Regan's wedding dress too?"

"She's an awesome seamstress. She should be in New York, she could be famous."

"She likes it here in Wright City just fine." He kissed her forehead. "That still doesn't explain why you're driving a black SUV instead of your little tin cup."

A wide grin split her beautiful face. "I bought it. I traded my car for it."

"Why?"

"Because the more I drove Regan's SUV, the more I liked it. The more I was tired of getting in and out of my little car. Your mom and Regan are right. Everyone does have to take her own emotional journey. I think mine started today." She kissed him softly on the lips then rose. "Come on, dinner is on me tonight."

Kevin stood slowly. "Now, baby, you know I can't let you pay for dinner."

"If you ever want to make love with me again, you'll let me buy you dinner."

Kevin mulled over his choices in his head. Okay, it was a no-brainer. "Okay, if you're paying, then I'm seducing you later."

"I was counting on that."

"What do you mean, Kyra bought a SUV?" Elias asked Regan after kissing her within an inch of her life. He didn't know what it was, but Regan looked more beautiful to him every day.

Regan was propped up in her bed, smiling. "Just what I said, Elias. She liked my SUV so much she traded her car in and bought it. She got money back on the deal."

Elias caressed her hand. "I thought she loved that car."

"Baby, she's on a journey. That car was her old life and she is starting fresh. She's changed so much in the week she's been here. That car represents her old life and the things she used to hold dear. You know, like clothes, shopping, designer purses. Those things don't hold a candle to the new and improved Kyra Chase." She motioned for him to get into bed next to her.

There was a time Elias would have thought twice about sliding in next to Regan in bed in her mother's house, but now with the new and improved Brenda, he didn't have to worry. He lay next to Regan, facing her. "Kevin did that to her?"

Regan smiled and moved closer to him. "Kevin and the town. Actually, I think they've had a profound effect on each other. She puts a certain something in his life. I don't quite know what it is, but Kevin acts different now. He still loves being a sheriff, but it's not so life-consuming anymore. He's enjoying life. When he was married, was he happy?"

Elias shrugged. "I'd always thought so. It wasn't the best marriage, but I thought it was good enough. Kevin finally admitted that he'd been unhappy for years."

"He's such a sweet person. He needs someone to take care of him."

"And you think that someone is Kyra. She doesn't strike me as a nurturer." He kissed Regan softly on the lips. "Now, you are a nurturer. I can't even imagine what would have happened to me if we hadn't run into each other. I love you, Regan."

"I've always love you, Elias. And I always will."

"What are we going to do about Kevin and Kyra? You know he's thinks she's heading back to Austin the minute the story is done. He doesn't want to put his heart on the line again."

"They'll be just fine," Regan said confidently. She laid her head on his chest. "They still have some mountains to climb, but they'll be fine."

He didn't question Regan's logic. Well, not any-more. If she felt his conservative brother and the free-spirited reporter with the millionaire dad would get together, then he regarded that as the truth.

He and Regan lay in the quiet of her bedroom. He thought of the future, mostly, the near future. When he and Regan would be husband and wife. He'd waited his whole life for the right woman and she'd been in Wright City all along.

Miguel arrived in Wright City earlier than expected. Why hadn't he thought of this sooner? He could have saved his family $3 million by doing the job himself. He hadn't made the mistakes the others had. He'd researched the small town, and knew a pricey import car would stand out to law enforcement.

He bought a cheap used car, and clothes from

Goodwill somewhere between here and Austin. His tracks were covered. This town was a joke. There was only one motel, handful of places to eat, and only a Super Wal-Mart to do any shopping. How on earth could Chase's pampered daughter stand it in this backwater place? Seemed like you had to leave town for just about anything. He'd had her credit cards monitored and she hadn't used them since hitting the small town a week ago.

He sat in the diner, looking over the crudely printed menu. Everything listed on it had too much fat; there were no healthy options listed. *Haven't these people heard of high cholesterol, heart attacks, diabetes, or any other life threatening disease?*

"May I take your order?" a young man asked, pad in hand.

Miguel looked at him. "Sure, kid. What's good?"

He smiled, revealing braces. "Everything."

"How about a salad?"

"We have chicken, tuna, or egg."

Miguel sighed. This was about as good as he was getting. "Egg salad and a glass of unsweetened tea."

"We don't have unsweetened tea. We have water."

This place had to be in the Twilight Zone. "Water, then."

The young man nodded and scurried away from the table. Miguel glanced around the restaurant, noticing that it was packed to capacity. Apparently these people didn't mind having a heart attack or three.

Finding Kyra wouldn't be hard. He already had her address. In fact, he'd given it to the last hitter he'd contracted, for all the good it did. He was going to take his time to make sure the job was done this time. He couldn't wait to see Chandler's face when he heard the news that his precious daughter had finally been eliminated.

He'd noticed Miguel Ditano the minute he entered the diner. Never would he have figured Miguel for a cleaner. This was a big mess he would have to make disappear. Too bad he wouldn't succeed. Miguel created disasters for his mob daddy to pay to have cleaned up, not to actually do the cleaning himself. There was only one reason for him to be in this town. He was going to take Kyra down himself. Or so Miguel thought.

He hated to have kill another person, but it was either Miguel or him. Miguel could blow his cover. By killing Miguel the hit would be called off and he'd lose out on $3 million. If he didn't kill Miguel, and somehow Kyra evaded his grasp, the hit would be called off. What a decision.

He pondered his decision as he ate dinner. Miguel would have to die. Then he'd kill Kyra Chase just because she's been so much trouble.

He followed Miguel to his car and to the motel. This was going to be easy. Miguel parked on the side of the building. Amateur move. He got out of his Mercedes, stuffed his favorite nine mil in his gun holster, and walked toward his prey.

"Excuse me, Miguel," he said, approaching the young man.

Miguel stopped immediately. "How do you know my name?"

He shook his head. "Not important. I just wanted to welcome you to our town." He inched toward him with each word he spoke.

Miguel stepped back out of range. "Thanks, buddy. I'm a little busy right now. Beat it." Miguel opened his car door and got in, ignoring his visitor.

"I'll beat it, all right." He pulled out his gun, fired two shots into the driver's side window, and walked back to his car.

Kyra Chase was next.

CHAPTER 27

Saturday morning, Kyra's eyes popped open at the sound of footsteps on her front porch. Kevin was asleep beside her, and no one in the sheriff's department would dare disturb him, so it had to be some unwanted company. She slipped out of bed, glanced at her man with a smile on her face, and pulled on her bathrobe. He rocked her world several times during the night. He was going to be a hard habit to break.

She heard the unmistakable sound of someone shaking the doorknob. She went to investigate.

As she entered the living room, she heard the prowler utter a curse then stomp across the wide porch. Kyra knew this was a very determined person and she needed to be in some real clothes, plus, she needed to wake Kevin.

She went back to the bedroom, surprised to see Kevin sitting up and smiling at her. "I thought you were coming back with breakfast."

"Good idea. No time," she whispered. "We have company. Unwanted company." She slipped on her jeans commando style, then struggled into a sweatshirt. She reached back into her closet for the gun she never wanted to use.

"Kyra, I have a gun." Kevin stood and dressed in record time. "You don't know what you're doing."

She looked at him as she slipped in a clip into her gun. "Your gun is in your truck, which is at your house. Remember, I wanted to show off my new SUV yesterday? I know how to shoot. Daddy taught me years ago. In fact, he bought me this gun."

He did the eye roll thing, then shrugged. "Give it to me, I'll do the shooting." He held out his hand. When she didn't give it to him, he simply said, "Baby, it's what I do."

Well, he had her there. She tossed him the gun and he motioned for her to get behind him. Kyra didn't want to, but good sense prevailed. Especially since she'd never fired the gun before, except on a shooting range.

"And be quiet," he ordered.

She was about to tell Kevin where to go when a figure paraded in front of the bay window. "It's not any of your guys," Kyra said. "I can't make out who it is."

"He's too short and thin for one of my deputies," said Kevin, moving further into the living room. "Maybe he's another assassin for you."

"That's so not funny," Kyra grumbled. "Whoever is after me should be broke by now and can't afford any more hitters." She wondered who could want her this dead.

Then the slight body came into view.

Kevin turned and motioned her to go back into the bedroom. And that was his mistake.

The glass in the window shattered the quiet of the room with the piercing of the bullet. Wind whirled in the open area and cold invaded the the room, circling them. It happened too fast for Kevin to react. The bullet caught him in the back and he fell face down on the floor with a thud. He moaned in pain. Kyra stood frozen in terror. What was she supposed to do? He moaned again, bringing her back to reality. She hit the floor.

"Kevin?" Kyra crawled over to his very still form and carefully turned him over on his back. But he was silent.

Kyra quickly felt his pulse. She had to concentrate really hard, but she finally felt it. She sighed in relief. He was still with her. Kyra pried the gun from his limp hand, ready for whatever was going to happen next. She had to stay alert and protect them both.

She didn't have to wait long. Carter Record stepped through the broken window with his Glock aimed directly at her.

Then it all fell into place. "You're the assassin?"

"Not strictly speaking," he said. "I'm retired."

Kyra knew she had few options to come out a winner in this situation. She kept one hand on Kevin's pulse to make sure he was still with her and the other on the gun, waiting for the right moment.

"You've been killing the other men who came to kill me. Why did you come back to Wright City anyway?"

"You obviously didn't know my family," Carter snorted. "No one knew I was a contract killer for the government. My small-town parents thought I was some kind of paper-pusher in DC. When Dad died, I had to come back to run that infernal paper that has been in the family forever. I was in the process of selling it to a big New York conglomerate when Cotton found out. He had the nerve to want to buy it. Like he had any real money. But he was making too much noise, so I had to silence him."

Kyra let the information sink in. "You had him killed? Why didn't you do it?"

"I'm a highly paid assassin. Cotton was too easy, plus, someone else wanted those honors. I had nothing to do with his death."

Kyra could actually see the straw that Record was clinging to. "But you had everything to do with his death."

Record stepped closer to her. "Being back in Hicksville wasn't for me anymore. I was dying of boredom here, so I took odd jobs when I could to keep my hands in the pie, so to speak."

"So you've been taking jobs over the years? The Brunner killing in Dallas six months ago." Kyra remembered the case well. Judge Brunner was killed right in front of his three young children as they prepared to leave for school.

Carter scratched his chin. "Yeah, that was some of my best work. He made it too easy. He was too predictable. Your father was a problem. Old man Ditano felt a loyalty to him and didn't want him killed, but you, on the other hand, are expendable. If you were killed, Chase would have died emotionally. So you became the target."

Kyra still didn't understand who was after her father. "Why kill Daddy?"

"How do you think your precious father made all those millions?"

"My father worked very hard to get where he is," Kyra said proudly. "He's a good attorney." She also knew her father had a checkered past that no one discussed.

"Yeah, yeah. Spare me the platitudes. Well, let me tell you about Chandler Chase. There was a time he'd accept any kind of case just to keep food on the table and you in the finest schools. He was the legal counsel for the Ditano crime family."

"I don't believe you."

"Ask him. There was a time Chandler would have done just about anything for Mario Ditano so he could keep you and your mother living in style."

He raised his gun and aimed at Kyra. "You've been a pain in the ass since you came to town, but now all my problems are solved. After I finish you, I—" He stopped his speech suddenly. He raised his blood-covered hand and stared at it in amazement.

Kyra looked at him. She'd waited patiently for him to get too confident and take his focus off her. When she had him where she wanted him, she took a shot. When she saw the blood on his shirt, she knew she hit the mark. Why was Carter still standing? She'd hit him in the stomach and he should have been writhing in pain or something, but he just stood there with a murderous look in those blue eyes.

"Too bad you didn't hit a vital organ," he drawled, aiming the gun at her again. "You know, I should kill the sheriff for you trying to kill me."

Kyra shook her head. "No, don't hurt him. This has nothing to do with him. You're after me." The gun was still in her hand and her finger was still on the trigger.

"You know, you're a lot smarter than your father. Too bad you won't get to tell him how smart you were." He stepped closer to her. "Just so I don't miss this time." Carter laughed.

"Maybe." She took a deep breath, raised the gun, closed her eyes, and fired. She heard him fall to the hardwood floor, then she opened her eyes. This time she had shot him directly in the heart and he fell to the floor without so much as a gasp. She felt like clapping, but she turned her attention to Kevin.

In those few minutes, his pulse had weakened, his breathing gotten shallow, but he was still with her. She looked around the room for her phone. Finally, she spotted her cordless on the coffee table. She stepped over Carter's body, careful not to contaminate the crime scene. If she did, Kevin would kill her. She laughed at the thought. What a difference a week made in her life. A week ago, she could not have cared less about contaminating a crime scene. She dialed 911 and before she could tell the dispatcher to send an ambulance, there was a knock at the door.

"Kyra, it's Nick."

She threw down the phone and ran to the door,

pulling it open. She flung herself into Nick's arms. "Oh, Nick, Kevin got shot in the back. Help him."

"What?" Nick's handsome face remained stoic as he surveyed the room. "I came here to tell him we found another body. This time it was Miguel Ditano." He kneeled next to Kevin, checked his pulse, then looked at Kyra. "He's pretty bad off, Kyra. Get a pillow so I can ease the pressure off his back, and bring a sheet or something to stop the bleeding." He dismissed Kyra, pulled out his walkie-talkie cell phone, and began barking orders to send an ambulance pronto.

Kyra ran to the bedroom, and returned with the pillow and a clean bedsheet. She watched Nick with amazement. He moved Kevin's large body with precision and skill. She hadn't realized she was holding her breath until she heard Kevin gasp with relief.

Nick watched her with dark eyes. "Okay, Kyra, what the hell happened? Why is the owner of the newspaper dead?"

Kyra knew she'd have to explain, but she didn't want to start now. "It has to do with my father. Carter used to be a contract killer for the government. There was a contract on my father, but they couldn't touch him, so they put a hit on me instead. That's why my editor sent me here, to keep me out of harm's way. I just didn't know it at the time. Carter gave me the willies every time I went to the paper for research. I did some checking on the paper and it's not making any money. Yet, his mother's lifestyle hadn't changed since his father passed away, and he drove a brand new Mercedes and wore designer suits. He had to have money coming from somewhere. I suspected but I couldn't prove anything." She took a deep breath and almost choked on the odor of death in the room. "So Carter killed the three hitters and came after me himself. He was going to kill Kevin and I couldn't have that."

Nick's hard gaze was unyielding. "So, you knew Carter was a hitter and didn't bother to tell Kevin or me? If we'd had that info a little earlier, Kevin might not have to be fighting for his life right now!"

"You know I would have told. I suspected there was a local person doing the killing, but I had no idea until this morning it was Carter when he burst into the house."

Nick nodded, turning his attention back to Kevin. "His pulse is weak. What is taking the EMT so damn long?"

Kyra was about to answer when the wailing of the ambulance filled the silence of the quiet neighborhood. "They're here." She ran to the door. She knew she probably looked a hot mess, but didn't care. The only thing that mattered was Kevin.

As if she didn't matter, the paramedics filed past her with the stretcher, and quickly assessed Kevin's injuries. They ripped off his blood-soaked shirt, tossing it on the floor. Before she knew what was what, they had Kevin loaded on the stretcher and headed out the front door.

Nick followed. "Call his folks," he barked. "I'm going with him. See you."

CHAPTER 28

Kyra was stuck. She wanted to be with Kevin. She also had to stay until the other deputies got there to take Carter's body away. She watched through teary eyes as the ambulance took off.

She sat on the couch, trying to gather her courage to call Dorrie and David Sr. and tell them that their son was almost killed and it was her fault. She thought of her yoga exercises, hoping that it would calm her. What she really needed was some good karma.

Suck it up and just do it. Kyra took a deep breath and dialed Kevin's parents. With a trembling voice she recited the past events to his mother. "He's at the hospital."

Dorrie took the news like a trooper. "We're on our way. Thank you, Kyra. I'm sure you did what you could." She ended the call.

Kyra looked at the phone as it buzzed at her. When this was all over she was going to have a really good cry. Deputy Hall walked through the open front door. "Hi, Kyra. I came to take your statement." He glanced at Carter's body. "The ME will be here shortly. I know you're anxious to get to the hospital."

She nodded. "I—I called his parents." She wiped her eyes with the back of her hand. "It's my fault. I should have been able to figure this out. I could have saved him."

The young deputy shrugged. "I'm sure this isn't your fault. Now tell me what happened."

Before she could recite the events again, the medical examiner entered the house, shaking his head at the scene before him. He glanced in Kyra's direction. "I guess this is your doing? Carter's been nothing but trouble since he came back. I was wondering when his mouth was going to get him in trouble."

"Self-defense. He was going to kill the sheriff," the deputy said on Kyra's behalf. "I'm sure Ms. Chase won't be charged.

"Good. Let's get Carter out of here, so she can go to the hospital." He motioned for the two assistants to enter the house. "I heard it over dispatch," he told Kyra.

A little later, Kyra entered the waiting room. She had no idea how she got there, but she now faced Nick. "Any word?"

Nick shook his head. "Nope, his family is down the hall in the family area." He stood and walked toward her. "Dorrie asked me to bring you."

She wasn't ready to face them. "Oh, no, I couldn't intrude on them."

Nick sighed. "You don't understand. What Dorrie wants, Dorrie gets. So you might as well come on or otherwise I'll have to take you by force. But understand this, you are going to the family waiting room."

His voice left no room for negotiation and she didn't have any fight left in her. The events of the morning had taken all that away. "Okay, Nick, you win." She rose and followed him down the hallway.

In the week she'd been in Wright City, Kyra had never been in the small hospital. Now as she walked to meet Kevin's family, she felt as if she were on death row and this was the last mile. She tried to calm her nervous heartbeat but it was useless.

As she entered the room, Nick quickly deserted her. She was face to face with Kevin's mother, father, brothers, and nephews. Even Regan and her mother were seated in the waiting room.

"Hello," she whispered.

Kevin's father saw her first. "You're here." He rose from his chair and led her to sit by Dorrie. "We were beginning to get worried. Kevin is still in surgery."

Kyra took the seat offered and nodded. "Did the doctor say anything before he went in?" She wanted to know the smallest detail.

David Sr. shook his head. "Not a damn thing. I hate hospitals."

Even though David Sr. was a retired surgeon, Kyra knew why he hated hospitals. Elias had had an accident last year and the family was in this same position. "I hope we hear something soon. Kevin will be back on his feet in no time, I'm sure." Kyra hoped with all her heart that it was true.

It was almost nightfall by the time Kevin was out

of surgery. This really didn't bode well with Kyra. The doctor entered the waiting area and headed directly for Dorrie and David Sr.

"Mr. and Mrs. Johnson, Kevin is out of surgery."

Dora wiped her eyes. "What exactly do you mean?"

"The bullet entered through his back and it nicked his spinal column. I won't know the extent of the damage until I perform some tests."

"Will he be able to walk?"

"Yes, Mrs. Johnson. The damage isn't severe, so I won't go into the worst-case scenario. I don't want to give you false hope, either, because he might have some trouble walking in the first few weeks following surgery. That's where this dynamic family comes in. I know with all the love for the sheriff in this room, he'll be just fine. He's going to need your patience and understanding." He walked out of the room and Dorrie sobbed.

Kyra felt like she didn't have the right to be in the room, let alone in Kevin's life. It was her fault he might not walk again. What if he couldn't perform his sheriff duties? This was her doing and she had no way to fix it.

When she was finally allowed to enter Kevin's room, guilt had almost consumed her. He was lying in bed, asleep, with all kinds of tubes running to and from his body. His mother was still at his side, holding her son's hand. She rose, vacating the seat by the bed.

"Why don't you sit here? He's been asking for you." She walked to the door. "Take your time, dear. We're going to get some coffee."

Kyra nodded and took the chair. Kevin was so lifeless. Unlike the man who occupied her bed this morning. And now he might not be able to walk. She wiped guilty tears from her eyes.

"Baby?"

She didn't think she heard him. It was probably just her nerves on edge. Surely, Kevin couldn't be speaking.

"Kyra." His voice with thick with medically in-duced sleep.

This time she knew it was him. Her eyes met his. "Hey, Kevin." She grasped his hand and caressed it. "How do you feel?"

His head turned toward her. "Dizzy. Hot. My legs feel strange. I think that bullet hit my spine."

She couldn't hold back her guilt anymore. Maybe Kevin would forgive her. "I'm sorry, this is all my fault. How can you even look at me?"

Kevin spoke in an even tone, trying to calm her. "Kyra, it's my job to protect the citizens of Wright City. I knew the danger of the job when I took it. So don't think any of this is your fault."

"If you hadn't spent the night, you wouldn't have been there. You wouldn't have gotten shot in the back. I could kill Carter again for shooting you."

"You shot Carter?"

"Yes, after he shot you. He was going to kill you as my punishment, but I got him first."

He smiled. "That's my girl. I knew you could do it."

"You're proud of me? After all the trouble I caused?" She couldn't keep the wonderment out of her voice. Her father had never told her that in her adult life. "That's the nicest thing anyone has ever said to me."

"You deserve it. You saved me. I owe you my life."

"No, you don't. You don't owe me anything but your love."

"You already have that."

"Right back at you, Sheriff." She watched his eyelids fluttered closed and she quietly left the room.

CHAPTER 29

Two days later, Kyra felt the walls of Wright City closing in on her. No one blamed her for getting Kevin shot, but she couldn't take the whispers anymore. She sat in Jay's Diner, contemplating her next move and not eating her lunch.

Since the news of Record's death hit the airwaves, Auggie had been blowing her phone up demanding that she return to her job. Her father had also called asking in his own way when to expect her for dinner. Then there was the love of her life recuperating in the hospital. Talk about pressure.

"Looks like you're doing a whole lot of thinking," Jay said as she sat down across from Kyra. "How's Kevin?"

Kyra sighed. "He's doing better. He's going to have to go through a couple of months of therapy, but I know he's going to make it."

"What about you?"

"Oh, Jay. I don't know what to do." Was that her sounding like a whining baby? Her father would have her hide for that. "I know I belong back in Austin, but I actually don't want to go."

"Why are you running back to Austin anyway? You could work right here if that's what you wanted to do. I know you don't really need to work. Kevin's going to need someone to take care of him."

"But that's just it. It was my fault he didn't have his gun. He's going to start hating me sooner or later for getting him shot. I'd much rather it be later." She knew she had to go back to Austin, and the quicker the better. She had to get Wright City and Kevin Johnson out of her system.

The next morning, Kevin knew something was going on. There wasn't much he could do about it at the moment, since he was flat on his back and still hooked up to the IV. He hated being on receiving end of hospital care.

He watched his mother arrange his breakfast tray and avoid eye contact. Kevin knew getting information out of his mother would be harder than questioning a criminal. He struggled to sit upright. Every move he made sent shivers of pain up his back. His legs were a different story.

"Mom, what's wrong?"

She sighed, took a deep breath, and finally looked at him. "Honey, maybe we should wait for your father to get here before I tell you."

"You know I hate waiting, Mom. Tell me."

"The good news is that they got the bullet out."

Kevin read between the lines. "The bad news is?"

"I really wish you'd wait for your father." She finally sat in the chair near the bed. "But I know you're just like your father in this respect. He hates to wait too. The bullet grazed your spinal column. I know you've noticed your legs feel numb."

Kevin sighed. He had noticed, his legs wouldn't work when he wanted them to. He couldn't feel his toes, let alone wiggle them. His life was over. "Which part of the spinal cord did it injure?"

Dorrie looked at her son in confusion. "I don't understand."

"Mom, the spinal column is made up of several different sections controlling different parts of the body."

She shook her head in amazement. "How do you know that?"

"Dad." After all, his father was a retired surgeon.

"They were saying the L3."

Thank God. It was still bad, but it wasn't that bad. He'd still be able to walk. Maybe. "Okay, is Skip assisting on this case?"

"No. You know he can't."

Kevin nodded. He wanted the best doctor working on him, but unfortunately the best doctor in town was also his oldest brother. "What's next?"

"Therapy."

"How long?"

"That's going to depend on you. It could take a few weeks, or it could take six months. Don't you worry about a thing. The mayor said your job will be waiting for you when you get better."

For once, Kevin's mind wasn't on his job as sheriff. It was on being in love. Kyra was used to a different kind of man. The kind he could never be.

Kevin wasn't a suit-and-tie kind of guy with a six-figure income, and that was what Kyra Chase needed.

"Kevin, didn't you hear what I just said?" His mother sighed. "I know right now things don't look so good, but it will get better."

He smiled at his mother. "I heard you, Mom. Dad kind of broke it to me as gently as he could, but it didn't sink in until just now. Where's Kyra? I need to talk to her."

"She went back to Austin," his mother said. "Ran out of here like a scared rabbit the day before Easter when she heard the news."

Although he wanted nothing more than her, it was good Kyra had the sense to leave town before things got really complicated. He didn't want her to stay with him out of pity. He was a man and could take care of himself. "Can you blame her? She deserves a lot more than I could ever give her. I'm not moving to Austin and she could never be happy here. Not permanently. It's just as well she left."

His mother patted his hand. "If you say so. She still could have come and said good-bye to your face."

He was glad she didn't. He couldn't take one of those dramatic break-up scenes. The last person he wanted to see was Kyra Chase. "This is better. A clean break is the best thing for both of us."

Kyra unlocked the door to her townhouse and took a deep breath. She was finally home. As she gazed around, the cozy upscale place didn't feel like home anymore. Everything was just as she left it nearly two weeks ago, but somehow everything was different.

Her heart was in Wright City with Kevin.

She had to shake off this impossible feeling. She felt like a first-class bitch for leaving him without so much as a good-bye. But teary good-byes weren't her style. She didn't want a scene in the hospital. He'd hate her more if she did that. It was bad enough she was responsible for getting him shot and now he was going to be in therapy for the next six months. It was all her fault.

She sat on her custom-designed couch and stared at the mail neatly stacked on her antique coffee table. Thank goodness the concierge had collected her mail in her absence. She wondered how Kevin was doing. She had to do something to get over this man. Maybe there was something interesting in the mail that would take her mind off her troubles.

Her phone rang and she froze. *Please, don't let it be Kevin,* she prayed as she reached for the cordless. It was her father. Kyra didn't know which was worse: that Kevin hadn't called or that she'd actually have to talk to the famous Chandler Chase.

"Hello, Daddy." Kyra sat back on the couch, settling in for a sermon of "I told you so."

"Kyra. I heard you'd left Wright City. Why did you run?"

She came up with a start. "I didn't run. My story is finished and I came back home."

"What about the sheriff?"

How on earth did her father know about Kevin? "What are you talking about?"

"I'm talking about my dear daughter, that I

know you're in love with the sheriff, and I know he's in love with you. How could you run away from your feelings?"

"Your snoops were misinformed. The sheriff and I were just working together to find out who was trying to kill me."

"Yes, we need to discuss that. Why don't we have dinner tonight? There're a few things about me you should know and I want you to know them. And, to set the record straight, the reason I know about the sheriff is because he came to pay me a visit a few weeks ago."

"Yes, he told me about his visit with you."

"He gave you information about an ongoing investigation?"

Daddy seems surprised that Kevin broke protocol.

"Well, I guess it's true what people say," her father said.

"What's true?"

"When a man's in love, he casts all logical reasoning aside. Based on all the reports I received on the sheriff, I would have guessed he'd never share that information with you."

Kyra didn't see it as such. "Oh, Daddy, he was just trying to get more information on the killers. He probably just figured I'd be more forthcoming with information if he confessed coming to Austin. It wasn't that big a deal."

"Oh, yes, it is, baby. We've been in constant contact ever since that first meeting. I called the office to find out what was going on, and they told me what happened and that he was injured."

Kyra couldn't stop the tears. "Yes, the bullet

nicked his spinal cord and he's going to need therapy. It was all my fault."

"Now, Kyra, it's not your fault. That's part of being a lawman. His job was to protect you and he did. Why did you run?"

This man was going to browbeat her until he got an answer, whether she liked it or not. "My job was over. My life is here in Austin."

"We'll discuss this over dinner. I'll make reservations and get back to you." He ended the call.

"Well, at least that's the same." Her father always treated her like the client he didn't really want. Kyra tossed the phone on couch and returned to her mail.

Four hours later, Kyra sat across from her father at one of Austin's premiere steakhouses. La Carne de Cuba had a waiting list months long, yet her father had gotten a reservation for dinner in one of the cozy alcoves. She knew he held most of his business dinners at the five-star restaurant, and apparently the management was very thankful.

He was dressed in a dark Armani suit that complimented his dark skin perfectly. Those dark eyes peered at Kyra, studying her like she was on the witness stand. "Now, you were telling me why you ran like a scared rabbit."

"I didn't run. My assignment was over." Kyra gazed at the menu.

"You left that man without so much as an explanation. In my book, that's running. And a Chase does not run."

"It was best to leave clean."

"Well, you look pretty miserable to me. Your eyes are puffy, from crying, most likely."

"I'm not miserable. I'm glad to be back. It was a nice diversion, but it's over and now it's time to get back to my life."

He smiled. "Keep telling yourself that and maybe one day you might actually start to believe it. I just want you to be happy and not end up like me. I know your mother didn't love me. We didn't have that love that a man and a woman are supposed to share after thirty years of marriage. And that was my fault. I drove a wedge between us because I let work dictate my life. I couldn't begin to count the missed dinner parties, missed vacations . . . I really let your mother down."

Kyra looked at her father in shock. Tears were actually running down his face. "Daddy?"

"I wanted a better life for you, Kyra. Yes, you do have a job, but that doesn't have to be your entire reason for living. I was married to your mother for over thirty years and wouldn't trade one second of it. She made it the best life I could ever have. It could have been so much more, but I thought life was about having money, and material objects. Now that she's gone, I would gladly give away every penny I have to have her back."

This man was not the Chandler Chase she'd grown up with. After her mother died, her father never let himself grieve for her. It was nice to know that her father was a human. "I miss her too, Daddy. I think about her every day."

"You have one life. Don't waste it. I loved your mother more than life itself, but I was too focused on being the best of the best to enjoy being married to my soul mate. I don't want you making the same mistakes I did."

Kevin hated his life. He'd been released from the hospital a week ago, and it had been a week of pure hell. A therapist came to his house every day, along with his mother and father, Regan, and her mother. He appreciated all the concern, but enough was enough.

This morning, his mother was fixing breakfast. His father had helped with his shower and dressed him. Kevin wanted some of his dignity back. He was forced to use a cane when he did walk, which wasn't often. His legs wouldn't allow him to walk over thirty minutes at a time and that was when he pushed himself.

His parents were waiting for him when he made it to his breakfast table. His body felt like he'd just run a marathon when he finally sat down. "Sorry you guys had to wait."

His mother placed in front of him a plate of scrambled eggs, bacon, hash browns, and toast, and a mug of coffee. "Oh, baby, it's okay."

Kevin shook his head at the amount of food on his plate. "Mom, I told you not to go to all this trouble." But he was so glad she did. All those medications he'd been prescribed had increased his appetite.

"Your father still has to eat." She placed a plate in front of his father before sitting down with her own. "It's never too much trouble to fix your meals, Kevin."

"Thanks, Mom. I really appreciate you guys coming over every day."

"I hear the paper is up for sale," she said.

This was his mother's attempt at being subtle. Kevin had heard the same news from Regan on her daily visits. Since Record had been killed, the family had decided to get rid of the paper. So many newspapers were being sold to larger companies that Kevin feared the *Wright City Record* might lose that homey touch. He instantly thought of Kyra and her love for those small town stories. He knew he was smiling; he only hoped that his very observant parents hadn't seen it.

"I know that look," his mother teased. "Why don't you call Kyra? I know she'd love to hear from you."

Kevin would love nothing more, but what good would it do? Kyra could never be happy in Wright City and he could never again be happy in a big city. He looked at his mother's anxious face and wanted to say something, anything that would please his romantic-minded mother. "She could call me. She's the one who left. I'm still right here."

Instead of his mother's usually understanding, soft voice agreeing with him, she turned on him like a mother lion defending her cub. Or in this case, the cub's girlfriend. "Kevin, don't be such an ass. That girl calls me every day to see how you're doing. I can hear the hurt in her voice, just like I hear it in yours. One of you has got to make the first move."

"Mom, you don't understand. What can I give her? Kyra's dad is loaded. I mean, millionaire loaded. Can I ask her to live in a town without a shopping mall?"

His mother waved her chubby hand at his questions. "Love doesn't know anything about class, careers, or much of anything else. If you love her, that should be your only concern. Everything else will come out in the wash." His mother resumed eating and effectively closed the conversation.

Later that evening, Elias came to visit. Kevin had noted the changes in his brother in the last few months since becoming engaged to Regan. Now, with only two weeks until the wedding, the excitement, or reality, of getting married was finally showing in his brother.

Elias sat on the leather chaise longuer, a gift from the mayor, and stared at Kevin as he reclined on the sofa. The day's events had totally drained him. Between thinking about what his mother had told him and the therapist working him within inches of his life, Kevin was spent. "What is it, EJ?"

Elias had the nerve to look surprised at the question. "Nothing, man. I just came by to see how my brother was doing."

"Man, quit playing. I know when you come home, you're spending every possible moment with Regan. The case is over. So what made you leave your fiancée's arms to come visit the non-walking?"

Elias shot up off the chaise and began walking around the room, looking at the pictures on the wall. Something was definitely on his mind and it must have been a major deal because he kept his back to Kevin. "That piss-poor attitude of yours, for one. Mom is worried about you. I guess I am too."

"Don't tell me you're here to get on the Kyra Chase bandwagon?"

"There's no harm in calling her," Elias said gently. "If there's nothing between you guys, then at least you'll have closure and can move on with your life."

Kevin sighed. Everyone made it sound so simple, but that one phone call would break his heart and no one seemed to understand that. "Easier said than done."

"I know this hurts like hell, Kev, but harboring all this sorrow isn't good, either. You've gotta confront your demons or you'll never be able to move on."

Kevin mulled over his brother's words. Yes, he wanted to move on, and, yes, he wanted Kyra back in his life, but could he actually do either of the two? He also knew his brother and Regan had been planning a wedding, and as far as he knew, Regan had finished picking bridesmaids. "Don't tell me Regan is considering asking Kyra to be a bridesmaid?"

Elias nodded. "They became really close in that short amount of time. Regan had asked her a few weeks ago if she'd consider being the maid of honor."

"And?"

"She said yes then, but with all that's happen between you two, Regan wants to make sure you're okay with Kyra still being in the wedding."

Kevin sat up with much effort, but he did it. He felt like crap. He looked at his brother sideways. "Why the hell does she need my approval to be in your wedding?" He couldn't keep the incredulousness out of his voice.

"Because you're the best man." Elias looked down at his brother. "You haven't changed your mind, have you?"

He had been mulling over the prospect of not being in the wedding, but didn't want to let Elias or Regan down. They'd been through so much the previous summer, helping him break his first major case as sheriff. "That's a lot of standing, EJ. You know, during the ceremony, than the reception line and stuff. I don't know if I'll be able to do it. What if I can't?"

Elias sat on the edge of the chaise, closer to his brother. "Kevin, the wedding is two weeks away. Regan and I talked about it, and if it comes down to it, you can just sit in the front row with Mom and Dad when you think you can't stand anymore during the ceremony. And at the reception, since Regan is also healing, we're thinking of doing away with the wedding party line." Then his brother added in a much lower voice, "I really want you to be in the wedding. It would mean the world to me."

Well, that did it. For Elias, this was as close to begging as it came. Kevin had to do it. "Okay, man, that will be my motivation for the next two weeks."

"Thanks, Kev." Elias wiped his eyes discreetly.

Kevin was man enough not to mention the tears. "And it's okay if Kyra is in the wedding. I'll just man up and hope for the best. Besides, what could happen in front of a crowd of people?"

Two weeks after leaving Wright City, Kyra's heart still hadn't mended. In fact, she missed Kevin and Wright City more than ever. She had to do something. She sat in her large corner office, relishing her much-deserved promotion for her coverage of the three hit men sent to kill her.

Being the senior editor of the community section would have been enough for most people. Kyra was finally editing the stories she wanted to write. But it wasn't enough. If only she'd never stepped foot in Wright City, she wouldn't have known what happiness or love was. Now that she had, there was only one option.

She walked into her boss' office and took a seat. Auggie didn't look surprised to see her.

"What's up, Kyra? Have you finished editing the stories yet? I need those by six to go in tomorrow's edition."

"Auggie, this isn't working for me."

He stared at her with those intense blue eyes. "So I guess you're telling me you're quitting and moving to that little hick town."

"How did you know that?"

He clasped his large hands together and smiled at her. "Because I've known you a long time. When you first got back, you had this glow about you. I had hoped it was just because you'd done such a great job on your assignment. As the days went by, the glow was gone, and I knew your heart wasn't in it anymore."

"I wish you would have told me," Kyra teased. "You could have saved me a lot of time."

Auggie leaned back in his chair, watching her closely. "It's the sheriff, isn't it?"

"No." And she wasn't lying to her boss and mentor. Partly it was Kevin, and partly it was the town.

"Kyra," he drawled. "Come on, this is me."

"Really, it's not just the sheriff. It's the town. Their paper uses all those stories we only use for filler."

"You know, the paper is up for sale. Record's family is getting rid of it for pennies on the dollar. Someone could talk to her millionaire father and convince him what a great investment it would be."

Kyra didn't have to ask her father. She had her own money, but she needed to check a few things out first. Even if Kevin wouldn't take her back, she still wanted to live in Wright City. "Thanks, Auggie," she said, rising from her chair. "I have some calls to make. I'll have the stories to you by deadline."

He waved her out of his office. "You just make sure I'm invited to the wedding."

It took another week to get all the ends in her life tied up all nice and proper, but it was done. Her father gave his financial blessing on the purchase of the *Wright City Record*. Kyra knew this was as close as he'd get to an apology or an explanation of all things he'd done, mainly putting her in harm's way in the name of being stubborn. He offered to be a silent partner in the paper, claiming that he wanted to retire in a few years and would need something to keep him busy.

Kyra couldn't imagine her father in a small town, but people changed. Her father's confessions about his life were certainly a start. She still didn't believe he actually admitted that he missed her mother. Kyra had also changed and it had only taken a few weeks. She came to town a cynic not believing in love, and now Kevin had shown her a rich and everlasting love, and his family welcomed her with open arms. Even the town had gotten under her skin. So many of the people had left their mark on her forever. She'd always remember Jay no matter where she lived. And Regan. She hoped they stayed in touch once Regan and Elias married and went back to Fort Worth to live.

As she packed the last box of her belongings, she took one last look around her townhouse and sighed. All she thought of was Kevin.

CHAPTER 30

In the middle of his bedroom, Kevin struggled to stand. It had been four weeks of hell, but he'd been able to stay upright without the aid of crutches, that dreaded cane, or a walker. He smiled in triumph.

"Oh, honey, you can stand!" his mother exclaimed as she walked into his bedroom with his breakfast tray. "This is wonderful! Elias will be so excited." She set the tray on his bed. "Have you called Kyra?"

He sighed. Every morning his mother asked him the same infernal question. Every morning he gave her the same answer. "Mom, it's better this way. I'm not a millionaire, I'm just a sheriff. She'd never be happy here."

She stood in front of him, her hands planted on her thick waist. "Did you ask her? 'Cause the last time I talked to her, I don't think she said anything about you asking her what she wanted. Money isn't everything."

"She was born and raised in the Austin limelight. Her dad has crazy money. You think he's just going to tell me to marry his only daughter and drag her out of Austin? He'd probably have me arrested."

"All that doesn't matter when you're in love."

His mother was a romantic. He wasn't. "Mom, love isn't everything. Some people can't let go of what they're used to. I can't see Kyra settling here in Wright City."

His mother had an odd look on her face. "Eat your breakfast, dear. My omelet is getting cold."

He sat on the bed and did as he mother said. Something was going on. "What's going on, Mom?"

"Nothing, dear. Elias wants to take you to Waco today to get fitted for your tux. He's coming over in an hour."

Kevin knew crap when he heard it, but his mother wouldn't elaborate. "Why didn't he tell me that himself?"

"He was with Regan."

"So?"

"He was helping someone move some furniture and lost track of time."

"Mom, the wedding is four days away. I know he and Regan are going to Hawaii for a two-week honeymoon. I know neither one of them is buying furniture since they're going to live at Regan's townhouse in Fort Worth until they have a house built in Arlington next summer, so what are you not telling me?"

"I'll just take these dishes to the kitchen so you can get dressed."

Kevin shook his head. That woman. Instantly his brain focused on Kyra. Another stubborn woman.

He missed her more every day. It was the only thing that kept him going through therapy. Soon he would be ready to face her. He only had four days to get ready.

He stood slowly, walked to his closet, grabbed some clothes, and went to shower. It felt good to be ambulatory again without the aid of anything.

As he walked down the hall, he heard the doorbell. He glanced at his watch. EJ was early. Maybe he could shed some light on his mother's strange behavior.

The doorbell sounded again. Kevin wondered what had happened to his parents. Usually his mother answered the door, but today, nothing. The doorbell rang again.

He walked to the door, ready to rip Elias a new one for ringing the bell so many times, when he had a key. He opened the door and looked in disbelief. Kyra stood in the doorway.

"Kevin, can I come in?"

Kyra looked Kevin up and down as he stared holes through her. He'd lost weight, but at least he was standing on his own. She didn't like the beads of sweat pouring down his face.

She had to say something. "I met your parents as they were leaving. They said you were getting dressed." Still he just looked at her. "Kevin, can I come in?" She hoped his mother was right and he still had feelings for her. Her heart wouldn't be able to stand it if he turned her away.

He just held on to the doorknob. Kyra decided she might as well have her say. "Kevin, I know I left without even saying good-bye and that was wrong. I can't tell you how much I've thought about you these last four weeks. I've thought of nothing else."

"Kyra," he whispered, leaning against the door.

She shook her head. Now that she was on a roll, she didn't want to stop. "Let me finish, Kevin. I love you and I know what I did was unforgiveable and I will spend the rest of my days making it up to you. I want you to know that I've moved back to Wright City permanently and I bought the *Wright City Record.*"

"Kyra," he mumbled.

She knew what those gorgeous lips were going to say. He was going to give her her walking papers. She deserved that, so she had to step up to the plate and take it like a woman. "All right, Kevin. I've had my say, now it's your turn."

"I'm going to pass out." And he crumbled to the floor.

"Kevin!" Kyra was his side instantly. "Oh, my gosh! I'm really bad luck for you." She lightly patted his face. "Please wake up, baby. Please." She tapped his face again.

It took a few moments, but he swatted her hands away. "Stop."

"Honey!" She helped him sit up. "Can you stand? You need me to help you?"

He breathed in and out slowly. "Give me a minute," he said between labored breaths.

She stepped back at the tone in his voice. She wanted to call someone to make sure Kevin was all right and hadn't reinjured his back. But she'd already taken away enough of his dignity.

"Okay, I think I can stand up."

She prepared to help him, but he waved her away and stood unsteadily on his own. "Close my front door. I think I've given the neighbors enough of a show already."

She closed the door as he walked slowly to the sofa and sat down. As she entered the living room, she saw that it was tidy as ever. Kevin stared at her as she stood in front of him. He didn't offer her a seat. The man with the excellent manners was gone.

This was her fault. "I can't take this anymore!" She paced the area in front of him. "I can't do this, Kevin. I came here and pleaded my case. I'm sorry I hurt you. But I've thought of nothing else but you and this place. I've come to love Wright City. If you can't forgive me, I get it. You'll just have to get used to seeing me around town."

"Did you say something about buying the paper?"

She'd poured her heart out and that was all he heard? "Yes, I did." She took a deep breath, willing herself not to cry. There would plenty of time for that later. "I'm sorry I wasted your time."

"Before you get your martyr act going, will you shut up for five seconds?" He smiled at her. "You waltz out of my life without so much as a good-bye then waltz back four weeks later and I'm not supposed to say anything but take you back like nothing has happened?"

Okay, she deserved that. "I know I handled it wrong. Kevin, it was my fault you got shot and have to have therapy."

"And I told you it's my job. If I was afraid of getting shot in the line of duty, I'd never have taken the job."

"Kevin, what do you want from me?"

"Some honest answers for a change." He looked up at her. "Sit down."

She did. "What are you talking about?"

"Why did you come back?"

"For you."

"Then why did you leave?"

"Because no matter what you or anyone else in the town says, I feel responsible for you getting shot. I guess I was running from you, from me, and from us. But I decided I'd much rather be with you no matter what you think of me or how long you want me."

Kevin sighed. "What if I can't work?"

Kyra shook her head. "Doesn't matter. You can help me at the paper."

"Baby, your father is worth more money than I'd make in five lifetimes. Can you really be happy here in Wright City? The nearest mall and Starbucks are in Waco."

"Have I been to Waco?"

"No."

"You make me happy, Kevin. The things I thought were important to me, weren't. You made me see that. When all those men were trying to kill me, you made me feel totally safe." She moved closer to him. "I know we haven't known each other long, but I feel so close to you."

Kevin leaned down and kissed her on the forehead. "You know what I missed the most?"

She looked up at him. "What?"

"Waking up next to you."

"I love you, Kevin." She moved closer and kissed him on the mouth.

"I love you, Kyra," he said against her lips. "I want to wake up with you forever."

"Regan made a beautiful bride," Kyra said as she got into bed with Kevin four days later. "The whole ceremony was just beautiful. I can't believe the dresses fit perfectly. Harriet is a gem."

He pulled her close to him. "I thought you were a beautiful maid of honor. Next to my new sister-in-law, you were the hottest thing in the building." He kissed her on the mouth. "I'm so glad you came back. I think I would have gone out of my mind without you."

"I was going crazy without you." She kissed him. "Austin wasn't the same for me anymore."

He wanted her to be sure. "But, baby, this is nothing like Austin, and I'm in therapy. You're giving up a lot."

She looked at him with those pretty eyes. "Kevin, there's nothing you can tell me that's going to make me walk away. Whatever you need, I can give it to you. I don't miss Austin. You're my journey, Kevin. You complete me."

He sighed. He'd had this big speech prepared in his brain and she'd just made him forget every single word of it. He cleared his throat. "You complete me too. You're the first woman I've had in my house. You made me forget how unhappy I was before you sped into town. I love you, Kyra."

"I love you, Kevin." Kyra grabbed his hand and kissed it. "You keep telling me to think about what

I'm giving up. What about you? I mean, are you sure you want me? I can't imagine life without you, but I do want you to be sure."

"I'm sure."

"Sure enough to get married?" She kissed his hand.

Kevin laughed. "That's supposed to be my line." He kissed her.

"Does it really matter who proposes?" She sat up in bed and stared at him, daring him to defy her.

He looked up at her, seeing the future for the two of them. *It would never be boring*, he mused. She'd probably surprise him every day for the rest of their lives together. "No, baby, it doesn't matter. When did you want to get married?"

"Next Saturday. A small wedding at the Safe Haven on New Year's Day with just our friends and families."

"You want to get married here?" Kevin didn't know how this would sit with Chandler Chase. "Why not in Austin? I'm sure your dad would like you to have it there. Are you sure?"

"Yes. This is where my heart is. With you."

EPILOGUE

New Year's Day
Safe Haven

Kevin would have paced the room, but he needed to save his strength for the wedding. He sat in a chair trying to think of something that would calm his jittery nerves.

He and Kyra had planned a small wedding and had hoped to keep it low-key, but that went out the window when Chandler presented his client list. Talk about clash of the titans. Luckily time was on their side and since the wedding was so sudden, most of the Austin people couldn't make it.

Elias and Regan had postponed their honeymoon, so they could witness Kevin and Kyra's special day. He walked inside the room and smiled his brother. "I can't believe you guys did something this outlandish. A wedding in seven days! That has to be a record somewhere." Elias was outfitted in a black-tie tux. "That Kyra is a whiz at planning."

"You don't have to tell me, Elias. I know she's the bomb."

"How's her daddy handling all this? His baby girl having a small wedding, living in this small town, and being married to a sheriff?"

"Pretty good. You know, he's footing the bill for the honeymoon. I think he'd do anything she wanted right now, just to make up for the Ditano hit fiasco." He and Kyra were joining Elias and Regan in Hawaii for two weeks, then they were off to Canada for another week.

Elias gasped. "Please tell me you're kidding."

Kevin shook his head. "When Kyra mentioned that you guys postponed your honeymoon to be in our wedding, he made some calls."

"So that's why the airline called us and offered us first-class seats and accommodations, and my boss is telling me to take as long I need."

"That would be correct."

Elias laughed. "So that's what it feels like to be well connected."

"Apparently." Kevin stood and walked around the room. "I was afraid he was going to insist on us having some kind of reception in Austin, but he's cool with the way things turned out. Since Kyra is thirty-five and I'm thirty-four, he wants to know how soon I can get Kyra pregnant."

Elias laughed. "He really doesn't mince words, does he?"

"No."

The music started playing. Elias opened the door. "They're playing our song."

Kevin nodded. His nerves had settled down and he was ready to get married. "Yes, they are."

* * *

"Kyra, I know I don't say this nearly enough, BUT you grew into a beautiful woman, and you make a beautiful bride," her father said as they prepared to walk down the aisle.

"Thank you, Daddy." She kissed him on the cheek. She was dressed in a Harriet Miller original. The strapless white floor-length gown made her feel like a queen getting ready to marry her king. Harriet really earned brownie points with that dress. Tiny white pearls and clear rhinestones had been attached all over the front of her dress and train. She also wore the diamond necklace Kevin had given her the night before. "Thank you for not making a fuss about me having the wedding here."

"This is your home now. Here with Kevin. I told you I didn't want you repeating my mistakes. This place brings back memories of a happier time in my life in Corpus Christi."

Kyra laughed. Maybe her father was on his journey. "It's time, Daddy." She held on to her father's arm and started to walk down the short aisle to Kevin.

He stood with Elias at his side, and Regan was her matron of honor. Kevin smiled at her as she made her way to his side. He took her hand.

"You look beautiful."

She tried so hard not to cry, but it was useless. Happy tears streamed down her face as she recited her vows to Kevin. When it came time for the kiss, they both had tears of joy.

"I now present Kevin and Kyra Johnson."

The crowd erupted in applause.

"See, you always cause a scene," he whispered, putting his arm around her.

"Just wait until tonight," she promised, "and I'll show you a scene that will make your teeth rattle."

"Oh, I can't wait."

She winked at him. "I love you, Sheriff. You showed me a different side to love. The good side. With you I know I have found what I was looking for."

"You gave me a reason to believe in spontaneity. There was a time I'd have run from a woman like you, but I'm glad I didn't. I love you, Kyra, and I really love your freaky side."